# RISING
## *from the*
## SEA

CRISSI MCDONALD

# RISING
## *from the*
# SEA

### CRISSI MCDONALD

Lilith House Press

Lilith House Press
Estes Park, Colorado

**eBook ISBN:** 979-8-9913374-1-0
**Print ISBN:** 979-8-9913374-0-3
**Library of Congress Control Number (LCCN):** 2024927282

Cover and Interior Design: Jane Dixon-Smith / jdsmith-design.com

Editors: Susan Tasaki, Kara Stewart
Sensitivity Reader: Maryann Flett
Cover art: Carissa Sorensen

Author Photograph: Lindsey Sutherland www.lindseysutherlandcreations.com

Published by Lilith House Press
Lilithhousepress.org

Printed in the United States of America

First Edition: January 2025.

# CHAPTER ONE

"I can't believe I let you talk me into this," I yell into Andi's ear. Jostled by the heaving, Friday-night Seattle bar crowd, bass vibrating in my chest, I bump into Andi and slop my overpriced Manhattan on my skirt. The couple dancing in front of me are grinding on each other's thighs.

"Isn't it great?!" she yells back. "I love all this energy!" She sways back and forth, sipping from her drink as neon bands of purple, pink, and orange flash across her silver hair. Closing her eyes, she shifts from swaying to bouncing. I watch, mystified as to how she's able to keep every drop of her gin and tonic in her glass.

Someone pushes into me again, but this time I'm prepared and shift to the side. Protecting my drink, I turn to see who's run into me.

"Shorry…," he slurs. I wonder if I'm getting to the age where everyone in their twenties looks like babies. "Wanna dance, Grandma?" He laughs at his own joke, then stumbles toward the bar, ricocheting off people as he goes. At first irritated, I laugh as I realize I wouldn't take all the land in my home state of Texas to be in my twenties again.

Now Andi's in the middle of a pulsating conflagration—sweat-slicked skin, tattoos on arms and hands and bellies, laughter and smiles and the smell of sweat and cocktails. I gulp the rest of my drink, enjoying the burn as it goes down my throat, then wade into the mass of bodies.

"Andi! I'm going to Uber back to the hotel."

She opens her eyes and moves closer to me, yelling in my ear.

"Already? Nolee, we're supposed to be celebrating!"

Andi had been promoted to general manager of the animal shelter where we both worked, so we'd planned this weekend in Seattle together. It was a dual celebration, also marking my new part-ownership of a local pet supply store that my business partner, Ava, and I bought last year.

"A hot bath and a quiet room are my kind of party right now," I yell back.

Andi smiles and gives me a thumbs up, dancing to the heavy beat swirling through the room. Edging my way back to the bar, I put down the glass and head to the exit, eager to leave the fug of sweat and ear-ringing music behind. Once outside, I slam the door behind me, relishing the quiet. My breath fogs in Seattle's chilly spring air, the pavement shiny from the rain earlier that day. I open the Uber app and find a driver. He arrives in a Prius, and I scoot into the front seat, giving him a smile, smoothing my hair away from my face.

"Calling it quits early on a Friday night?" he asks. He turns down the volume on the classical music that's playing.

"I guess I'm officially old." I turn toward the window, watching as the lights of downtown Seattle and the darkened buildings slide past. There's a full moon, but I can see only its blurry edges through a sky thick with clouds. It reminds me of a dream I used to have in the months after I left Texas. In the dream, a man stood waist-deep in black water, the full moon shining down on him, a searchlight on a dark and watery stage. The recurring dream turned out to be an augury, a hint at the reality of my partner, Keet Noland.

I'm jolted away from memories of Keet when the driver asks, "You're going to the Fairmont?"

"I am."

"Nice place."

As he accelerates through the yellow light, I say, "It is. Nicest one I've ever been to. My friend convinced me that a girl's weekend in the city should include a fancy place to stay."

"But you're leaving early." He signals and turns right.

"I thought it would be fun, but it was loud and overcrowded."

Letting out a burst of laughter, he glances at me. "I've felt that way about this city since I was a kid."

"You grew up here?"

He nods, gliding to a stop as the light changes to red.

"What was that like?"

"Too loud," he says with a smile. "But I like the rain."

"Why do you do this?"

"Driving people around?"

I nod.

"It's a good way to meet folks."

"And fewer people than a nightclub," I reply.

He laughs again, the sound filling the compact car. I laugh with him.

"I live on Lopez.  It's as quiet as I could want. Most weekends, I come into the city so I can run errands and earn extra money driving."

"I live on Camas. It's as quiet as I could want, too."

We're silent for a few moments, and then I recognize where we are through the rain sluicing down the windshield. After exchanging well wishes for the weekend, he pulls away from the curb and I enter the elegant hotel and head for the elevator.

The idea of a girl's night out with Andi seemed perfect a week ago: escape the island for a couple days of fun. But as the elevator doors close, I yearn for the sounds of Osprey Bay at night, and the comforting shape of Keet sleeping beside me. *Is it a product of age or knowing myself better, I wonder, that's changed me into someone who no longer likes crowds or loud music?*

Once in my room, I shower, put on my pajamas, read until the words start to blur, then turn off the light. I know I'm dreaming, but I can't wake up. The air is thick around me, a black tide holding me. I spin in slow motion, blind in the darkness.  I sense space behind me, and—moved by an unseen force—my body bending and folding as I'm drawn toward it. I try to move my arms, but nothing happens. Holding my breath, I push against the paralyzing force. As I twirl for the final time, I know I'll be lost in eternal blackness. Then a spotlight shines behind me, casting my undulating shadow on a tall stone door. I see it through a scrim of liquid, a dark rectangular shape, darker than the sea I'm swimming in. But my shadow is not of a woman—it's an orca. The dorsal fin is behind my head and my arms are long pectoral fins. I try to scream, and a watery heat fills my lungs.

Opening my eyes, I fumble in the space beside the bed and turn on the light, which reminds me that I'm in a hotel room. Disoriented, legs shaking, I stand up and go to the window. The city is quiet, the streets shiny where car lights hit the wet pavement. A few commuters pass by below me. On the skyline, a thin thread of early morning light sneaks under the cloud cover.

I'd had nightmares as a child, and they'd returned during the last years of my marriage as it imploded in slow motion. I'd hoped my new life would put an end to them.

Letting the curtains fall closed, I get a drink of water and sit on the edge of the bed. Knowing I won't be able to sleep again, I shower and dress, then sit in an overstuffed chair in the anonymous silence that only hotels have and read my newest book. The nightmare fades as words fill my head with another world. Then, glancing at the clock, I see there's time for me to have breakfast before I meet Andi in the spa.

"My body is a big noodle," I say as we wait to be seated at our table for lunch. Despite myself, I feel my eyes drift closed.

Andi nudges me with her elbow. "Wake up. You're drunker than you were last night, only this time it's from a massage."

"I wasn't drunk last night."

"You're right. That was me."

I open my eyes and smile as the server, a young man dressed in black, says, "Ladies, may I show you to your table?" He turns without waiting for our answer.

"How'd you find this place, Andi? It's the fanciest hotel I've ever stayed in." When I was married to Nathan and living in Texas, places like this couldn't be found, even if Nathan and I'd wanted to spend that much time together.

"I used to live in Seattle, and this is where I stayed when I had big business meetings. It was a perk the company I worked for offered and I took them up on it."

The carpet is so thick, I can't hear my own steps. "What business were you in?"

The young man pulls out one of the floral-upholstered chairs for Andi as she says, "Corporate development."

We order tea and pastries—Darjeeling for me, orange pekoe for Andi.

"What does that that mean??" I ask.

Andi shrugs. "The short answer is, I was hired by big companies to improve productivity and show them ways to implement strategies that would increase their competitiveness in their chosen markets."

"That sounds like an answer you've given a few times."

"A few," she smiles. "I like my current job better. Dogs and cats aren't worried about profit margins and stockholders."

I laugh. "But I bet the board of directors of the shelter are."

"They're a good group of people. We need to make money, and they also realize that rescuing and adopting animals has value. I see myself as able to walk in both those worlds."

Our server sets down two teapots and delicate cups on matching saucers, then gives us detailed brewing directions (and an egg timer) for each pot. When he leaves our table, I say, "They take their tea seriously here."

"They do. I should've ordered a Mimosa." She gives me a sly smile.

"Why didn't you get one?"

She shrugs. "I had enough to drink last night."

"Looks like you were having a great time."

"I was. Why'd you cut out early?"

"Too loud. Too many people. And some guy called me 'Grandma.'"

"Wait—twenty-something with a mullet? Sloshing his drink all over everyone?"

"That's him."

"If I had a dollar for every time someone called me Grandma," she smiled.

"It doesn't bother you?"

"Used to. I really don't care anymore."

"What'd you do?"

"I took his drink, downed it, then danced with him. He has a different definition of Grandma now." She pours her tea into her cup and swirls in a splash of milk. The server arrives again with a three-tiered cake stand filled with small sandwiches and pastries. My stomach growls.

"Wait—did you bring him back here last night?"

Setting her spoon in the saucer, she takes a sip of tea. "God, no. Too young."

"Dancing was enough?"

"More than. Besides," she slides her fork under a small triangle of cucumber sandwich, "I'm not into hooking up anymore. I still like a good time, but it's easier for me to be on my own."

"I preferred being on my own. Especially toward the end of my first marriage."

"Nathan, right?"

I nod, and surprise myself by almost smiling. Andi catches the glimmer.

"What was that?" she asks. "An actual good memory of your horrible ex?"

"Not a good memory, a realization: If he hadn't been who he was and made the choices he did...."

"Like having an affair and falling in love with another man?"

"Yes, like that." Now I *am* smiling. "Even though he was lying to me while we were married, he followed his heart. Doesn't make the lying right. But a part of me understands what he did. It took courage."

"It took nerve. You're the one with the courage, moving all the way from Texas to an island in the middle of nowhere."

"Yeah, but I was comfortable in my misery. It'd gone on so long that I thought being numb was the same as being content." Lifting the fragile teacup, its heat seeping into my chilly fingertips, I take a sip. The tang and sweetness soothe my jangled nerves, wiping away more of the early-morning nightmare.

"I think there's something about Camas that cultivates contentment," Andi muses, after taking a sip of her tea.

"Definitely."

We each take a pastry from the stand, eating in silence until Andi says, "But didn't you mean to stay independent?"

I rest my fork on the porcelain plate and think for a moment before replying. "I had every intention of never being with anyone, ever again."

"What changed?"

Now my smile isn't almost appearing; it's beaming full force across the table at Andi, who smiles back.

"Stupid question, Nolee. I know you and Keet met. But I mean, how did you decide you could try being with someone else again?"

I shake my head. "Would it be an easy out to say that I trusted my feelings?"

"Way too easy. C'mon. You'd just left a marriage where your husband treated you like you were invisible. You knew you could get by if it was just yourself. What changed?"

Instead of answering, I fire a question back at her. "Why the sudden interest in my love life, Andi?"

With a nervous laugh, she takes a bite of cake and a sip of tea. When she sets down the cup, it rattles in the saucer. "I met someone. A guy—"

"Andi, that's wonderful! How did you meet him?"

A pink flush creeps up her cheeks before she says, "Online. His name's Mason."

"And?"

"And he wants to fly out here and meet me."

"Where does he live?"

"New Mexico. Albuquerque."

The smile fades from her face, and the lines around her mouth deepen.

"What's wrong?"

The waiter leaves our table after we assure him we have enough hot water. Andi says, "Nothing's wrong. Everything seems right. We FaceTime almost every night and text during the day. He seems like a nice guy."

"And?"

Andi laughs. "You're trying to distract me from you and Keet."

"We can get back to that. Right now, I want to hear why you're hesitating about Mason."

"Shit. Caught."

"Spit it out! You're the one who had this idea for an amazing girl's weekend."

Andi drains the tea from her cup. "I've been on my own for a very long time. I like it."

"How does that affect your concern about Mason?"

"I'm incredibly attracted to him. But we've only texted and FaceTimed."

"Don't you think it's possible you'd be more attracted to Mason in person?"

"Look at you, smiling like you have a juicy secret."

"No secret, Andi. That's why Keet and I got together. Mutual attraction."

"And?" She throws my question back at me with a smile.

"And nothing!" I flush, knowing that in addition to our mutual attraction, Keet and I do share a secret—that he's Keykwin, one of a dwindling race of people who can also change into orca, or, as they call themselves, Blackfish.

"Nolee Burnett. Are you blushing?"

Mouth suddenly dry, I drain my teacup. "Maybe. What I was going to say was that attraction turned into something much deeper. A relationship with him was going to be different than with any other person I knew."

"It was love at first sight?"

I shake my head. "Not exactly. Keet intrigued me. He still does. He sees the world and interacts with it in ways that I've never even imagined."

Realizing that Keet's secret is hidden in the words I've chosen, I want to take back what I just said. Instead, I take the last bite of chocolate cake and watch Andi, her expression thoughtful.

"Like?"

"He's calm in situations that rile me up. He reads me like an open book, even when I don't want to look at myself. He's gentle, and strong."

My heart races as I remember Keet's kisses. The ache of missing him these past weeks is embedded like a splinter in the middle of my chest. I understand why he chose to accompany his sister Zelka to return the water clock, but that doesn't make me miss him any less.

"But you didn't know that when you first met him."

"I didn't know the details, but I felt them all the same."

"Felt what?"

Shifting in my chair, I move the empty cup and saucer away. "I could be myself with him. I've kept myself buried for most of my adult life, Andi, and I'm not doing that anymore. Keet was the first person I knew I could trust."

"Even after he left you last winter?"

I look out the window at the rain, hearing its soft patter against the glass.

"When he left, I was more determined to not lose everything I'd gained for myself."

"You were also a wreck. How'd you come back from that?"

Then it hits me. Andi wants an entry and exit plan, a Guide to Relationships. I laugh more loudly than I mean to and notice people at the other tables looking at us. I ignore them and watch as Andi smiles, then chuckles.

"What's so funny?"

"You! Me. Look at us, trying to come up with surefire ways to protect ourselves from being hurt by another person."

"I wasn't—"

"Maybe not on purpose, Andi. But isn't there a part of you, a part you don't want to listen to, who wants assurances no one can give?"

She pauses, then nods, looking down at her empty plate and cup. The silver light outside matches her hair. "Maybe. Probably. But you still didn't answer my question, Nolee."

"About how I trusted Keet again? Well, I had two choices. I could be alone and wonder, or I could believe what he told me and try again. This time, from a place of trusting myself."

"That easy?"

"That simple. Wasn't easy."

Andi digs through her purse, grabs her phone, and swipes it open. She spends a few moments tapping at the screen before turning it toward me. On it is a photo of a man with salt and pepper hair, laugh lines around his dark eyes, and a broad and inviting smile. He's holding a black cat with bright green eyes.

"This is Mason?"

"That's him. Stunning, right?"

I smile. "Most definitely. Helps that he likes animals, even if it is cats."

Andi laughs and tucks the phone back in her purse.

I pause, then ask, "The only question you need to answer now is, 'What's next?'"

"You sound like me."

"Great minds."

"What's next is a visit with Mason," Andi says.

"Is he staying at your place, or a local hotel?"

"I thought I'd take him to bed as soon as he got off the ferry."

I choke on a piece of cake.

"You deserve that, poking into my business. He'll stay at the North-sound Inn."

"That's a good place." I take a sip of water to clear my throat.

"They serve a nice breakfast…," her voice trails off as she looks out the window at the rain.

"What? You're not making breakfast for him?"

Andi tosses her napkin across the table as I laugh. "Dammit, Nolee," she says, laughing. "I think you want me to get laid more than I do."

We laugh through the rest of our meal, and I'm still smiling as I take the elevator up to my room. Andi and I agree to meet later for our final dinner in the city, so I opt for a bath and a nap. I check my phone to make sure Sylvie is doing okay with my dogs, Fae and Wallace. No texts. I lob the phone on the bed and walk into the bathroom.

As the tub fills, I undress, catching glimpses of myself in the mirror, noticing my droopy upper arms, the fullness of my hips and thighs, the disappearance of my once-small waist. When did I get so much gray hair? Who is this old woman staring back at me? I look away from my reflection, vowing to watch myself in the mirror less often.

# CHAPTER TWO

After hugging Andi when she dropped me off at home, I open the door into a quiet house. It was only a weekend, but Andi's companionship and our activities in Seattle filled a void I didn't know I was living in. I've been keeping busy during Keet's absence, but apparently, not busy enough. The silence crashes into my chest, so heavy that I collapse onto a kitchen chair.

A sudden longing hits me. *I wish I could change into an orca, so I could've gone with Keet and Zelka to the Water Canyon House.* Flashing behind this thought is the nightmare I had in the hotel. I push that aside, along with the memory of the water clock that Keet and his sister Zelka returned to their distant Keykwin relations.

Why aren't they back? Has something happened?

I shake myself, dislodging my anxious thoughts before getting up and looking out the window. Fae and Wallace sniff along the beach, accompanied by Keet's grandmother, Sylvie. I decide to join them. As I walk out the door, I see Keet's 4Runner parked in front of the garage and it makes me smile.

I was amazed that Keet had allowed Sylvie to drive it home from our trip to Neah Bay. Keet's words come back to me. That last night before he and Zelka left, swimming as orca to return the water clock to its people, he'd said, "She's kept that blue truck of hers safe all these years. My car isn't that important to me. Besides, maybe it will sweeten her up and she'll let me get behind the wheel of her truck sooner."

As a sigh chases away my smile, Sylvie turns, sees me watching, and waves. The dogs run toward me, white teeth flashing in huge grins, tails thrashing their sides. I kneel and throw an arm over each of them, all of us snuffling with pleasure.

"I'm going to make fish stew, Nolee, using that halibut we bought from the fisherman on the dock. Do you want to share it?" Sylvie asks.

"I'd like that. I have a loaf of sourdough bread, and some greens I could bring."

Sylvie's attention is already sliding away from me as she turns to go back to her cabin. I glance at my phone and see that it's the dogs' dinner time, so we go back to the house, and I feed them, then gather up the bread and greens and let myself into Sylvie's cabin.

"Sylvie, do you want me to start a fire?" I call out as I walk inside. Seeing her bent over in front of the woodstove, a match in her hand under the kindling, I say "Never mind." Once the orange flame catches, she tosses the wooden match inside but leaves the door propped open and makes her slow way into the kitchen.

"Happy to help with the prep for the stew," I offer as I set the food I'd brought on the table. She shakes her head.

"I promise not to spy on you." Her look tells me my attempt at humor has fallen flat. Sylvie's halibut stew is legendary in their family, but she keeps the recipe a secret. "Okay, well, I'm going to go home and unpack. Text me when you're ready." I turn to leave.

"Nolee?"

I turn. "Yes?"

"Thank you."

My first instinct is to ask why she's thanking me, but then I see the pain in her eyes and nod. Like me, Sylvie is grateful she's not in Osprey Bay alone.

After Nolee leaves, Sylvie walks to the woodstove and stands with her back to it, the heat smoothing the knots from her aching spine. She hears Fae's yip of excitement and watches as Nolee lets both dogs out for another beach run. Her face softens, and the sharp dagger that threatens her heart moves a short distance away. Sylvie knows that Keet's girlfriend is family, and not just because Keet loves her. Not just because Nolee accepts them whether they wear the orca cloak or their human skins. Nolee is family for many reasons: her mysteries intersect with their own, she's proven herself willing to stand in the middle of a storm that isn't hers, to honor and share her life and her clear vision. Sylvie decides it's time to ask Nolee a question, one she hopes Nolee will answer with happiness. Of the two issues bothering her mind, this is the easier one. The difficult decision will come later. Now it's time to make dinner.

First, she prepares the marinade for the halibut, then adds the fish to the bowl and covers it. Standing on tiptoe, she stretches to reach the battered stock pot she'd brought from home months ago and sets it on the stove. After taking the rest of the ingredients she needs from the refrigerator, she moves to the pantry, where she's tucked her secret ingredient behind the cans of cream of mushroom soup.

Putting everything in the pot, she stirs in gentle circles, watching the colors swirl together, a spiral of nourishment to share with a woman she's grown to admire. Sylvie sings a blessing over the food, closing her eyes and inhaling its intensifying scent. She adds a pinch of her secret ingredient and stirs again, then turns the heat down and puts a lid on the pot.

While she waits for the stew to cook, she adds wood in the woodstove, closes its door, then opens the damper. The fire crackles as it devours the wood, the wind rushing through the pipe like a low sigh. *The house is too quiet*, she thinks. Back into the kitchen, she lifts the lid; as the steam caresses her face, she thinks how much she'd miss having a sense of smell.

With the stew needing another few minutes, she decides to start a load of laundry. Since Zelka and Keet left weeks ago, she's avoided washing Zee's things. Sylvie likes seeing Zee's clothes thrown all over her bed. Pausing with one of Zelka's shirts, she crushes it to her chest, and memories of her granddaughter and the Keykwin words that form a prayer knot together like the material in her hands.

Climbing the stairs to her bedroom with its two twin beds, Sylvie stands looking out the sliding glass doors, her gaze lingering on the sea. She remembers Zelka's gasp of amazement the first time Keet stood with her out there, the day she walked out of the sea and into their lives. Sylvie smooths the comforter on Zelka's bed, moving aside a pair of jeans and socks, and sits on its edge, still gazing out at the gray light disappearing from the sky. Then she catches a waft of the stew, finds her phone in her pocket, and texts Nolee.

My phone pings with a text from Sylvie. *Stew is ready.*

*Be there in five,* I answer.

When I walk into the cabin, I smell the aroma of fish and a savory broth. I don't see Sylvie, but thumps overhead tell me she's in the bedroom. I put together a simple salad, then take the bread from the wrapper and slice off several chunks. When I hear the stairs creak, I look up to see Sylvie shuffle toward me holding a length of colorful material, soft strands of different shades of blue interspersed with black and white. Down the middle, a thin strand of red has been knitted in. Before I can ask about it, Sylvie stops in front of me.

"My grandmother spent much of her time knitting. She made this scarf for me after I gave birth to Keet's mother, Hazel." Sylvie runs her hand over the smooth wool, rubbing each stitch between finger and thumb. "I would like to give it to you."

"Sylvie…"

"Nolee, will you call me Grandmother?"

I'm already on the verge of tears, and this request sends them spilling down my cheeks. I nod as I wipe at my face. Sylvie wraps the scarf around my neck, her weather-worn hands lingering on my shoulders. I lean in and kiss her cheek. My own grandparents had died before I made any lasting memories of them, and I didn't realize how much I'd been missing the presence of an elder, someone to guide and help me. I know Sylvie's gift is an honor, and as I look into her eyes, I see the happiness my acceptance brings her.

"Thank you, Grandmother."

She brushes the remaining dampness from my face, then cups my elbow in her hand and walks with me to the kitchen. I hold an end of the long scarf in my hands, wondering if I'll ever risk wearing it outside. "This is so beautiful."

"The blue is for the oceans we swim in as Keykwin, and the sky and air above it. The black and white represents our Blackfish body."

"What does this red thread mean?" I follow it with my eyes, feeding the soft weave through my hand, tracing the red yarn that runs through the middle with my thumb.

"The red represents the blood we shed as women, from maiden until wise elder."

My laugh escapes in a puff of air. "I hope someday to be wise, Grandmother. Like you." Sylvie's eyes glow and she gives me a broad smile.

"Wisdom is hard-earned, Granddaughter." My heart flutters hearing this endearment from Sylvie. "And it's also hard given, because it walks with truth." Removing her warm hand from my elbow, she flicks off the burner under the stew.

As I watch her ladle the stew into bowls, I feel the first stirrings of unease about Sylvie. The old me would've shrugged it off, labeling it as anxiety about losing someone I'd grown to love. The new me accepts this information, this trembling in my chest. I suspect that Sylvie is contemplating a change and remember asking Keet when she first arrived if she meant to take her Walk Into the Water, a ceremony by which she would leave her human life behind and spend her remaining years as orca. At the time, Keet said he didn't know.

Every instinct I have is telling me this is what she's thinking about. Although I don't like this knowledge, and it brings me deep sadness, it also reminds me to cherish the time we have together.

As she sits, Sylvie catches me looking at her, and smiles. "What is it, Granddaughter?"

"I love and appreciate you so much." I reach across the table to hold her hand, avoiding putting pressure on the delicate bones beneath the skin.

She pats my hand. "I love and appreciate you. Eat before the stew gets cold."

# CHAPTER THREE

A black abyss stretches behind Keet as he swims upward, clicking as he speeds toward the surface, toward the bright water churning overhead. Four strong strokes of his tail and he's there, the water refracting sunlit shafts into the dark below. Spy hopping, he draws air into his lungs, then twirls in place on the gentle swells, listening to the gulls calling above him. He knows it's morning, just as he knows the pull toward Camas Island, and Nolee. He dives, pointing his rostrum down, sounding for the Water Canyon House, singing his sister's name.

A black void fills the canyon's boundaries; the sounds of the people, the sound of his sister's voice, are gone. Without Zelka's help, he knows that if he tried to swim back to the Water Canyon House, he'd run out of air before he could find the door. Now, happy to be free of its stifling presence and mystery, he dives and turns east, swimming toward home, the cold air against his dorsal fin sinking into the warmth of the water. The mysteries of the Water Canyon House and its people aren't as strong as his desire to be with Nolee.

Keet scans for fish and finds a school; following them, he slices through the middle and grabs a tail as it flashes by. Hunting, eating, swimming, he finally rests when he reaches the Strait of Juan de Fuca. Behind him, the songs of humpbacks. Above him, a cloud-shrouded sun. Before him, the rumble of watercraft, a distant hiss where the sea meets land.

On the second day of his swim, Keet and his pod reunite. He sings their names, and their squeaks and whistles of excitement connect them as they join him in twirling flashes, bumping alongside as he swims back to Camas Island. Nana is next to him as he surfaces. He hears the strong thump of her slow heartbeat. George is ahead of them, sliding against his mom and aunties, launching out of the rough waters as he chases waves.

When the sun disappears, they swim through the channels that separate the islands. *Patos and then horseshoe-shaped Sucia,* Keet thinks to himself. In the distance, sounds of Bigg's orcas — their mammal-eating cousins—can be heard; as one, the pod angles away from them. Then come the sounds of water slapping against the buoys that mark the shallower waters of Osprey Bay.

As the moon rises, he and his pod brush their bodies against one another, the black of their skin melting into the black sea, the white patches a monochromatic mosaic. Keet nudges Nana one last time, then swims into the bay, twirling slowly at first, a relaxed glide until he sees the ground rising to meet him. Head down, he pushes almost to the silty bottom, then twirls faster, contracting into himself. In the spin, his tail disappears, his long legs take shape, and his arms pull against the cold water. He flips and opens his eyes, pausing to admire the moonlight spilling across the surface of the water. As the oxygen in his blood thins, he kicks without urgency, reaches up, fingers wide. Using the water like a rope, he pulls himself to life, to Nolee—to home.

It isn't the dogs' nails ticking against the floor that raise me from my dreams of stone doorways and twisted orca shapes, it's the deep voice greeting them that rockets me from the warm bed, down the hall, and straight into Keet's dripping arms. Startled, he laughs at first, his breath warm against the top of my head. As his arms tighten around me, I rest my forehead against his chest. The dogs nudge my legs, their paws tap dancing on the floor. Behind my closed eyes, the dark veil of fear I've grappled with since Keet left softens to the palest of sunrise pinks, pulsing in time with my slowing heartbeat. I feel Keet's heartbeat against my cheek, then move my head so I can open my eyes. I see the moonlight on the sea through a window streaked with yesterday's rain, then shift so I can see his eyes, black as the moonlit sea.

In their depths, I release the memory of my violent dream. Touching his face with my fingertips, I feel the soft wrinkles around his eyes, the stubble along his jaw, the lips that are now moving closer to mine. I tilt my head back to welcome his mouth, and our kisses are slow. Our hands twine together and part, nighttime flowers in a sensuous dance, as we walk to the bedroom.

When I wake hours later, the light is muted. Closing my eyes again, I tune into Keet's slow breathing and am grateful to have his warmth beside me once more. I roll over and look at him, his dark hair spread across the pillow, the shape of his face. I kiss him, remembering the intimate silence of our lovemaking.

"Good morning, Lia." He smiles, his eyes still closed.

"Good morning yourself, Keet Noland."

He runs his hands through my hair, opening his eyes, his smile fading.

"When did you dye your hair?"

"After Andi and I got back from our weekend in Seattle. Do you not like it?"

He smiles again, though this time, it's a little forced.

"I like it if you do."

"It's the color it was when I was younger. I couldn't stand the gray anymore."

"I liked the gray," he says as he catches sight of my face. My uncertainty masked by bravado isn't fooling him. "I like this too, Nolee." He kisses me, then gets out of bed to let the dogs out, making his way to the kitchen.

After we eat, we sit at the table going over the loan paperwork for the pet store Ava and I are opening. The front door opens and Sylvie walks in, touching the doorframe to steady herself. Keet and I exchange a quick glance, then he rises and pulls out a chair for her. With a sigh, she sits and asks if there's any coffee. Keet walks into the kitchen, then returns with a steaming mug, setting it in front of his grandmother.

As Keet and I shuffle the papers into manila folders, I ask, "How are you today, Grandmother?"

Out of the corner of my eye, I see Keet turn his head so quickly I think he may get whiplash. With all the excitement about his return, I'd forgotten to mention the change in my relationship with Sylvie.

She chuckles at Keet's expression, but the smile fades as she says, "I miss Zelka. That cabin is too quiet."

Keet clears his throat and says, "You're always welcome here. You can sleep in the guest room."

She shakes her head. "I'm fine." Taking another sip of coffee, she sets the mug on the table. "Keet, when will she be back?"

"I don't know. She wanted to spend time with her cousins, but said she'll come home."

Sylvie grunts, then pushes up from the table and sets the mug in the sink. Taking a breath as though she wants to tell us something, she instead thanks us for the coffee and turns to leave.

"Grandmother?" Keet calls. She turns toward him. "Are you sure you're okay?"

"I will be glad when our family is together again. Don't worry about me."

We're silent as the door shuts, then begin to clean the kitchen.

"I have the down payment," I say, "and I'll finish filling out the loan paperwork at the bank with Ava."

"Your appointment is tomorrow, right?"

I nod. "I'll leave early in the morning and meet Ava at the ferry landing. I think we're going to do some grocery shopping while we're in the city."

Taking the folders off the counter, I slide them into my backpack. "Do you want to come with us, Keet?"

He folds me against his body, swaying side to side. My head empties of numbers as the thrill of memories from last night play in my head. My therapist would've said that not feeling where you end and someone else begins is dangerous, but at this moment, I don't care. The sense of oneness is addictive; I don't want it to end.

Keet's voice draws me back. "I've had enough of being gone. You go, I'm going to stay here and do some home improvements."

"What's on the agenda now?" I flash back to last year, when he fenced the back yard for the dogs; stained the deck; and, after I moved in, remodeled the guest room.

He squeezes me, kisses the top of my head, then walks into the kitchen and puts his hand on the butcher-block countertop. "I'm going to sand and oil this. It's pretty beaten up."

"That should keep you busy."

"It'll be a good day then."

# CHAPTER FOUR

Hearing Keet sing her Blackfish name, Zelka moves to the door through which he had vanished. Smiling, she takes a step closer and touches its rough stone surface before Byree, the matriarch of the Water Canyon House People, pulls her back to the fire. "Sit and tell us stories from the land," she says.

Zelka starts by telling them that she'd spent the first three decades of her life as orca, living a life with her mother beside her. To her surprise, her mother never disclosed that she was, in fact, also Keykwin, a being with the ability to transform between human and orca at will. Her mom also kept Zelka's brother Keet a secret, until last year when Zelka found him living in his house on Camas Island.

Time passes as Zelka describes cars, airplanes, and cities; how money works; food and the stores that provide it. The people laugh—they can't imagine a life without purpose or having to fend for themselves. Zelka is familiar with their way of living. It's the opposite of what little she knows of the human world. Although she's come to rely on her own close-knit family to help her learn to be human, she's aware that some people feel they are independent and don't need anyone. Conversations at the local market float back to her, and one, she remembers, puzzled her more than most. A heavily made-up woman with stiff hair said to her friend, "I don't need anyone, I've got me." Zelka wonders how it feels to go through life with only yourself.

She watches the conversations around the fire; as its warmth fills the House, the circle around it has grown. Zelka feels welcomed by these distant relations and is glad, once again, that she and Keet returned the water clock to its rightful place. She sees it nestled in Byree's lap; though it's empty of water, it glows. Her belly full, Zelka yawns, and the shapes made by the orange firelight become the outline of dancing women reaching for the sky. She glances at the stone walls rising into darkness, sporadic glimmers where stones sparkle in the firelight. They remind her of stars.

"Come, Zelka, let me walk you to your sleeping place."

She rubs her eyes as Arogem takes her arm and lifts her to her feet. She gives him a slow smile, letting him steer her away from the group. Moving his hand from her arm to her waist, he draws her close. She's too tired to protest, idly wondering if she wants him closer or farther away. It does feel good to be held against his strong body. But when she sees her bed, she moves away.

"Peaceful sleep to you, Zelka."

She nods, turns away, and says over her shoulder, "To you as well, Arogem."

Gathering extra blankets from Keet's empty bed, she arranges a soft nest, then burrows into the middle of it. Before drifting into a dreamless sleep, she hears the laughter of her new friends by the fire.

The next morning, as she helps Yiskal gather plates from last night's meal, she feels a light brush of fingers against her ankle and looks into Arogem's upturned face. He's sitting cross-legged, not smiling. His eyes blaze. She pauses, noticing the way her belly loops and her heart races. Yiskal breaks the spell by calling, "Zelka! Keep up!" Zelka smiles at Arogem, who removes his fingertips from her skin. Rebalancing the heavy stone plates, she follows Yiskal.

As Yiskal rubs the plates with a fine white sand and rinses them in a large water-filled urn, she asks, "Do you want him to touch you that way?" Zelka, squatting next to her and mimicking her actions, replies, "I don't mind it."

The dry rasp of sand against stone tickles Zelka's ears, and she smiles at the sensation, remembering Arogem's breath against her neck. Then a blade of uncertainty pierces her reverie. "Yiskal, are you and Arogem together?"

Yiskal barks out a laugh. "No!" Standing, she shakes the plates before stacking them on a low shelf, then scowls at Zelka before pulling the shawl she wears over her robe around her neck and walking away. Zelka watches until Yiskal turns a corner.

Later, Arogem brings Zelka a bowl of fish broth and sits beside her as she tips the bowl to her mouth, drinking so she doesn't have to talk to him. She notices he's keeping his distance, and though his eyes are softer, in the dark depths the burn is still there, waiting.

"Tell me of your life on the land, Zelka."

Setting the bowl on the floor in front of her, she says, "You didn't hear enough yesterday?"

"I want to hear what you didn't tell anyone else."

Needing space, she averts her gaze and says the first thing that comes to mind. "I live in a cabin with my grandmother."

"What's your grandmother's name?"

Zelka smiles, remembering her grandmother's halibut stew and her soft nighttime snoring, a comfort in the darkness. "Sylvie."

"What an odd name. What does it mean?"

"It's a good name, for a good person." She picks up the bowl and drinks until it's empty, swallowing her irritation with the broth.

Arogem takes the bowl from her hands. "Let me get you more. You have an appetite this morning."

Zelka blushes, knowing his words hold a hidden fire. When he hands her a full bowl, he sits in the same place, his muscular arms wrapped around his knees. Zelka shifts on the hard ground, then swirls the amber broth in the bowl.

"I didn't mean to say that your grandmother's name is terrible. I've not heard those sounds together."

She nods, swallowing the rich, salty broth, enjoying the warmth it brings to her belly.

"Sylvie is your mother's mother?"

Zelka nods again.

"What was your mother's name?"

"Hazel." Now she swallows twice, but the lump in her throat has nothing to do with the broth.

"You miss her," Arogem says, his voice becoming softer.

"I do. Every day. I wish she was still in Osprey Bay with us."

"That's the name of where you live?"

She nods.

"Is there anyone else there besides you and your grandmother?" Arogem leans closer, still not touching her. She realizes he's doing his best to not scare her, which softens the mix of feelings his presence provokes in her.

"Keet, my brother, lives in the other house with his girlfriend, Nolee."

"It's strange to me that you don't live together, in the same place."

Zelka sets the empty bowl in front of her and dares a look into Arogem's eyes. "Maybe to you. But for them, it works."

Arogem grunts, straightening his legs and leaning back. Confused by the swooping sensation in her gut, Zelka tries not to look at the muscles in his torso. Instead, she says, "Keet is my older brother, and he's a great cook. He's a land Keykwin. He and Nolee only met a couple of years ago, but I can tell they're very close. It's funny, even though Nolee is human, she has this ability—." She stops, unsure whether she should tell Arogem about Nolee and their way of communicating through touch.

Arogem waits. In the silence, Zelka feels calmer, and without thinking, says, "She and I can communicate almost like Keykwin do when we're Blackfish."

Arogem looks toward the central fire. Following his gaze, Zelka sees the now-familiar sight of children running in and out among the adults, who are sitting or standing, eating, and talking. Some of the children are stringing black and white rocks on sinew, then tying them around one another's wrists and necks.

Still not looking at her, Arogem says, "That's very interesting. You must be good friends with this Nolee."

Zelka nods, smiling. "She holds a special place in my heart. She feels like family to me, even though we don't share the same blood."

"Where did you say Osprey Bay was?"

Zelka pauses, unsure where this line of questioning is going. In her confusion, she fails to notice that Arogem's body has tensed, or that his focus has changed to the gathering of people around the main fire. "Camas Island, in the Salish Sea," she answers.


Waking again to the disorientation of not knowing whether it is night or day, Zelka runs her hands through her hair and knots it behind her head, then picks her way through the sleeping children to sit by the main community fire. She aches for the sight of the sun and moon and stars. She wants to be back on land with her brother and Nolee, to sit next to her grandmother as they eat a meal together. She wants to be on the beach where she first set foot as a human. She looks upward again at the shining stones in the gray walls and distant ceiling of the Water Canyon House. They aren't the starry sky, but she appreciates their beauty.

Zelka approaches Byree and Yiskal. On a rumpled pile of blankets on the raised platform Yiskal sits, cradling the water clock in her lap as Byree feeds more wood onto the fire.

Zelka sits down, and Yiskal hands the water clock back to her mother.

Byree pours the water into an urn, then dries it with her own robes before rising and taking it to its resting place, a carved niche in the dark stone wall by Yiskal's bed.

Zelka picks up a garment with frayed ends. "Yiskal, would you show me how you're repairing this?"

"Why?"

"I want to do something to contribute."

"We don't need your help. We were doing fine before you came, and we're even better now that you've returned our water clock."

She wants to remind Yiskal that the cold, quiet house Keet and she had entered—soaking wet, unsure of their welcome—didn't look like a family that was doing fine. But she swallows her comment, listening to the meaning under Yiskal's words.

"The water clock will always be yours. No one will take it away again," Zelka says.

"Unless you and your land family change your minds."

"It's not ours to take. We don't want it."

"Why not?"

"It's a sad thing, but I think modern ways have replaced the wisdom of the water clock."

Yiskal doesn't answer, looking down instead at the robe she's hemming. "I don't understand what could possibly replace Earth's wisdom."

Yiskal is right, Zelka thinks, watching the rhythm of the bone needle in Yiskal's agile fingers as she pierces the fabric, leaving behind a smooth line of small, straight stitches. Yiskal notices Zelka watching. "There's a needle threaded here in front of me. Take it. You're driving me crazy with your staring."

Zelka smiles to herself as she picks up the needle, careful to not jab her fingers. Yiskal takes the robe from Zelka's lap, trims the frayed edge with a small knife, and makes a finger's-width fold. She shows Zelka how to knot the thread, and where to stitch.

As Zelka begins, she asks, "What are these robes made of?"

Yiskal cuts her eyes sideways at Zelka, who has her head bent over the cloth, concentrating on pushing the needle through without punching holes in her fingers.

"Why do you ask?"

Zelka looks up and shrugs. "I'm curious."

"Seaweed."

"What? How?"

It's Yiskal's turn to shrug. "You'd need to be apprenticed as a Cloth Weaver, like I am, to find out. Your job right now is to make your stitches straighter." She reaches over and gives the bunched hem a tug. "You'll have to wear this robe yourself. I wouldn't ask a member of my family to wear something so crooked!"

Yiskal's laughter softens her words. As the two women sew together, Yiskal's occasional criticisms hit Zelka's ears with fewer barbs.

When Zelka is done with the garment, she holds it up, smiling. The bottom undulates and puckers. She loves it. "I'm happy to wear this one. I think it looks unique."

Yiskal shakes her head, slanting a small smile at Zelka. "That's one word for it. Enough sitting around. I'm going hunting."

"I'll join you—"

The smile leaves Yiskal's face, and the hardness of her expression returns. "No. You stay here."

"I can't leave?" A surge of panic brings Zelka to her feet, but she's distracted by a soft touch at her elbow. Turning, she sees Byree. "Zelka, will you walk with me?"

Zelka looks toward Yiskal, who's already joined the group gathering near the door, readying themselves for the hunt. Nodding to Byree, she takes a breath and walks with her to the far end of the House. Here, away from the fire and its smoke, the stone walls glitter more brightly, though the light is dim. Despite the dimness, Zelka's surprised to see the faint outline of a door, a narrow slash of black against the gray stone walls.

"There's another door? Where does it go?"

Byree takes Zelka's hand in her own. Byree's skin is like thin parchment over her bones. Zelka feels an ache in her chest as she remembers her grandmother's hands.

"Our Council of Elders has been talking about you, Zelka. We would like to invite you to be initiated into our Water Canyon family," Byree says.

Faces swirl through Zelka's mind: Nolee, whose kindness helped her transition from sea to land; Keet, whose strength made her feel safe; Grandmother, whose presence comforts her in the nighttime. But the last image is a knife through her heart: Hazel, her mother, kneeling on the wet dock, keening as long silvery strands of her hair are cut away, then as Blackfish, her body limp and empty of life, sinking into the dark reaches of the ocean.

She feels Byree squeezing her hand and opens her eyes, surprised that she'd closed them.

"They are the people you love?" Byree asks.

Zelka nods, pulling her hand away to wipe the tears from her eyes. She'd forgotten their shared way of communicating through touch. It was a comfort with Nolee, but less so here, and Zelka realizes she must be on guard. Although she feels welcomed by these distant relations, she's still a stranger. She wonders if she would be a stranger after the initiation Byree has asked her about.

"Why did you bring me here, to this part of the House?" Her eyes are again drawn to the narrow door.

"It is a token of trust, Zelka. I cannot tell you where this door goes, and it won't open for you if you aren't a member of our family. But if you choose to become a part of us, we will share this, and more of our ways with you."

Zelka thinks of Yiskal. She thinks of the happiness she feels in the company of these people, the safety of being part of a whole. *Is that enough?* she wonders. And would it allow her to continue to discover her human form? Her time as a human had been short compared to the thirty years spent as orca, swimming with her mother and a small, adopted pod.

"You look as though you have more questions," Byree says.

Zelka thinks. "How does this House have air, and why can we have fires?"

Byree laughs, patting Zelka's shoulder. "Even I don't know the answer to those questions, Zelka. Just like life, this House has its mysteries."

Zelka nods. "Do I have to give up my family on land?"

"No. You give up nothing unless it's your wish. You commit to nothing, unless it is your calling."

"How do I find my calling?"

Byree turns and looks at the door again, then walks to it and runs her hand over it. The door is so black that Byree's skin seems to glow against it. Then she turns toward Zelka. "When you realized that the water clock wasn't yours, what did you do?"

"I knew we had to give it back, no matter what it took."

"You couldn't ignore that feeling?"

Zelka shakes her head. "It wasn't ours. I couldn't keep it, knowing its home was here with you."

"That's a calling. The Ancestors knew the water clock belonged in our

Water Canyon House. Through it, they called to you so you could return it to us."

Now Zelka joins Byree at the door, putting her hand against its rough surface, feeling the cold of ocean and stone through her fingertips. The door, like the walls, is impenetrable.

"I understand. Now that we've returned your water clock, what is my calling?"

Byree lays a gentle hand on Zelka's arm. "There is never any doubt when the Ancestors call to us. This Initiation ceremony has not been held in three generations' time. It's a sacred rite that many of us have only heard about in stories. In returning our water clock, the heart of our people, you have become one of us, Zelka. We perform the Initiation ceremony with our gratitude. We honor the great mystery of life, and how you came to us. The old traditions have a new life in you."

Zelka reaches for Byree's hand. Cradling it in her own, she's conscious of the waves of emotion engulfing her heart. Then she nods and releases Byree's hand. "What else do I need to know of your ways, Byree?"

"Has anyone told you of our history with humans?"

"No."

"Many generations ago, our people would entice humans into the ocean, then swim with them to this door. Once they were in the Water Canyon House, they became Keykwin."

Happiness floods Zelka as she imagines life with Nolee as Blackfish. But Byree's next words extinguish this feeling.

"Unlike Keykwin who chose to be initiated into our family, the humans we changed had to stay here and could only visit those on land for a small amount of time once every sixth moon."

"Are their descendants still with you?"

Byree nods. "Yes. But some rebelled and went to live back on land."

"What happened to them?"

"They died."

The floor spins under Zelka's feet, and she sits down, her trembling legs unable to support her. She feels Byree sit next to her, and the weight of her hand on her shoulder.

"This doesn't happen if you're already Keykwin, Zelka. We don't understand why the Water Canyon House has this effect on humans. Long ago, we chose to stop these abductions, and instead, to live outside of the human realm."

"But you're human, too. You live on the same earth, swim in the same waters."

"We're different. You're different. It's how Creator made us."

"How long has it been, Byree?"

"Been? Since what?"

"Since you've seen the blue sky and the moon?"

Byree sighs. "Many fire cycles. Many hunting cycles. Since before my hair turned white."

"You don't miss that part of the world?"

Her hands now resting in her lap, Byree smiles, and Zelka can see the woman she was through the wisdom of the Elder she's become.

"I didn't have the luxury of missing anything. My calling was to bring our water clock home. As it was my mother's calling, and my grandmother's."

"But now?"

Byree's smile disappears. "I've forgotten their light."

Zelka stands, holds out her hand to help Byree up. "Let's go see them now."

"We cannot."

"Why? You just said I can come and go as I please."

"Only if you choose to be initiated."

"If I choose not to, am I a prisoner?"

"No, Zelka, you're not our captive. But the Water Canyon House may have other ideas."

Zelka frowns, then walks toward the door. Placing both hands against the cold stone, she closes her eyes and imagines pushing through it into the water beyond, swimming as Blackfish. She inhales as much air as her lungs allow, closes her eyes, and pushes harder. The door stays shut. When she looks at her palms, she sees deep indentations; the stone had almost split her skin.

# CHAPTER FIVE

By the time I return home from signing the loan papers with Ava, night has dropped around Camas like a black cloak. As I walk to the kitchen, I inhale the mingled scents of wood and oil from the countertop, which is now a gleaming golden brown. Keet is leaning against it, a glass of Scotch in each hand.

"I thought we could celebrate both your new business and the beauty of this newly reconditioned countertop."

I smile, go up on tiptoe to kiss him, and take the glass, clinking it against his.

"Here's to Paws and Suds Pet Pantry."

"That's the name you and Ava decided on?"

I nod, unable to hide my pleasure. "We'll also offer doggy day care and dog walks, but that's for the future. First, we remodel."

I run my hand over the countertop's smooth surface, enjoying its golden sheen. "It looks great. It must've taken you all day."

Keet nods, covering my hand with his. "Worth it, though." He finishes his whisky in one long drink and puts his glass in the sink. "Want me to draw a bath for us?" The whisky sits soft in my empty belly, as does the new direction my life is going. For the first time, I feel as though my life is what I want it to be. Keet must sense this. Stepping closer to me, he kisses my smiling mouth. "Or dinner first?"

"Dinner first. I think we could both eat."

After dinner, we lie together in the bath, water lapping around us, Keet's cheek against my head and his breathing steady.

"Keet?"

A low hum begins in his chest, then tickles my ear with his breath. Taking this as acknowledgement, I ask, "Do you think I could try..." and stop. Fear of his answer silences my voice.

"Try what?"

I sit up, steam rising from my skin when the cool air hits it and turn to face Keet. "Remember when you said you wished you could show me your world when you're orca?"

"Yes."

"Can we try it now?"

His half-shut eyes open.

"I know you can't change here in the bathtub! I meant, could I try…"

"You want to see if you can experience what I'm experiencing."

I let out the breath I was holding and nod. Keet opens his arms, inviting me to lie back against him again, and I feel a rush of warmth when my skin meets his.

The house is silent, the only sounds are those of water settling and our breathing. I want to be in Keet's world to the point of obsession; every muscle in my body vibrates with this desire. I shake out my shoulders and settle into the place our bodies meet. My attention shrinks to the warmth of the bath, the heat of his skin, and the weight of my head against his shoulder. I relax again, this time letting my attention expand to encompass both of us, spiraling outward like a vine around a trellis.

"Keet?"

"Hmm?"

"I'm not getting anything."

"Not even absolute contentment? Try again."

A misty veil of steam rises around us, and I try to relax. I sink into the warm water around us, and the solid comfort of Keet's body behind me. Outside I can hear the faint crashing of the high tide on the beach.

"I bet you'd have to be orca for me to experience anything," I say.

Keet kisses my temple.


In bed, after Keet has rolled away from me, I lie awake, watching the moonlight through the open bedroom window. I try breathing myself into a calmer space, hoping the goddess of sleep will find me. Keet's lying on his side, and I move so my back is against his. He moves closer, and I feel the familiar rhythm of his ribcage. But even this favorite sleeping position doesn't lead me into somnolence.

Shifting back to my side of the bed, I throw off the covers; I feel as though I'm sweating on the inside. I stretch to find a cool spot, and sigh when I find one, ready for sleep at last.

Minutes or maybe hours later, I hear someone call my name. When I open my eyes, Fae is watching me, eyes glinting in the moonlight. She gets up with me, as does Wallace. Pulling on a pair of yoga pants, one of Keet's sweatshirts, and my battered down jacket, I consider—then reject—socks and shoes. Defying common sense, I want to sink my feet into the icy water of the Salish Sea. After easing closed the front door behind us, Fae runs to the shore and stands looking out toward the buoys. Wallace sits behind her, his hackles raised.

I follow his gaze and see a large male orca swimming in lazy arcs, then spy hopping as though he's watching us as well. When he releases an explosive breath then dives, I can't see the outline of a saddle patch behind his towering dorsal fin. He must be as large as Keet. Rolling my pant legs above my knees, I walk closer to the tideline, a squiggle of kelp and small branches denuded of their bark, left by the thundering water.

The intensity of my focus on this new orca is so strong that even the cold water against my calves doesn't stop me from wading deeper. He swims closer, gliding on the surface and I step farther into the roiling tide, feeling its pull across my knees. Behind me on the shore, the dogs' whining grows louder. Without thinking, I unspool my awareness toward this new orca, wondering if he's ill, or lost. The moonlight reflects off his black skin, and beneath the white of his eyepatch, I see that he's watching me.

He doesn't look ill and shows no signs of confusion. My pants, now drenched up to the thigh, stick to me, and I'm suddenly aware of how far I've strayed from shore. But something inside is tugging me forward; the water doesn't seem so cold, or the unfamiliar orca as unknown. My heartbeat slows, and I close my eyes, breathing in the chilly night air until it fills every bit of space in my lungs. As the current swirls around my legs, I imagine my body enlarging.

"Nolee!"

Keet's shout startles me, and I slip on a kelp-covered rock. Flinging out my arms out to rebalance myself, I'm caught by a wave and pulled farther from the shore. Spitting out salt and sand, I take a breath and kick back toward Keet, who's striding toward me through the water. I hear aloud exhale, and glance over my shoulder as the male orca submerges. With him goes the magnetic pull I felt in his presence. Then Keet's arms are around me, tugging me upright, and the cold finds me. My entire body quakes so hard that I'm surprised Keet's able to keep hold of me. I'm even more surprised that I'm not swimming with the strange male orca who moments ago had been gliding toward me on the moonlit, black-silk water.

"What were you doing out there?" Keet strips Nolee's wet clothes from her and drops his soaking pajama bottoms on the pile, leaving everything in a sodden heap by the door. Towel around his waist, another around his neck, he dries Nolee, then hands her a thick blanket to wrap up in. The dogs retreat to their beds, heads on paws, eyes and ears alert.

"Keet, stop!"

But he can't. He grabs another blanket, as though more layers will shield her against the fear he felt when he saw one of the Water Canyon orcas swimming toward her, hypnotizing her into the moonlit waters. He drops the blanket on the sofa and sinks into it, taking the towel from around his neck and rubbing his head, avoiding Nolee's gaze.

"What's the big deal?"

He realizes she doesn't know what almost happened to her. Until tonight, he thought the stories his grandparents told him were so far in the past as to be almost forgotten.

"I'll be right back." He gets up and goes into the bedroom to find something to wear. When he returns, Nolee's in the kitchen, standing by the stove. Holding the blanket closed against her with one hand, she turns on the burner underneath the kettle with the other.

"Do you want something hot to drink?" she asks. He shakes his head. "I'm going to put on something warmer, too. Be right back."

She passes by without touching him, her bare feet soft on the wood floor. The dogs watch her go, then lower their heads back to their paws; their eyes are closed, but four ears tilt toward the bedroom.

When the kettle shrieks, Keet turns off the heat, then pours the hot water over a ginger teabag in Nolee's favorite mug. When he looks at the clock, he sees it's almost four in the morning. Nolee's soft touch against his back startles him. Taking the mug from the counter, she sits down at the table and looks at him through narrowed eyes.

"What's going on, Keet?"

In the time it takes him to move from the counter to the table, he hasn't decided whether to tell her everything he knows. Would it scare her or entice her? She seems to be fixated on knowing what it feels like to be orca. Her desire to change herself mystifies him, and he wonders if what she has is enough: the new business, her family here on Camas Island, her friends. Him.

"I woke up and you weren't beside me. I got nervous."

"Why? My car is in the driveway. I couldn't sleep so I wanted to walk on the beach."

"Your pant legs were rolled up to your knees; it looked a lot like you were planning on going in the water."

She pauses, sips her tea, and sets her mug on the table with extra care.

"I was having a hot flash. I needed to cool down."

Her answer doesn't lessen the intensity of his feelings.

"Keet, tell me what this is about. I'm a little lost here."

He gets up and paces between the living room and the table.

"That bad?" she says, trying to laugh, trying to inject some levity into a situation she knows nothing about.

"I was worried when I woke up without you. When I came out into the living room, the first thing I saw was you in the water almost to your waist, and that orca swimming toward you. I didn't like that."

"Why?"

He sits again, agitation flickering through his limbs like heat lightning.

"Because I don't know who that orca is. Isn't that enough?"

She takes another sip. "What I don't get is why I don't feel anything with you, but when I was out there with an orca neither of us has seen before, it was as if I could slip into his consciousness as easily as blinking my eyes."

Keet, trapped between wanting to tell her the truth but not wanting to tempt her to seek another dangerous encounter, drums his fingers on the table. He remembers seeing Uncle Jerry do the same thing when what he knew that he *should* say and what he *wanted* to say were at odds.

"I don't get it either," he says.

"I'm not sure I believe you, Keet."

"I'm being as open with you as I can—"

"Which isn't the same as being as truthful as you need to be."

Trapped again, Keet gets up and resumes pacing, grateful she can't share the intensity of the conflict that has him in its jaws. He knows he needs to tell her more, at least enough to resolve her questions. Wiping a hand across his mouth, he begins. "Do you remember the story Grandmother told us, about Janadsila and the water clock?"

She smiles. "How could I forget?"

Keet tells it again the way he remembers it, focusing the story on the difference between the land-dwelling Keykwin and the underwater

Keykwin—people who subsist by relying on their orca natures to live together and hunt together, a tight-knit community in which survival depends upon the contributions of each member. They live deep in a canyon, in the Water Canyon House, and it is from this house that Keet had, two months earlier, returned. His sister Zelka remains there still.

"That male orca who almost coaxed you into the water with him is a member of the Water Canyon House."

"How do you know that?"

"Like Zelka, none of them have a saddle patch behind their dorsal fins."

Nolee drinks the last of her tea, looking at him over the rim. She sets the mug on a side table, then pushes her hair away from her face. "What else? You're not this rattled because they're a different part of your extended family."

Resolved to keep the biggest secret he knows about the People of the Water Canyon House, Keet says the first thing that occurs to him. "You could've become hypothermic again. You put your life at risk, and it was thoughtless."

Her green eyes narrow and her forehead creases in a frown. Keet moves to sit beside her; he'd like to take her hand but doesn't want to disturb the anger he senses rising inside her.

"The water was cold at first, but then I stopped noticing it. I was so close to feeling what it was like to change into orca. You took that away from me."

"Nolee, you don't understand."

"What don't I understand? If you'd left me alone, I would've found out." Her eyes harden, challenging him to doubt the truth of what she's saying.

He stares at her in disbelief. Instead of hearing that he thinks he knows the orca who was swimming in the bay, she focuses on having what she wants. She doesn't realize how close she is to discovering a secret that could threaten their lives together.

He stands and says, "I don't want to talk anymore. I'm going to the marina. We can talk when I get back."

"Keet—"

He raises his hands, defending himself against his own confusion. "I'll see you this afternoon." His head full of centuries of stories, he turns and walks to their bedroom to dress. Fearing its impact on the woman he wants to spend the rest of his life with, fearing that if he told her everything, it would only inflame her desire to become Keykwin, he still wonders why he's withholding crucial information from Nolee.

# CHAPTER SIX

"Four days of preparation, and four days of ceremony?" Zelka looks at Byree and Yiskal for confirmation. Seated across the crackling fire from her, they nod.

Zelka shifts, the cushion beneath her not thick enough to offset the floor's hardness. She wonders whether her perceptions will change if she accepts the invitation to become a part of the Water Canyon House family. Will the stone cavern's walls and the floor feel warmer?

Byree gives her a small smile and says, "An Initiation ceremony hasn't honored us in our lifetimes. If you embrace becoming a member of our family, you won't only become one of us. You'll also be remembered as the woman who reintroduced a cherished and ancient tradition into the lives of many."

Zelka stands, the sudden weight of responsibility bearing down on her like giant waves of an ocean storm. "I need to walk."

She retraces her steps to the tall stone door where she and Byree had spoken the day before. The smells of cooking disappear, as does the low drone of firelit conversations. She runs her fingers across the door, caressing the stone. A flutter of longing for it to open bursts behind her ribcage. She takes a breath and utters a single word. "Please."

The door stays closed. Zelka lowers herself to the floor, legs folded underneath her. Memories of her arrival, of telling Keet that she wanted to stay and connect with these people, these distant family members, dampen the urge to escape. The longer she stays, the more appealing she finds it being part of a bigger group. Her singular needs are woven into the needs of a race of people who were inhabiting this House before she arrived and will continue to live within its walls long after she's gone.

Zelka understands that her life is only a grain of sand amongst the numerous grains of sand that make up humankind. The people of the Water Canyon House are inviting her to share their world.  As much as she longs to return to the sea and the sky above it, as much as she wants to be amongst her own land family, she's also aware of a growing sense of belonging among the Water Canyon House people.

Standing, she touches the door and whispers, "Thank you." As she walks along the passageway, the ocean's chill seeping from its walls, she wonders if the House had, without her noticing, opened her eyes to a larger perspective about her kinship with these people.

Zelka enters the cavernous main room, scanning the faces around the fire, looking for Byree. Then, caught by their laughter and the firelight's soft glow, her longing disappears. She knows from the depths of her heart that she wishes to be one of them.

Byree is speaking with the younger men and women who will soon leave the House to hunt. When they disappear through the door, Byree turns to her, smiling, and Zelka speaks before she can change her mind. "Byree, I accept your invitation to become a member of your family."

Byree, beaming, says, "Then it shall be done."


After eight days of activity and very little sleep, Zelka feels a curious mix of exhaustion and elation. She sits and watches the flames dance around a log in the fire, listening to the soft conversational drone of her new family members. Her eyes are drooping with fatigue, but the sense of pure belonging makes her heart feel as light as an air bubble. She's been shown through the whole Water Canyon House, the narrow passages that lead to storerooms and workshops, and the well of fresh water that bubbles up from the floor.

She feels a warm shoulder against hers and turns. Arogem is smiling at her.

"Zelka, you're one of us now. Your cousins are happy you've joined us."

Nodding, Zelka leans into Arogem's warmth and rests her head on his shoulder.

When he doesn't finish his sentence, she raises her head. "What about you, Arogem? Are you happy to have a new cousin?"

Touching her face, he runs a finger along her cheek, then down her neck, stopping where her robe crosses her chest. "I don't want to be your cousin."

His dark gaze extinguishes the sparkle of joy she'd felt, and she shifts away from him.

When she doesn't answer, he takes her hands in his. "I want to be your beloved. The one who shares your bed at night."

Nervous, Zelka laughs, and he stops her laughter with a kiss. When he puts his hand on her thigh under her robe, she pulls away. "I'm not ready for that, Arogem."

He removes his hand, smiling as though he knows something she doesn't.

"You'll be ready soon enough, Zelka." He leans toward her again, but this time, she's ready. Wrapping her arms around herself, she walks toward Byree's fire. When she's sitting next to Yiskal, she finally takes a breath.

"Are you all right, cousin" Yiskal asks.

Zelka runs a shaking hand across her mouth. "Can I have some water, please?"

Yiskal hands her a stone tumbler and Zelka takes it and drinks, wetting her dry throat. Yiskal watches Arogem as he walks to the small group of men and women gathered in front of the door, readying to go out.

Zelka turns her attention toward the fire. "Is Arogem always this intense?"

Yiskal laughs. "Not always. You've caught his eye, it seems."

Zelka doesn't answer Yiskal's smile, instead pulling loose threads from the bottom of her robe, running her fingers over the pucker in the material. She feels Yiskal's warm hand on her shoulder. "Have you been with a man yet?"

Zelka shakes her head. "I haven't been with anyone, not that way." She wants Yiskal to know that although she's inexperienced, she's not ignorant. "I know what sex is. But I thought it would be easier because I would want to—"

Yiskal laughs. "There are women here who would give up their hair to have a chance with Arogem."

Zelka stops picking at her robe "What do you mean?"

"He's one of our best hunters. He's an artist, and…" Yiskal's voice drops to a whisper, "according to several women here, he's a skilled lover."

"Then why am I confused every time I'm near him?"

Yiskal shrugs. "Get over it, Cousin, and have some fun." Yiskal stands, pats Zelka's shoulder, then walks away, leaving Zelka's confusion and shame in her wake.

Later that night, hearing murmuring voices by the door, Zelka sits up in bed. When she forces open her sleep-heavy eyes, her family members are rising, some pulling their robes around their shoulders and others rubbing their faces to wake up. Yiskal is bent over the community fire, feeding it bits of dry wood, coaxing the flames higher. Arogem is wrapping his robe around his waist, knotting it above one hip and tucking a small knife into the knot. His hair still drips with water. As though he's felt her gaze, he looks over at her.

Heat suffuses Zelka's face, and she turns away, tugging her own robe higher on her chest, tightening its thick layers around her shoulders, hoping he sits anywhere other than next to her.

"May I sit with you, Zelka?"

She pushes the blankets she's slept in behind her and nods. *Why*, she thinks, *do I always lose the power of speech around him?*

She sits straighter and wills herself to speak. "Were you out hunting?"

A small, secret smile appears on Arogem's face, half of which is in shadow, half softened by the firelight. "You could say that."

"What does that mean?" Her voice is trembling, and she doesn't like what she's feeling in the pit of her belly.

"It means," he pauses. "I found enough, but not as much as I wanted."

Zelka's gaze drifts to Arogem's full lips. Another swirl of confusing emotion silences any reply she might make. She can't decide if she wants him or if he scares her. He's older than she is, and more experienced in every way she can think of. Especially—she stops that train of thought after an image of Arogem, naked above her and bathed in firelight, pops into her head. She looks away, afraid he'll be able to guess what, in a moment of unguardedness, she saw them doing.

"I have something for you." He rests his closed hand on her knee as he moves closer to her.

She leans in, consciously trying to relax.

"I remember you telling me that you missed the sun and stars, Zelka." When she glances into his eyes, Yiskal's words of encouragement float into her head. Before she can give in to her fear, she puts her lips against his. Arogem turns toward her, his arms snugging their bodies together. She breaks from his kiss with a gasp, blinking as though she's woken from a dream, churned by an emotion she can't name.

She talks so she doesn't have to kiss him again. "I do miss them. I miss everything."

Arogem moves in for another kiss, but Zelka leans away. He smiles and opens his hand. Four small, round stones—white and light gray, with holes in the middle—shine against his palm. As he moves his hand, they sparkle in the firelight.

"They're only stones, but I thought they might remind you of the stars." Supporting her hand with his, he pours the stones into her palm.

Zelka blinks again and tries to move away, but Arogem restrains her, his thumb stroking her hand in slow motion. Freezing as he leans in close to her, she feels her breath falter.

"I could give you much more than shiny rocks, Zelka," Arogem whispers against her ear.

Zelka feels an emotion she now knows surge through her, riding on a wave of anger. "I don't feel that way about you, Arogem." She yanks her hand away and the stones fall to the floor and scatter. "It's time for me to leave."

She stands and strides toward the door, all that separates her from the ocean and her family on Camas Island. She's alone; no crowd of friendly people are pushing her toward it, as they did with Keet. She closes her eyes as she gets closer, willing it to open. But when her hands meet the rough surface, it might as well be a wall.

She balls her hands into fists, exhales, and runs to the narrow door at the other end of the House. No one follows her. Before she reaches the door, she sees small pools of water on the stone floor. Looking closer, she sees that they're footprints, and that they begin at the door. Hope flaring once more, she takes a deep breath and rushes toward the dark rectangle, but it, too, refuses to open.

Turning, she once again tries the main entrance, closing her eyes, her will to swim free lending strength to her approach. No more begging or pleading. She's getting out.

The shock of her open palms against the immovable stone startles Zelka, and her eyes fly open. Agitated, she pushes again, then stops when she hears Arogem.

"You can't return to the sea unless you leave something of yourself here. With us."

She turns toward his voice, frowning. "I don't understand. Keet left. Why can't I?"

"You are now part of our Water Canyon family," Byree says, stepping away from the circle around the fire. Her hair hangs loose past her shoulders, waves of silver and white floating next to the darkness of her face. "The House knows this and requires that some part of you remain here when you leave, so that the circle of family isn't broken."

"I'm happy to do this. Tell me what I need to leave."

"I don't know."

Zelka breathes heavily, thinking. She turns to Arogem, holding out her left hand. "Your knife, please, Arogem."

He moves toward her, face guarded. As he places the hilt in her hand, he tries to stroke her palm, but she closes her hand before he can. Bringing the knife upward, with her other hand, she lifts a lock of hair from the nape of her neck, tilts her head, and slices off a silken skein. As she holds it clenched in her fist, the black tendrils sway in the current of her breath. Handing the knife back to Arogem, Zelka gives the hair to Byree, nods, then motions to the door.

Again, she breathes deeply and holds her hands in front of her, heady with the anticipation of being freed from a house that the sun never touches. But the door doesn't move.

"The Water Canyon House requires more of a sacrifice than a puny lock of hair, Zee." Zelka whirls from the door toward Arogem, facing his taunting gaze and the use of her familiar name, saying it as though he's wiping his feet on it.

She places her left hand to her shoulder, where the robe is held closed with carved bone. Commanding Arogem's gaze, knowing he cannot look away from what she's doing, she slips the point of the bone across one finger as she loosens it from the material. Raising her hand, she sees the firelight's sparks in the dark red blood running from her finger to her wrist. The robe falls to the floor, puddling around her ankles, and she steps out of it. Hair cascading around her hips, blood dripping from her elbow in a thick rivulet, Zelka takes a step toward Arogem, sees his eyes absorbing every inch of her body, thinking it's his. She pauses for a moment and feels power bolt through her. This time, surely, she will escape this House and return to the salt-laden air and the embrace of her family.

Whirling in place, she goes once again to the door, running her cut finger along its rough surface, silent through the jagged pain of the stone against her raw flesh. Feeling the people's gaze on her, she takes a deep breath and pushes, willing her body to expand outward. She closes her eyes, breathes again, and pushes harder, driving her cut finger into the stone.

The door doesn't open.

Zelka drops her hands to her sides. She wants to hang her head and slink away, or rage against the door and the twisted magic of the Water

Canyon House. Instead, she steps back and gathers her robe around her body, sharp needles of pain shooting from her cut finger. Looking at the jagged cut, she realizes another, smaller hand is gently holding her own. Yiskal.

"Come, cousin. Let me take care of your hand."

Zelka follows Yiskal to a fire, where Yiskal bathes her hand in a stone basin filled with warm salt water. That night, she sleeps with Byree and Yiskal, her back against the chilly wall of the House. Gathering her thick hair in front of her, she clutches it to her chest, taking comfort in its softness. She's like that still when she wakes in the morning. As she rises from dreams of sunlight and trees, Zelka knows exactly what she must give into the Water Canyon House's keeping.

# CHAPTER SEVEN

Keet leaves without eating breakfast. The door clicks shut behind him, and when he starts his 4Runner, I can hear the strains of guitars and drums as he throws the vehicle into reverse.  He backs out of the driveway, the lights of his vehicle swaying as he travels down the road. I want to run after him and apologize and kick the tires flinging mud behind them. The old Nolee would comply. The new Nolee, a woman I've coaxed out of hiding, will do what she damn well wants.

Filled with sheer rebelliousness despite Keet's concern, I put on some shorts and a sweatshirt and take the dogs out to the beach again. Legs stippled with goosebumps, I wade into the water, looking out at the horizon, hoping the orca will appear again.

As my toes go numb, a shiver starts at my feet and goes to my head; I'm freezing from the inside out. I stomp out of the sea. After a hot shower and breakfast, I see I have two texts. Swiping open the phone, I hope one is from Keet, but am still too angry to admit it, even to myself.

One is from Abbie, asking about summer dates to visit. I flip the calendar hanging on the wall, calculating the time it will take to open the shop and my hours once we do. I text her back, saying July might be best. This gives Ava and I several months to get things up and running. As if she's read my mind in advance, the other text is from Ava, asking when I'll be in today. Breathing a sigh of relief, I text back. *Within the hour. See you soon!*

The exclamation point seems like a lie, taunting me with its false humor. Telling me that arguing with Keet has left me feeling worse than I'm willing to admit. After hovering over Keet's name, wondering whether to text an apology, I drop the phone on the table. What could I say that I haven't said already?

"C'mon, dogs, let's go to our new store."

Grabbing my backpack and car keys, I leave the house in a flurry of canine excitement and a slammed door. I drive too fast down the dirt road, distracted by anger and worry, ignoring the light returning to the forest and skies. My anger feels like a bomb, obliterating any worry about the argument Keet and I had.

Later that morning, I stand, hands on hips, panting for air. Ava and I have moved two sets of tall wooden shelves, painted the walls a pale green, stacked three pallets-worth of dog food, and emptied everything out of the storeroom in the back. Sitting on boxes, we have some water as we wait on the builders and plumber scheduled to arrive that afternoon.

"You alright?"

"I am, you?"

She laughs, wiping a hand across her brow. "Great. I'm really excited about our store."

"Me, too." Though I smile, the dark cloud of the earlier argument—our most serious ever—leaves me with a sense of disconnection from everything going on around me.

Ava puts a hand on my arm. "Just want to be sure you're okay, Nolee. You seem a little distracted."

I cover her hand with my own. "I'm good, Ava. Just have some family things on my mind." Releasing her hand, I move toward the front of the store. "Let's paint these shelves."

Rather than letting my thoughts run back toward Keet, and the expression on his face when he said he couldn't talk anymore, I vow to focus on what Ava and I need to accomplish. But I keep seeing the hard line of Keet's shoulders as he walked out of the door, hearing the quick silencing of his favorite music from inside his car. I don't want this tangle of anxiety sitting in my stomach, reaching for my heart and making it ache. But if I shut that part of myself away, I might never find out what it's like to be an orca, unbound by gravity, living in a world reflected in waves of sound. The desire for that experience is bigger than any desire to become invisible again—bigger, even, than my fear of having alienated Keet.


Later that afternoon, I groan as I unfold myself out of the car. Even though the drive home is short, I feel stiff. Stretching my arms toward the sky to loosen up, I let Fae and Wallace out of the back seat, then kneel to scratch their backs and chests. As I laugh at their exuberance, I forget for a moment the discord with Keet.

"They're glad to be home." Keet's deep voice shatters my momentary joy. I stand and look at him, feeling the smile fading from my face.

"So am I," he says, trying for a smile.

I force a return smile. Uncertain how to start, I glance at the dogs, taking solace in their wagging tails and the simplicity of this moment.

Then Keet says, "You're right. I wasn't being honest with you."

"Okay."

"I've made some dinner. Are you hungry?

My smile is easier after the mention of food; Ava and I worked through lunch and my stomach makes its emptiness known, rumbling in answer to the mention of food.

"I'm starving."

Keet's smile eases, too. His hand on the small of my back, we follow the dogs inside. In the center of the table is a platter of pink-fleshed salmon, accompanied by roasted potatoes, golden and sprinkled with rosemary, steamed broccoli, and a loaf of my favorite sourdough bread from the Sugar Bear bakery in Northsound.

Keet notices me scanning the kitchen for the dogs' bowls and says, "Fae and Wallace are eating in the laundry room."

"Thanks." Dropping my backpack next to my shoes, I sit at the table. Keet pours water for each of us, then sits across from me, and we pile our plates with food. Minutes go by. The sea's distant pounding and faint birdsong fill the silence between us. I concentrate on my plate, uncertain and still a little anxious about where this conversation will lead.

"I haven't shared all my knowledge about the people in the Water Canyon House."

"Okay."

"We keep secrets, and we hold promises, Nolee."

His use of my first name rather than the intimacy of Lia, my nickname, concerns me. The only thing worse would be if he called me by my full name, Magnolia.

I set my fork down and wipe my mouth. "What else do I need to be aware of?"

Keet shifts in his chair as he taps his plate with his fork. He places his fork on the table and then speaks.

"I don't want to keep anything from you. But my desire to share everything about myself is at war with the promises I made to my grandmother."

"Keet, if this is a secret you promised to keep—"

"It is. But if I don't share it with you, you'll never understand why I'm upset."

"Do we need to include Grandmother in our conversation?"

Keet brings his gaze up to mine and tries to smile. "It still surprises me when I hear you call her that."

"Me, too. But I like it."

"She asked you to call her Grandmother. That means she considers you family. And as family, you have a right to any knowledge we have."

"If it helps, I'll promise not to share it."

Keet, still looking at me, sets his jaw, sits up straighter.

"The Water Canyon House Keykwin have the ability—or they used to—to change humans. Into Keykwin."

I don't quite drop my fork, but a blaze of curiosity and excitement burns as I imagine being able to join Keet in ways I can't do as a human woman.

"The orca we saw this morning was going to do that?"

Keet shrugs, his eyes on his plate. "I'm not sure, but the way you were oblivious to the cold tells me he was doing something to you."

"Why me, though?"

Keet looks at me, a half-smile offsetting the worry that wrinkles his forehead.

"I don't know. And I don't like not knowing."

"Do you think I'm in danger? I'm strong enough to resist."

"Nolee, he hypnotized you somehow. Besides, I think the Water Canyon House Keykwin don't need to change humans anymore."

"Why?"

"Long ago, they needed to increase their community. But while I was in the Water Canyon House, I heard that changing humans into Keykwin isn't part of their recent memory, or even in the memories of their Elders. That knowledge might have been lost."

Through the window, the sky is growing darker, blue shading into night, the fog dropping down like a pewter curtain

"That would explain the sensations I had when I saw the orca."

"What were they?"

"My body felt bigger, and the water was almost warm."

"Once they turn you into one of their own, you are, for the rest of your life, bound to them and their house in the Water Canyon."

"What does that mean?"

"Nolee, you stop being human. You're Keykwin. For six months of the year, you have to live with them to stay alive."

I look across at Keet. His brow is still wrinkled, and the dark skin under his eyes tells me he didn't get much sleep, either.

"Does that mean you and I couldn't live together for six months?"

He nods. "That means six months in a row. You'd be imprisoned in a deep canyon, in a cave where the only light is from fires, and with only strangers for company."

"You'd join me in this Water Canyon House, right?"

He shakes his head. "It almost killed me getting there the first time. If it hadn't been for Zelka…" He shivers, and I ask him what he'd remembered.

Keet rubs his eyes. "The experience of almost drowning, which is still a little too fresh."

"Every year, for six months, I'd have to live in the Water Canyon House? I wouldn't be able to go back and forth as I chose?"

"Your life would be different than the life you've always known, Nolee. You'd become a prisoner. The life you're building here would be over." He pauses, then says, "I think the reason you connected with that male orca this morning is because he knew what he was doing."

"Your branch of the family doesn't do this?"

"We don't. It's not our way. Which is why there are so few of us, and so many of them."

I push away from the table, moving to sit next to Keet. He takes my hand in his.

"Why didn't you tell me?"

Keet shifts in his chair, keeping his eyes focused on mine.

"Some knowledge must be protected." His voice trails off, and I see uncertainty cross his face.

"I understand, Keet." He gives me a quick smile, squeezing my hand. "But I thought we'd become close enough to be able to share more. I guess besides being confused about what made you so mad this morning, I'm also hurt."

Before he answers me, he lets out a slow exhale. "I was mad, and scared."

"Because?"

"Because I was aware you were being manipulated into doing something without knowing the consequences. Those consequences affect me, too. I would lose you for the rest of your life."

Without knowing how I got there, I'm in Keet's arms, his head buried against my neck. Squeezing him, I inhale the wind and salt of the sea, and the deeper musk of his skin.

"I'm sorry, Keet. I had no idea. It was so seductive. That feeling of becoming orca, of being able to experience what you've been your whole life—"

"So far."

We break into nervous laughter at a joke we'd shared when we first met. There's the gentle pressure of his lips as he kisses my neck and my jaw, then puts his hands to either side of my face. His face only inches away, he whispers, "I'm sorry, too, Lia."

I shiver, as much from relief as from the warmth of Keet's body next to mine. I've never experienced this: what it's like to reach a resolution after an argument and, almost impossibly, love the person even more afterward. A fierce longing surges through me as we hold each other. "Let's go to bed."

"I promise to be more open with you," he murmurs against my ear. As we topple onto the bed, Keet's kisses set alight my longing.

# CHAPTER EIGHT

"Cousin, I'd like to return to my land family, with your blessing."

At first, Byree doesn't reply. Then, putting her hands behind her back, she looks at Zelka. "You have my blessing. But, my child, the Water Canyon House needs more than that."

"The House has my blood, my promises to return, and my desire to return to land. I have one last offering."

Zelka searches Byree's dark eyes; like her own, each brown iris is bordered by a thin lavender ring.

"Before you make that offering, talk with Arogem. Make your peace with him. Our House protests when there is conflict."

Zelka looks over her shoulder and sees Arogem watching her. Sighing, she tightens the soft robe around herself and strides toward him, doing her best to understand his emotions. Although she doesn't want to be with him, her realization that at the core of his need is a loneliness she too has carried, softens her heart toward him.

Arms folded around herself, she faces him, then relaxes when she sees the look in his eyes. Being rebuffed seems to have extinguished his desire, but she has no idea what to say in response to his pain.

Finally, she takes a breath and gives Arogem a soft smile. Words fall from her mouth before she can think of them. "When I witnessed my mother's lifeless body descend onto the ocean floor, I was by myself, despite being surrounded by my Blackfish family."

Arogem's eyes glimmer and he looks away from her. She resists the urge to reach out and comfort him; solace is not what he wants from her.

"My mother was the only one I had for a long time. She knew me in ways no one else ever will. Now I have new families, one here," she sweeps her gaze around the room, "and one on the land. I'm not alone, Arogem. My time here is over for now. I need to see my land family again."

Arogem returns his gaze to hers, taking her in as though seeing her for the first time.

He reaches for her bandaged left hand, then stops himself.

"I don't understand this, Zelka. I don't understand you. But I would have to be blind to not see that you are a woman of both sea and land."

"You don't need to understand, Cousin." Arogem winces at the word, hurt by its use. He's a family member, not a beloved. Though they stand eye to eye, the distance between them grows. The other members of the clan tend to their fires and children, indistinct murmurs of conversation humming around them.

Zelka pauses, wanting to lighten the mood between them. "They sound like bees, don't they?" she says.

"I've never heard bees." Though Arogem steps away, he holds her gaze, seeing eyes that are so like the rest of his family's, knowing she is also unlike any of them. Softening his voice, he adds, "Maybe you could show them to me. I'd like to hear their sounds."

"There's a hive at a farm on the island where I live. There are so many bees, and the honey is the sweetest thing I've ever tasted." She pauses, considering her next question, taking an inevitable step closer to doing the thing she least wants to do.

"Arogem, do you still have the little stones you carved for me?"

He nods, dipping his hand into a pocket and pulling out the stones.

"I have an idea that might appease the Water Canyon House, and I'd like to include those stones."

He nods and drops the stones into her outstretched palm. She shakes off the bandage, laying her still oozing finger against each stone. The rock shines red as her blood finds the surface, then absorbs it, returning to a white that sparkles brighter. Zelka bends to pick up the cloth that was wrapped around her finger and stanches the blood, then closes her hand around the stones.

"Thank you, Arogem. May the waters always embrace you."

"Zelka, one day I'm going to change your mind. You'll come back to me."

Zelka looks away before her eyes can reveal the pity she feels for him. Instead, she walks to Byree and Yiskal, who are sitting near the fire sharing a steaming bowl of fish broth from the previous night's meal. Lowering herself to sit between them, she looks at Byree first.

"Grandmother, I have a gift for the House."

Byree eyes the stones nestled in Zelka's palm before looking up at her. "What is your intention, child?"

Yiskal bumps Zelka's hip as she moves closer and reaches for the cloth bunched in Zelka's hand. She removes it and, bringing a bowl of warm saltwater close, guides Zelka's hand into it. Zelka's eyes don't leave Byree's, even as the sting bites into her oozing flesh.

"My intention is to leave my hair with the Water Canyon House, with you as its guardian."

Byree's eyes open wide. She touches Zelka's chin and turns her head. Zelka feels Byree's hands on her hair as she strokes it, then lifts it from the ground where it lies in a shiny pile. "Are you sure?" she asks.

"I am."

"If this doesn't work…" Byree doesn't finish the sentence. Zelka knows what comes after. If it doesn't work, she will be trapped by some ancient binding. The same magic that shelters its people within the stone walls will keep her here. Her hair will be gone, and she'll continue to live away from sunlight.

Zelka feels the weight of Byree's hand on her shoulder as she stands, before walking to a shelf set deep in the wall. Eyes closed, lips moving in a silent prayer, she reaches until her body is pressed against the shelf. When she pulls out her hand, she's holding a stone knife as long as her forearm.

"Mother, not that one." At Arogem's voice, the rest of the clan turn, firelight reflecting in their eyes.

Byree stands in front of Zelka. "Stand up, Zelka."

She looks at Yiskal bent over Zelka's hand, which she's dried and wrapped in a clean bandage. Laying her forehead against the top of Yiskal's head, Zelka whispers her thanks, then turns and faces Byree. The stone knife glitters in her hand.

"I give my hair into your keeping, Byree, guardian of the water clock."

Byree holds the stone knife as though she's holding a platter, much like her brother had held a platter of fish he'd baked. The longing for home expands, pushing against her ribs.

Behind her, Yiskal puts both hands on Zelka's shoulders. "May I braid it for you?"

"Yes. Please include these." She opens her hand holding the stones. They glitter in the firelight. Is it her imagination, or do they grow warmer? Are her eyes deceiving her, or do they take on a deep red shimmer, her blood glowing at their center? She blinks, and the crimson disappears. When she tries to sit, Yiskal stops her. "We'll stand."

Zelka watches as each member of her new family also stands. Mothers cradling infants at their breast, men and women, young and elder. They form a large circle framed in firelight against the shadow of the House beyond. A young woman, the lavender ring around her dark eyes thick and bright, breaks away from the circle and opens her hands to receive the stones from Yiskal.

Yiskal combs her fingers through Zelka's hair, running the strands into a smooth sheet that billows across her shoulders and down her back, brushing her thighs. Tears bloom in Zelka's eyes; raising her chin, she tries to blink them back. But they spill across her cheeks, falling to the floor, diamonds in the firelight, small dark circles like raindrops at her feet.

Singing, Yiskal begins to shape the braid. Zelka closes her eyes. Despite the tugging on her scalp, the song and the warmth of Yiskal's touch soothes her, and her tears stop. A memory of her mother swimming beside her rises, her mother singing as she slept and swam. She hears something of her mother's song in Yiskal's.

Zelka knows she will swim away from the Water Canyon House and return to her land family. She feels it in each racing beat of her heart.

Yiskal plaits the braid, her rhythm punctuated only by the click of a stone added to her hair. Her voice breaks through Zelka's trance. "Zelka, please tear a small strip from the bottom of your robe." She holds the rope of Zelka's hair so she can kneel. Finding a frayed edge, she tears the soft material, then holds it over her shoulder. Yiskal takes it from her, and the hypnotic singing and tugging returns. Zelka hums the song with Yiskal, then listens in amazement as the rest of her family takes up the song—voices high and low, the shared sound weaving around them as Yiskal weaves Zelka's hair.

The tugging stops. Byree walks behind Zelka and stretches the braid. The pull of her hair is like sharp needles in her scalp.

"Do you willingly give your hair to us, Zelka William Eils Noland of land and sea?"

Zelka swallows, wanting her voice to sound strong and true.

"Yes."

"Do you promise to return to this House of your own free will and desire to be with us?"

This promise has more weight than Zelka expected. Closing her eyes again, she descends into her mind and sees every face of her new family, hears their breathing. Opening her eyes, she says, "I promise."

She lifts her chin toward the ceiling as the pull at the back of her head grows stronger. She hears a ripping sound, and the needles in her scalp tingle in protest. Studying the fire-blackened ceiling, she wonders if it's her imagination or if the ceiling is higher than it was. Suddenly, the tension is released.

Byree stands, stone knife in one hand, Zelka's long braid in the other. Even raised above her head, the tip of the braid almost touches the floor. Stones sparkle within its tight weave, and the white cloth that snakes through it reminds Zelka of the white-on-black curve of her mother's belly. Zelka touches the back of her head, feeling its bristly surface. Focusing her attention on the beauty of her hair in Byree's grip, she lowers her hand.

The people draw closer and form a path to the door. Zelka turns and walks toward it, then stops in front of it, her family silent behind her. This time, when she undoes the bone clasp, she is gentle. Stepping out of the robe, she places the clasp on top of the garment, then unwraps the bandage from her left hand and drops it as well. Cool air runs up her bare skin, casting its chill hand on the back of her thighs, her waist, her exposed neck. All sound disappears as she walks toward the door.

Holding the sense of her Blackfish form close to her aching heart, she takes a deep breath and plunges forward. The last thing she hears is Arogem calling her name.

When she breaks through the galloping waves in orca form, her cries of joy and anguish mix with the shrieks of the gulls wheeling overhead.

# CHAPTER NINE

I take my tea to the beach. Some pink sky mornings, the sea whispers to me and the breeze that touches the whitecaps caresses my face. Today, it's crashing into the shoreline and punching the rocks, flinging its frothy waves into the air. The neighboring islands are coated in gray fog, and where the sun is supposed to be looks like a dimmed spotlight. Finishing my tea, I go back inside and flip the calendar to March wondering when Zelka will be home. Given what Keet has told me about the Water Canyon House, I wonder if she'll be allowed to come home at all. My impression is that they prefer to keep their family close.

As though thoughts of Zelka have conjured her from the dull gray water, when I look out the window, I see her crossed arms on the dock and the rest of her body submerged in the water below. Her head rests on her arms. I blink, but if I had any doubts, Wallace's whining presence at the door dispels them. His front paws dance as he waits for me to open it.

"Zee's back! Go say hi." A gust of wet air hits me as Wallace streaks out, followed closely by Fae.

Bundled into my old down jacket, I wrap Sylvie's scarf around my neck and grab a towel and terrycloth robe. Jogging over the rocky ground, I hear Zee's laughter and Wallace's joyful exclamations as he licks her face. His front end is down, and his hind end is up in the air, long tail whipping from side to side.

"Wallace, let her out of the water." Briefly, he turns toward me then sits on the edge, his eyes never leaving Zelka. I put the towel beside him.

"I'm so glad you're here, Zee…" I say, my sentence cut short as she boosts herself onto the dock. She bows her head, and I see her bare neck, the frayed ends of short hair clinging to the curve of her skull. Sitting with her feet still in the water, she wraps the towel around her head, throwing me an embarrassed glance. I hand her the robe.

"What happened to your hair?"

She ties the belt around her waist and lifts her feet from the water, and my gaze is drawn to her ankles. "The lines around your ankles are black."

Her silence unnerves me, as does her reluctance to make eye contact. Instead, she kneels to enfold Wallace in a hug. I realize I may be coming on too strong and try to dial back my curiosity.

"Sorry about all the questions," I say. "Let's go inside so you can get changed, and I'll heat up something for our lunch." Fae trots behind me as I walk back to the house, but when I glance over my shoulder, I see that Zelka is still kneeling on the dock, her arms around Wallace.

As I lower the heat under the bubbling potato soup, I hear the door open and the click of Wallace's nails on the wood floor. I put two bowls of soup and a plate of buttered bread on the table, then sit down and wait, watching the fog swirl along the surface of the water outside the window. Within minutes, Zelka sits next to me; the towel is still wrapped around her head, but she's changed into black sweatpants and a purple sweatshirt.

"Keet and Sylvie drove to town, but they'll be back soon."

She nods, gazing down. We eat in silence, the only sound the clinking of our spoons against the bowls. Finally, Zelka puts down her spoon and tips the bowl to her mouth. After she finishes, she sighs, then puts her open hand on the table in front of me. I take it and feel the tremor running through her fingers.

Zelka says, "I can't show you everything, because my family under the waves asked to hold the ceremony sacred. The power is diluted if we talk about it too much." I nod, understanding. I close my eyes, and the pictures that flow into my mind are as clear and bright as a movie.

A dark, cavernous space fills with smoke, and I hear occasional laughter or cries of children. Zelka's voice interrupts the blackness. "That's cedar smoke, to signify the air, and purify our thoughts and hearts. We fasted this whole day and had only the main fire burning for warmth."

The scene in Zelka's memory changes into a burst of light and warmth. People are dancing and singing around the many fires and their orange and yellow lights. Shadows bend on stone walls, elongated figures that wave like kelp beds. Laden trestle tables are piled with food, most of which I don't recognize except for the bodies of fish. I see platters heaped with meat, stone bowls overflowing with greens, pitchers of liquids of all colors. When a question arises in my mind, Zelka answers, "Those are different kinds of fish broths, as well as water from the House's spring. This is the day of fire, of purification, of giving thanks for its warmth."

The fires fade, and the scene grows darker. People lie or sit with closed eyes; some splay their hands on the floor. "This is the day we honor the Earth and all she gives us. We spend the day in quiet reflection, hearing her rhythms and giving thanks for her care of us."

I shift in my chair, adjusting my hand in Zelka's. A question runs through my mind again: *why can I experience Zelka's inner world, yet not Keet's?* I push away that thought as the next scene floats into my head with such clarity that I gasp.

Dozens of orcas surround me, swimming between beams of sunlit water. I sense the bump and slide of the young orcas nudging me to play. Their mothers send out intermittent whistles for them. When I breach, the slap of waves echoes in my own body. The water cocoons me, rocking me back and forth as I swim. I dive into black depths, where my vision is expanded by the clicks I send out from my head. A tickle along my lower jaw transforms into the image of a rocky ridge, and I follow my pod members, chasing the low echo of squid hiding in waters deeper even than the Water Canyon House. With their short tentacles and arrow-shaped heads, they're easy to find. We are hunting for a feast that marks the end of the initiation ceremony.

"On that day, I had to swim deeper than I ever had. It was a test of my endurance and skill to hunt for a meal for my new family. Before returning to the House, I caught six squid, honoring the water from which all life springs."

Zelka continues, her soft voice startling after being bathed in the sound of clicks and whistles. The sunlit water is gone, the giant pod of orcas fades into blackness, and now there is only Zee's voice filling the void.

"We ate and drank that night. The very last drink was broth laced with a plant from farther north in the canyon. I fell asleep and had wild dreams. When I woke up, the lines around my ankles were pitch black."

In my mind, beams of bright light part the blackness with a shimmering amorphous shape at its middle. Before I can think why it looks familiar, it's replaced with the face of a square-jawed and handsome man, black hair reaching past his shoulders. The face moves closer, and a feeling of repulsion shoots through me before the face shatters into a thousand pieces and scatters. A woman with long white hair emerges, her face wrinkled and brown. In one hand, she holds a stone knife. The other holds a long rope of black hair woven with stones and a piece of pale material that suggests the undulation of white on an orca's belly. Zelka releases my hand and the woman disappears. I open my eyes.

I smile into Zelka's eyes, thanking her for sharing her initiation experience. The disagreement Keet and I had regarding my close encounter with the male orca comes to mind. I'm beyond mere curiosity about becoming Keykwin myself. After experiencing Zelka's time as orca, I want to *be* Keykwin, consequences be damned.

Zelka seems unaware of my thoughts. "That's where my hair ended up. That's why the lines on my ankles are darker. I'm now a member of the Water Canyon House family."

"You're also a member of this family, Zee."

"I know. My heart is here, Nolee, with you and Keet and Grandmother."

My hand flies to my mouth as a thought occurs to me. "Zee, do you have to live in the Water Canyon House for six months of the year?"

Her eyes drift away from mine. She chooses her words after a long silence. "I come and go as I wish. Why do you ask?"

My voice shaking, I tell her about the unfamiliar male orca who visited, how Keet had dragged me back to land, and what he said would've happened had I gone into the water with the orca. The longer I talk, the angrier Zelka's expression becomes. Her eyes darken, the lavender ring around the iris shading into dark purple.

"You need to stay away from the Water Canyon House people, Nolee. Unless you're familiar with the Blackfish you're seeing, stay away."

"Zee, you don't need to convince me. Losing the life Keet and I have is enough incentive."

But a traitorous longing to experience what it's like to become something else, to perceive the world from inside another skin, roils in me. I stomp on the thought, kick it away, focus on the young woman across from me who's become a second daughter.

"I'm so glad you're back."

She gives me a smile. "Me, too. But I'm kind of overwhelmed. It used to be just me and my mom. Now I'm related to dozens of people." Unwinding the towel, she runs both hands through her hair, a sigh escaping from her downturned mouth. "Can you help me do something with this?" She starts to cry, and I embrace her while she sobs, feeling her fear and loss, and another emotion I can't pinpoint.

"Zee, what is it?"

She shakes her head against my shoulder. When she answers, her voice is muffled. "Is it stupid that I'm crying about my hair?"

"No, honey, it's not. People can be sad about lots of things."

She sits up, using her napkin to wipe her face and dab at her nose. "Losing my mom was the saddest I've ever felt, but this is different."

"Are you sad about your choice to not be with Arogem?"

She barks out a laugh, shaking her head. "No! He's not for me, but I couldn't leave the House until he and I had no conflict between us."

"The House wouldn't let you out?"

She shakes her head again, tucking the few longer strands of hair behind her ears. "Byree…" She looks at me. "Did Keet tell you about everyone?"

"He did. He also mentioned Yiskal's efforts to get him into her bed."

Zelka flushes. "That's where Arogem wanted me, too. In his bed."

She shifts in her chair, turning to face me. "I'd tried to leave the House the day before. I left my robe, cut my finger, and traced my blood around the door, but it didn't work."

"Were you trapped there?"

Zelka nods. "That was my impression. But Byree told me that the Water Canyon House doesn't like unresolved conflict in the family. I made my peace with Arogem and left my hair with Byree."

"And you aren't sure which act was the one that the House accepted?"

She dabs at her eyes with the napkin again. "I'm not. Could've been both, I guess." She rubs the back of her head, then looks at me, a light of understanding dawning in her eyes. "My hair was the only thing that was mine alone."

I wait to hear what else she's realized.

"My mom claimed everything about me. The first thing I did to get to know myself was change into being human. After that, it was my hair. I didn't cut it when she died, and I had no intention of ever cutting it."

"And now it's gone."

She cradles the back of her skull in both hands, her silence more deafening than her grief. I place my hand on her back.

"Your hair is still yours, Zee."

She looks up at me, tears drying on her cheeks.

"It's a different length, but you can cut it or dye it purple or shave it all off, for that matter. It's still yours."

She gives me a hesitant smile. "Amethyst." I laugh, remembering how fascinated she was by a stranger's purple hair.

"Will you help me choose how to cut my hair, Nolee?"

I pull my phone toward me and flick open a web browser. "We can do that right now."

Keet, Nolee, Sylvie, and Zelka sit in Keet and Nolee's living room. Sylvie sees the path of the blade used to cut Zelka's hair, the ends ragged and uneven. She turns Zelka away from her and softly touches her head.

"It will grow, Granddaughter."

Zelka nods. "It will. I want to dye it purple."

Sylvie laughs, joy lighting up her face. "Like the young woman in Bellingham?"

Zelka smiles, remembering her first trip into the world. Boarding the ferry in their car, the loud noises and crowded surroundings had thrown her into a panic. Her grandmother never left her side. Once off the ferry, they traveled to a squat gray building and answered many questions. In the end, Zelka left with papers that displayed her name and date of birth. The person who had given this interview and taken Zelka's information had a silver nose ring and purple hair. Of all the memories of that trip, the purple hair made the greatest impression.

"How fast does hair grow, Nolee?" Zelka asks.

Nolee shrugs. "It's different for everyone. But to get it back to the length it was, maybe years."

Zelka gasps, and her hand returns to the back of her head, the blunt ends bristly against her fingers.

"Zelka," Sylvie says. Her grandmother's use of her name rather than the usual endearment stops the rush of tears that threatens to overcome her again. "Releasing our hair allows us to also release the past."

Like her realization in the Water Canyon House, Zelka feels her grandmother's words shift something inside her. "What do I have left, besides memories?"

"Memories aren't life, Granddaughter. They are part of it. Just as your hair was a part of you."

"But my hair is a part of who I am!"

Sylvie chuckles. "One part. Who you are is far bigger than your memories, good or bad, or your hair."

"But what about the wonderful memories?"

Sylvie takes her hand. "Those are also in the past. As your hair grows, it will keep the record of your new joys, your new sorrows, and all that you are and will become."

Zelka nods, and the smile she gives her grandmother is stronger. She strokes her grandmother's hand, the firm joints of each finger stable and warm. A question floats into her head, and she remembers her talk with Arogem.

"Grandmother, what does your name mean?"

"Which name?"

"Sylvie."

"It means 'spirit of the wood.' But I found that out after I chose it."

"How did you choose it?"

"Until I was thirty-three, the only name I had was the birth name my mother gave me. We were hiding from the government. They were putting Indigenous children into boarding schools operated by the government and religious groups. Not only were we Indigenous, but Keykwin as well, so we spent our lives in fear that we would be found—that my sister and I would be taken away from our family."

Keet says, "I had no idea you had a sister."

Sylvie looks at Keet and nods. "Her name was Regalia. I've been thinking about her a lot."

Nolee touches the back of Sylvie's hand. "Where's she now?"

Sylvie's shoulders slump. She straightens and looks at Nolee.

"She took her Walk Into the Water when she was twenty. I was eighteen and so angry that she was leaving me. I never said goodbye to her. But now I think I understand her reasons better."

Keet and Nolee look at each other, but Zelka's eyes remain on her grandmother.

"What were her reasons?" Zelka asks.

"She said she was tired of living in fear and didn't want to hide anymore."

"Do *you* live in fear?" Nolee asks, but she can see the question on Keet and Zelka's faces as well.

"I haven't for a long time. But we still must hide who we are. Sometimes I wonder …"

"…what it would be like to remain Blackfish?" Keet finishes her question.

Sylvie shrugs. "Sometimes, yes. I wonder that."

Zelka thinks for a moment. "I was Blackfish for so long, and it was wonderful. But it's even more wonderful being with my family."

Sylvie smiles and then squeezes Zelka's hands in her own. "It is wonderful having you in our family."

"I agree," Nolee says as she pulls out her phone from her hip pocket. "Zee, we'd better get going—your hair appointment is soon."

# CHAPTER TEN

Zelka is surprised when Nolee parks on the main street in Northsound, the largest town on the island. "Is this where I'm getting my hair cut?"

Nolee jumps out of the driver's seat and walks around to the sidewalk. "No, this is where we get a treat for ourselves. At my favorite bakery."

As Zelka gets out of the car, she notices the store's carved wooden sign: Sugar Bear Bakery. The smell that envelops them when they walk inside is enough to stop Zelka in her tracks. Running her eyes along the glass cases, she sees a colorful array of pastries of all shapes and sizes. Standing wide-eyed by the case, she inhales the fragrances of sugar, flour, and rising dough.

"Would you like something, Zee?"

Nolee's voice, tinged with laughter, broke her out of her reverie. "Two of everything."

"Two?"

"Of course. I'd share with you, Keet, and Grandmother."

The laughter Nolee had held back escaped. "How about we pick two of everything that looks good to you?"

Zelka notices the white box that Nolee's holding. "What's that?"

"This is our birthday cake."

Zelka shakes her head and feels the cap on her head waggle, a reminder that her brother's head is bigger than her own. She reaches up to straighten it.

"You were gone during your birthday, and mine. We're celebrating tonight."

"But the day of our birth has passed."

When she and her grandmother went to the city of Bellingham to document who she was, her grandmother selected her February birthdate, the month when the ocean raged with anger, as Zelka recalled. But here now, in the sweet depths of the bakery, Zelka couldn't remember ever celebrating a day of birth.

"Zee, the older you get, the longer you celebrate. Who cares if it's March?" Nolee bumps Zelka's shoulder, then turns to the bakery counter again, and the man waiting behind it.

"Graham, can we also have two chocolate croissants, two chocolate lava cakes—"

"Do you want the raspberry coulis with that, Nolee?" His accent, deep and melodious, sounds very odd to Zelka's ears.

"You have to ask?" They share a laugh as Graham places more pastries and cookies inside the box. "Graham, this is Keet's sister Zelka. She's here from Alaska."

Graham places a piece of tissue paper on top of the pastries and closes the lid.

"Hello, Zelka. Lovely to meet you. I'm from England, a little town called Biggleswade." Zelka's brow furrows.

"North of London?"

Zelka looks at Nolee.

"I'll show you later on a map."

Graham reaches across the counter, and Zelka takes his warm hand in hers. She says, "It's nice to meet you, Graham."

Another man comes through the swinging steel door, interrupting Graham as he says, "I didn't realize Keet had a sister—" The man puts his arm around Graham's waist.

"Sweetie, are you selling everything we have to these two beautiful women?"

Graham turns his head, pecking the shorter man on the cheek.

"Nolee, Zelka, this is my husband, Steve."

They repeat the handshaking ritual. When Zelka looks at her right hand, she notices smudges of flour across her brown skin. She raises her hand to her nose. It smells like the bakery they're standing in.

After Nolee pays, they wave to Graham and Steve and make their way through the line of people that has formed behind them.

"Now it's time to get your hair done, Zee. Are you excited?"

Zelka snugs the baseball cap on to her head. "I'm nervous."

Putting the bakery boxes in the back seat, Nolee slams the door shut, then slides into the driver's seat and starts the car. Beside her, Zelka buckles her safety belt.

"We don't have to go if you don't want to."

"I want to, but …"

"Keep in mind that hair grows. And like most things in life, it changes."

"This is wild." Zelka runs her hand over the back of her head. Her short black hair feels like soft bristles. It reminds her of the hair on top of Wallace's head. She smiles, looking forward to getting home so she can play with him on the beach.

"It suits you." Nolee smiles back at her.

In the car, Zelka pulls down the visor and examines her reflection in the small mirror. She turns her head left and right, pushing her hands through her hair, mussing it in different directions, then smoothing it down. It's a little longer at the front of her head and angles slightly upward toward the back. Zelka has no intention of keeping it this short; she misses her long hair.

"Those purple highlights really pop," Nolee says, reaching over to touch the hair framing Zelka's face. "You look like a rock star."

"The way you say that tells me that a 'rock star' is something good, right?"

"It is. I know you like classical music, but there's some great music called rock and roll. Well," she pauses, "it used to be called that. Ask your brother for a history of rock music. He knows way more than I do."

"I think I'd rather eat cake." Zelka glances in the back seat, eyeing the white box tied with multi-colored ribbons, thinking of Graham and Steve and how happy they looked together.

"How long have Graham and Steve been at the bakery?"

"They own it. If I'm remembering correctly, Keet told me they've been there at least fifteen years."

"They look so happy together."

Nolee glances away from the road to Zelka.

"What's on your mind, Zee?"

Zelka pauses, then decides she might as well say what she's thinking, because even if it sounds wrong, Nolee won't hold it against her.

"I've never seen two men together."

Nolee holds her eyes on the curving road.

"Well, people can be together any way they want, no matter their gender."

"But all I've seen are a man and a woman."

"Now you've seen something different."

Zelka nods.

"Zee, my ex-husband Nate left me because he fell in love with someone else. A man."

"That sounds …" But Zelka can't think how to say what it sounds like.

"It was a shock at first. I haven't met Nate's husband, Carlos, but I understand they're happy together. And I'm thrilled to be with Keet. I'd say that out of a very painful situation, something beautiful happened for all of us."

Zelka stays quiet, watching the green fields and forests passing in front of her eyes. She thinks of Arogem, and his insistence, and how, after her curiosity about him waned, she didn't want to be near him. She thinks about her mother keeping her away from male orcas. Preventing her from being part of a community and family.

"Nolee?"

"Yes?"

"How do you know if you like someone enough to be with them?"

Nolee laughs. "Oh, Zee, it's different for everyone."

"What was it like for you and Nate? Or you and Keet?"

The car slows down, the blinker clicking as Nolee makes a right at the dirt road that leads home. She coasts the car to a stop at a wide spot in the road and puts it in park. "Keet and I've had a lot of great talks in this spot." She unclicks the seatbelt and turns toward Zelka. "I married Nate because I thought it was what I should do. I was young, I'd been to college, and getting married seemed to be the next thing. It's what everyone around me was doing. And Nate was so in love with me—it was difficult to not be in love with who he thought I was."

"Arogem likes me like that." Zelka experiences a sudden drop in her internal temperature, as if her heart is turning to ice. "But after I wasn't curious about him anymore, I didn't want him."

"How did he handle that?"

Zelka laughs, a short bark that has no humor in it. "He didn't. But there was nothing he could do. It was my choice."

"When you talk about Arogem, what is it like?"

"Like the rocks in the Water Canyon that have never seen the sun."

"There's your answer, Zee." Nolee leans over and kisses her cheek. "When you find someone who brings out the sun inside you, you'll know."

Zelka smiles as Nolee shifts into gear and drives down the dirt road that seems to grow potholes for sport. But no amount of rocking soothes Zelka's fear that she'll never find someone who warms her like sunshine.

# CHAPTER ELEVEN

Spring on Camas Island comes and goes in fits of rain followed by blue skies, an augury of summer days. Keet and his employee and First Mate, Alex Zhou, have freed *The Salish See* from her berth, and they're taking some early-season guests out to a spot where Keet has heard reports of Biggs orcas.

Listening to the snap of the sails in brisk May breeze, Keet adjusts course as the cross currents cause the hull to shudder under his feet. Zelka, black-and-purple hair flying in the wind, is talking to a guest, a tall blond guy. Shoving her hair out of her face as she pulls an orange watch cap on her head, she catches Keet's glance and waves before returning to the conversation.

After finding the Biggs and giving his talk, Keet turns the helm over to Alex and makes his way to his sister, who's now standing alone at the rail, hands crossed over her thick orange life preserver.

"Hey."

She turns toward him, a small smile on her lips. "I'm glad we were in the boat and not in the water when we saw those Biggs."

"Why's that?"

Zelka lowers her voice. "They're fierce hunters. Mom and I always left the area when we heard they were close. I figured it was because they were dangerous."

"I've not had any unpleasant experiences with them."

Zee looks at him, surprised.

"Neither have you," he continues. "Just Mom's fear of them."

"She was afraid of a lot."

They stand with their arms on the rail, watching an island slide by. Keet reflects on his mother and how she left him to be raised by his grandmother. How she showed up forty years later, bringing chaos to his life before she returned to the sea as orca. The picture of her black and white body sinking into the depths of Puget Sound flashes in his mind. He shakes his head, trying to dislodge the memory and all the conflicting emotions that go with it.

"Do you miss her?" he asks his sister.

"I do. I had more time with her. She was a mystery in so many ways, but she was a wonderful mom to me."

Keet nods, looking down at his clasped hands. "I'd better get back. I want to show Alex how to dock the boat."

Zelka smiles at him before returning her gaze to the viridian water.

All the guests have left the boat, and as Keet checks his phone, a text from Trish, his office manager, pops up. *Your next tour starts in an hour. There are only three people on it.*

Keet smiles, hearing the tone in Trish's voice through the words on a screen. It's the word "only" that points to the ongoing disagreement between him and Trish: that he should do more to market his business. She wants a robust social media presence and a website where people can make their own reservations. Keet trusts that those meant to find him, will. Besides, it's early in the season. It'll get busier now through August, with some consistent but not full sails in September.

Zelka bounces off the boat onto the dock. "Keet, I'm going to say hi to Trish."

Keet raises his hand in acknowledgement and turns his attention back to his boat—throwing away the trash that always seems to accompany people, checking the weather and tides app on his phone, reviewing his maps for the next trip out.

"Hello?"

Keet turns from his contemplation, his heart stuttering when he sees the woman standing on the dock, smile bright against her dark brown skin.

"Maris—" Keet stops, realizing too late that he's not supposed to know her name.

The sight of her brings a surge of memories. Two years earlier, after being illegally captured while he was an orca, he was shipped to a rundown aquarium in southern California. Marissa was an intern there, and her compassion was the reason he didn't give up. She went out of her way to be kind to Keet, sneaking him extra fish and speaking to him in gentle tones.

The woman in front of him cocks her head, her smile fading. "Have we met?"

"I don't think so." Keet, never adept at lying, turns away from her.

"I could swear you almost said my name."

"You surprised me—I thought you were someone else." Keet steps onto the dock and holds out his hand. "Keet Noland, captain of *The Salish See*."

"You're the one taking us out this afternoon."

Keet nods, then turns and steps back onto the boat. Thinking about his late mother and then seeing Marissa has set him on edge. He needs to calm down.

"I'm Marissa Smithson, by the way. I'm early."

Keet forces a smile, hoping Marissa doesn't notice his tension. "No problem. If you'd like to go up to the office, I'll meet you there. I can put you on the boat after you sign some forms for us."

As Marissa walks away, Keet retrieves his phone from the pocket of his windbreaker and sends Nolee a text. *It's been a strange morning. Can't wait to tell you about it later.*

He watches the screen, waiting for the three dots to materialize into a message.

*Are you okay?*

Keet smiles. *I am.* He pauses, unsure whether to text his news or wait. He taps the screen with his thumbs.

*Marissa Smithson showed up. She's on the final tour today.*

The next moment, Keet's phone rings, and a picture of Nolee on the beach by their house fills his screen.

"That's the young woman from OceanMagic, the aquarium where you were trapped, right?" Nolee's voice rises, and he can hear that she's agitated.

"It is."

"What's she doing on Camas?"

"No idea. She's a long way from her home in Oklahoma."

"This is shocking, Keet."

"Tell me about it."

"Let me know what happens."

"Will do. See you soon, sweetheart."

Ending the call, he hears voices from the deck outside the office: Marissa and Zelka, talking and laughing. He turns away, only looking up from his maps and the tide chart when he hears footsteps running down the stairs, then thumping along the dock. He turns to see Marissa standing beside his sister, who asks, "Can I tag along on this tour?"

"Sure. That'd be great."

Zelka bounces on to the boat, grinning more than Keet has seen her do in months. She kisses his cheek. "Thanks, bro."

"Bro?!"

"That's what Marissa said you were when I told her you're my brother." Marissa gives him a wink as she follows Zelka to the life vest locker. He hears them laughing.

*I'm glad I can sail this boat blindfolded*, thinks Keet. *And that Alex is with me.*

The sense of unreality he felt upon seeing Marissa has increased, along with Zelka's laughter. She and Marissa are standing at the front of the boat, wind whipping their faces. They stop talking when he tells the other passengers about local history and the different populations of orca, but as the tour goes on, they sit closer together, shoulders bumping as the boat plows through the swell.

Despite his anxiety, seeing his sister connect to someone this way makes Keet feel good. He's overjoyed that she seems to have found a friend, someone she can laugh with. Laughter has been rare these past two months, as has her natural lightness of spirit.

The other part of Keet, the worn-out part, whispers that if the two become closer, Zelka will want to share their secret with Marissa. Keet understands the power of complete honesty with a loved one. He also understands the fear that arises when a person discovers that someone is not who they believed them to be.

He smiles, thinking of Nolee, and gratitude rushes through him. The only time Keet can remember Nolee being terrified was when he disappeared during a storm. She was angry when she found out he'd lied. The days of hiding who he is are behind him, but what aftershocks will Marissa's presence create?

Interrupting his train of thought, three orcas breach on the port side of the boat.

"Keet! It's our—"

He cuts Zelka off, not wanting her to shout out the word "family." He knows she's excited by her new friend but also feels a twinge of annoyance. She knows better than to shout about who they are in front of strangers.

"It's one of our pods of Resident orcas," Keet adds on the tail of Zelka's outburst. "These are the salmon-eaters I spoke to everyone about earlier. It's one of the oldest documented pods in the Salish Sea."

Keet wills himself to be calm as he glides the boat to a stop. The six orcas he and Zelka call their family play around the boat.

"We're required to keep a safe distance from them, but if they approach our boat, it's safest to remain still." He smiles when he hears the guests gasp, and Marissa looks as though she's about to jump in with them. A memory of her foot on his rostrum as he pushes her to the surface collides with another stab of irritation.

"Marissa, please keep both hands on the railing. We have calm seas this morning, but I don't want a rogue wave knocking you off the boat."

Eyes fixed on the orcas, she grips the railing with both hands.

Keet watches his family swimming around and under the boat, remembering the first time he and Nolee had gone out, when they named them. Nana, the oldest matriarch, is letting George, now four years old, bump into her and roll off her head. As loud talking erupts from the group of people, Keet savors his memories of that day, the day he realized he wanted to be with Nolee. He remembers her smile, and the other names she gave his family: Atma, Poppy, Belle, and Tia.

He also remembers the electricity he'd felt when he rested his shoulder against hers. When he looks at his sister and Marissa, he senses that same current passing between the two young women. Marissa glances back at him, then waves. He gives her a small smile before returning his gaze to the orcas. Then, after one last display of breaching, they disappear, leaving behind only the mist of their breath hovering above the swelling sea.

"I don't think your brother likes me," Marissa says.

Zelka glances at Keet, his profile tense as he checks the sails and runs his eyes over the people grouped on the side of the boat.

"Don't worry about him. He's a serious sailor."

"Do you take sailing seriously?" There's a sparkle in Marissa's eyes.

Zelka laughs, that same sparkle igniting in her own eyes. "Today is the first time I've been on the Salish Sea in a boat. I usually…" Zelka pauses long enough that Marissa finishes her sentence.

"You swim in it?"

Zelka nods, her smile fading.

"Didn't Keet say that even when the water is at its warmest, hypothermia can set in within minutes?"

"He did. But I'm from Alaska and used to cold water. Plus, I…" Zelka scrambles to come up with a reason, then remembers Nolee talking about wetsuits. "I wear a wetsuit."

"Okay." The notes she hears in Marissa's voice tell Zelka that her story is shaky.

Zelka wishes she didn't have to hide the truth. The discomfort erases her smile, despite the pod's antics in the dark green water and the splashes that land like cold fingertips on her face and chest. She has a sudden urge to dive into the water and follow her family, to experience the untainted truth of herself instead of hiding behind uncomfortable lies.

Zelka talks with Marissa until her brother and Alex have sailed the boat back to the marina and guided it into its slip. As they walk up the bobbing dock together, Marissa stares at Zelka's ankles.

"Cool tats. What do they mean?"

Zelka looks down. She's wearing scuffed white sneakers and no socks. The two wavy lines around each ankle, black against her brown skin, are as familiar to her as her own heartbeat. She smiles. And then wishes again that she could share the truth with her new friend.

"It's an ancient symbol of my People. It means water. From long ago, when they lived by the rivers and seas and oceans. Water is as much a relative as my brother." Zelka's heartbeat slows. She realizes she can tell the truth, just not all of it.

"That's cool."

"Do you have any…" Zelka searches for the unfamiliar word.

"Tattoos?" Marissa fills in.

"You called them 'tats.'"

Marissa beams a smile at her. "I did. My brother is a tattoo artist back in Oklahoma. And no, I don't have any."

"Why?"

Marissa shrugs. "I haven't found anything I want on my body forever."

They reach the parking lot, stopping next to a red convertible sports car.

"Do you like it?" Marissa asks, running her hand along the hood.

"It's beautiful." Zelka isn't interested in cars, despite her grandmother's long lessons about engines and body styles. For her, they're a way to get from one place to the other on land. She still prefers swimming as orca.

Marissa shoots her a puzzled look. "You have the same expression on your face as you did when you told me you swam in the Salish Sea."

Zelka's mouth is suddenly very dry. She looks away, watching Keet and Alex taking care of the boat.

"Zelka. What is it?"

Zelka wishes she had some water. Marissa's hand on her arm is warm. "I don't like cars, Marissa."

Marissa stares at her, undecided how to respond, before bursting into a throaty laugh, bending over with her hands on her knees. When she stands up, she's wiping her eyes. Zelka, frowning, is confused about the reason for Marissa's laughter.

"I thought you were going to say you didn't like me."

Zelka shakes her head. "Of course, I like *you*."

"Then what is it?"

"You like your car. I didn't want to hurt your feelings."

"If you not liking my car hurt my feelings, I'd be in bad shape. Be honest with me."

Zelka pauses, taking in this piece of information, recognizing that she needs to give it more thought. Maybe Nolee can help her sort out this confusion between her brain and emotions about Marissa.

"You need to drive over in this and meet my grandmother."

"Already?" The sparkle, Zelka notices, is back in Marissa's eyes.

"Why not? And what does 'already' mean?"

Marissa takes a step closer, her eyes searching Zelka's. "We just met. It takes a while in a relationship to meet someone's family."

"Oh." Zelka says, her face burning.

"Your eyes are amazing."

Zelka looks away. She usually forgets that a ring of lavender outlines her dark-brown eyes.

"If it would make you more comfortable, Marissa, we can wait two days, and then you can come over. Is that enough time?"

There isn't any pause between Zelka's comment and Marissa's laughter. Witnessing the delight on her new friend's face, Zelka bursts into laughter as well. When they stop, gasping, Marissa pulls Zelka into a hug, squeezing her hard before releasing her.

"I don't know where you came from, Zelka, but I like you, too."

Zelka smiles but says nothing, any words stolen by the warmth in her chest.

# CHAPTER TWELVE

The front door slams as I come out of the bathroom wrapped in a towel, hair damp against my neck.

"Nolee?"

"Just a minute, Zee. Let me get dressed." The cool wood under my feet is a relief after the hot shower.

"Can you get me a cell phone?" Zee yells.

I pause as I pull on my socks. Even though Zelka has asked me to show her how to use our phones, and has borrowed mine many times, she's never expressed an interest in having one herself. As I button up my flannel shirt, it occurs to me that this might have something to do with Marissa showing up.

"Be right there."

Halfway to the living room, I see Zelka bouncing toward me, a huge grin on her face. "I have a new friend, and she asked me for my cell number, and I told her I didn't have one, but she could text you or Keet."

I laugh.

"She laughed, too, then said she didn't want to text you or my brother."

Zelka pushes a crumpled piece of paper into my hand. Marissa's name and a phone number are written in neat, round letters and numbers.

"Of course she doesn't want to text us, Zee."

"Why?"

"Because she's interested in you, not us."

When there's no response from her, I take Zelka's arm and lead her to the sofa. Clear blue skies and sparkling water greet my eyes, a relief after months of pewter clouds and eternal twilight.

"When someone's interested in you, they want to find out more about who you are. Without other people around."

Zee remains silent as I take her hand.

"Do you like how you feel around Marissa?"

"Yes. I think we could be friends. She said something about a relation-ship."

"How'd that come up?"

"I told her she needs to meet my grandmother —"

Unable to stop myself, I laugh.

"Nolee! I meant because Marissa and Sylvie both like cars!"

"A friendship is a relationship, Zee. And a relationship can also be romantic. Meeting someone's family, whether as a friend or a romantic partner, is a big step."

"That's what she said, too." Zelka gets up and walks over to the window. "I know nothing about people," she sighs.

Moving closer to her, I stand with my shoulder against her arm. "I like her. Why can't that be enough?" Zelka says.

"It is enough."

We watch a log bob out in the channel, appearing and disappearing between the waves. A sailboat floats past and a gull glides on the spring breeze; I can almost hear its screech. "How about this, Zee. Tell her as much of the truth as you can. Tell her you're new to relationships. See where it goes from there."

Zelka nods. "I can do that."

I wait a moment before I ask her the question that's been worrying me the most. "Did Keet tell you about Marissa?"

Zelka turns toward me, brows pulled together, dark eyes narrowed. "No. What about her?"

"You need to ask him. It's not my story to tell. Where is he, anyway?"

"At the cabin. He said he wanted to talk with Grandmother."

"Do you think it's only coincidence, Marissa showing up here?"

His grandmother shrugs, soap bubbles floating on her brown arms as she washes the dishes.

"I think the only way you'll find out why she's here is if you ask her."

Grabbing a blue cotton dishtowel, Keet nods and starts to dry the dishes. "I'll find a chance to do that. Zee couldn't stop talking about her on the way home."

"Did you tell her about Marissa?"

Keet shakes his head as he puts the plate away in the cupboard. Picking up a mug, he watches his grandmother out of the corner of his eye, seeing her rub her swollen knuckles. He wonders how much they're bothering her.

"I will. Do you want to join us for dinner?"

Sylvie nods. "What are you making?"

"I'm not making anything except garlic bread. Nolee's making pasta primavera. I think she's ready for winter to be over."

"As am I." Sylvie shuffles to the woodstove and puts two more logs on the embers. As they catch, an orange whoosh beats against the glass door. Keet wonders how she can live in such heat; he's sweating just drying dishes. Finished at last, he folds the damp towel over the bar on the oven door.

"I'll get more wood for you, Grandmother."

He spends the next few minutes bringing in firewood and kindling, then sweeping around the fireplace, tossing the contents of the dustpan into the flames.

"Thank you." Keet turns when he hears his grandmother's voice. He puts his arms around her, a swell of all the day's emotions churning in his chest. Moving away, he says, "Join us whenever you're ready."

"I'll come with you now." She closes the stove's damper, and the bright-orange fire settles down to slow, tawny flames.


Keet sets a pitcher of water on the table, then takes his place beside Nolee. She rests her thigh against his and smiles at him. Glancing across the table at his grandmother's plate, he sees that she's taken only half of what she normally chooses. When she catches him looking, she takes a bite of food.

As he eats, Keet thinks through a dozen ways to bring up what he needs to say to his sister. He doesn't want to startle her, but he also needs to tell her the truth—he doesn't want to downplay the shock he felt at seeing Marissa. The best way is probably the shortest.

"Zee, do you remember me telling you about my experience in the tank at OceanMagic after being captured as an orca?"

Mouth full of pasta, Zelka nods. Before she can say anything, Keet continues. "Marissa was an intern there, and my only friend."

Zelka chokes and covers her mouth with a napkin, eyes watering, Sylvie's fork rattles against her plate. Keet takes another bite of pasta. It's as though his stomach waited for the words to leave his mouth before it would accept anything.

His sister clears her throat. "Nolee, did you know this?"

Nolee nods.

Sylvie pushes the food on her plate with her fork. Zelka tucks her hair behind her ears, fidgeting. "Why didn't you tell me this sooner, Keet?"

"I was in shock."

"Still—"

"Zelka, have you experienced isolation? To be orca for so long, you can't remember you're human?"

"No. Because I've only known I was also human for a year."

Seeing the confusion on his sister's face, Keet realizes that he's not shared any details of his captivity with her. He never mentioned the loneliness, the hunger, the cacophony of traffic on the streets and freeways that surrounded the aquarium. Even as he recalls the constant sensation of being overheated, the California sun making the water too warm, he shivers.

Nolee's touch sends a comforting warmth along his thigh. He covers her hand with his own. "I told you about being captured with my orca family and then setting them free. I don't regret doing that."

Zelka nods.

"Getting caught and transported was ugly. I was hungry and hot, and people handled me with hard hands. I wasn't worried because as soon as the people were gone, I thought I could change back to being human and return to Nolee."

"But it didn't work out that way," Nolee adds.

Keet shakes his head. "I didn't realize it, but there were security cameras around the tank. When I tried to change back to human, I couldn't because I was being watched."

"But you escaped," Zelka says.

"I did, eventually. But before that happened, I lived for months as a captured orca. They didn't feed me enough, it was blazing hot, and I was alone except for the lead trainer, who I didn't trust."

"Where does Marissa fit in?"

"She showed up after I'd almost forgotten who I was. Her accent reminded me of Nolee. Her kindness was exactly what I needed. She's the reason I didn't forget everything. She's the reason I'm sitting at this table with my family…" Keet stops, the full impact of his words hitting him. He holds Nolee's hand tighter.

"Keet?" Zelka's voice is soft. "Do you want me to stop being friends with her?"

Keet swipes at his eyes, pushes his hair back from his face. "I want you to do what your heart wishes."

Sylvie says, "Granddaughter, until we know this person, you cannot reveal the secret of our identity."

"Why not?" Zelka asks.

Nolee stiffens beside him. She has her own history with him in this enforced secrecy. Out of the corner of his eye, he sees her lean forward, waiting to hear Sylvie's reason.

"Because in the past, humans were afraid of us. And when people are afraid, they become angry. It is a very short distance from anger to violence."

"But that's not the world now, Grandmother," Nolee says.

"It is. I am afraid that if you do not accept the truth of this, Zelka will be hurt. Or worse."

"Keet, do you believe this, too?" He can see the pain on Zelka's face, dark eyes pleading with him.

"It's not a belief, Zee. It's the truth. One I've experienced many times."

"You didn't experience it with Nolee."

He and Nolee look at each other, a conversation with their eyes taking place in moments.

Nolee says, "Zee, there's a whole lot I could tell you, and maybe one day we can talk about the details. The gift I have of being able to experience what others are feeling isn't one many people are comfortable with, even though I believe that most humans are born with it."

"I still don't understand how that helped you accept who my brother is."

"Because before I met Keet, even in my darkest days, when my ex-husband and I were strangers to each other, that connection deep inside me never went away. At the time, it was with my daughter, and dogs. It's kept me open to the possibility of other mysteries."

Keet leans toward Nolee, kissing her on her temple. She closes her eyes and smiles.

"Other people aren't open to mystery?" Zelka asks.

With Nolee's head resting on his shoulder, Keet looks at his sister and says, "It's not something many are comfortable with."

Zelka nods. "Okay."

"Okay?" Keet watches his sister as she takes another helping of pasta.

"I won't tell Marissa we're Keykwin."

# CHAPTER THIRTEEN

I twist the key in the lock to Paws and Suds Pet Pantry, glad to be out of the rain that has been soaking the island for the past four days. Lowering the hood of my rain jacket, I brush damp strands of hair away from my eyes. Zelka walks in behind me, wet sneakers squelching on the floor.

Ava stayed late last night to finish painting the wooden shelves. I look around, pleased with the way the soft green walls are offset by white trim and the white shelves, pristine and unmarked.

"Zee, are you sure you want to help?"

She smiles, holding up her new cell phone in its bright purple case. "I am. I want to help, because you got me this." She stares at the screen, her eyes widening when facial recognition opens the phone.

"Which one is for texting?" She holds the phone out to me.

I point to the green icon with the white bubble in it.

"Tap that one."

Before I can glance away, I see three texts. One from me, one from Keet, and at the top, one from Marissa. I shrug out of my coat, leaving Zelka standing on the large mat inside the door, staring at her phone, concentrating as she taps each key, then smiling.

In the office, I hang my coat on the coat tree, also white but with wooden accents that make each long branch look like a large cigarette. I laugh about it. Ava found the coat rack but has yet to find the humor in my jokes about it. As I boot up the desktop computer, I hear Zee.

"Nolee?"

"Back here, Zee."

"What can I do?"

"Why don't you check all the shelves and make sure the paint is dry."

"How do I know if paint is dry?"

I often forget that Zelka has only been human for a year. She's learned a lot in some ways, less so in others. Paint, and the varying degrees of "dry," isn't something she's yet learned about.

"Come with me."

I lay my hand on a shelf, and she does the same.

"What do you feel?"

"It's cool, and solid."

"Good. Now bring your hand away and make a fist. We want to make sure your hand isn't sticky. That means the paint is still wet. You can—"

She raises her fist in between our faces, smiling.

The bell on the door rings and I hear, "No need for violence, ladies!"

Zelka squeals, "Em!" before running to hug the person who'd just entered, a tall, dark-skinned woman with a halo of curly hair. She sees me over Zelka's shoulder and smiles. Both turn toward me, and she holds out her right hand.

"Hi, I'm Marissa."

"Marissa, I've heard so much about you. I'm Nolee."

"I've heard so much about you as well, ma'am." In her voice, I hear what would've reminded Keet of me. Her Oklahoma accent is very close to my own Texas-inflected drawl.

"No 'ma'am.' Just Nolee. What brings you to Camas Island?

"I moved to Seattle to study marine biology. I'm here doing some research for my doctoral thesis."

"How did you decide on that area of study?" I try to feign ignorance, despite my partial understanding of who Marissa is. But as she talks about having been a summer intern at an aquarium called OceanMagic, I find it hard to listen like this is new information.

"It was anything but magical," she says, shaking her head. "My heart ached, seeing the animals confined in their filthy enclosures."

"That's how I felt when I went to a zoo when I was a kid. I get it."

"The worst was the killer whale enclosure. They put all this money into updating the stands for more people, but no money into improving the tank or the food they fed the orca. He was alone the whole time."

Afraid of giving myself away, I avoid eye contact and check the paint on the shelf next to me.

"After the killer whale was gone, I left, too. I thought I wanted a career as a trainer, then realized I could study the sea and all the life in it by becoming a marine biologist."

I can feel the flashes of her memories swim between us like a school of fish. Marissa breaks the silence first. "I miss him."

"Who's that?"

"Odin. The orca I helped take care of. It might sound weird, but he was my only friend there."

I nod and force a smile, trying not to display the shock I feel at hearing Keet's words reflected by Marissa.

"Anyway, I'm here for the summer, working on my thesis so I can graduate. And then I met Zee."

They smile at each other, beaming.

Before I can think about what I'm saying, I ask, "Why don't you come over for dinner some time, Marissa?"

"I'd like that. It would give me a chance to see Zee's grandmother's famous truck."

"We'll figure out a day." I reach out and touch Zelka's shoulder before walking away. I hear them behind me, voices hushed; then the bell jingles again as Marissa leaves. Zelka jogs over to the shelf I'm checking, which, it turns out, is dry.

"Where were we?" She has a wide smile across her face and her eyes sparkle. It's good to see her so happy. I hope Keet feels a fraction of that joy when I tell him I've invited Marissa to dinner. Which I should do sooner rather than later. Walking to the back of the store, I dial his number. I get out barely a dozen words before Keet interrupts.

"Did you think about asking me first, Nolee?"

"Marissa is wonderful. You should see her with Zelka. She hasn't been this happy since she first arrived."

"I *have* seen them together. On my boat."

Sighing, I watch Zelka checking each shelf. "We'll postpone the dinner invite."

Keet sighs.

"It doesn't have to happen tonight, Keet. Or even this week. Think about it."

"I'm sure Zee and Marissa have better things to do than hang out with us. Maybe they'll forget."

"Maybe."

"Nolee, I need you to talk with me about Marissa before you involve her in our lives."

"I invited her for dinner. She's not moving in with us." I feel myself digging in, defending my choice.

"From the sound of your voice, you think I'm angry with you."

"From the sound of *your* voice, I'd say you are."

I hear the bell jingle, look up, and see Ava talking with Zee. "I need to go, Keet. We can catch up later this afternoon." I hit the red button on the screen so hard the phone almost jumps out of my hand.

"Shit."

Ava says hello, then walks to the counter where the register will be and starts opening boxes. She pulls out what looks to Zelka like electronic equipment, only this is white, not black like her brother's stereo and cordless phone. Living as a human, she has never cared about their possessions the way they seemed to. Food and love and companionship fill most of her needs. She glances at her phone and smiles. This is one possession she wants, because it means staying connected to Marissa.

Zelka looks back at Nolee talking on her phone. Tension lines her face, and she crosses one arm over her body. As she turns to walk toward Nolee, Ava stops her.

"Zelka, can you help me unpack these boxes?"

"Sure." Out of the corner of her eye, Zelka sees Nolee jab at the phone and hears the quiet "shit." She hopes she isn't the cause of Nolee's distress. Moving around the counter, emptying each box, she glances up at the sound of Nolee's steps. "Everything okay?"

Nolee nods. "Let's get this system unpacked and set up."

"What does it do?"

"It's called a 'Point of Sale.' Meaning, it's where people pay for the stuff they buy."

Ava says, "It was clever of you to figure this out, Nolee."

She shrugs. "The company made it easy. I've already entered everything on their website online. We just log in."

Nolee turns toward Zelka. "Do you want to help set this up, or would you rather stock shelves?"

Zelka searches Nolee's face. It's closed, just like the sound of her voice. Nolee sees Zelka's concern and places a hand on her arm.

"Everything's all right, Zee."

Zelka nods. "I don't know what to do with all this electronic stuff, so why don't you show me what products you want out and where they go."

Nolee smiles. "Deal."

After locking the store for the night, Nolee gets behind the wheel, sighing as she slams the door closed. Zelka, beside her, wonders why Nolee feels so heavy, as though all the air has been sucked out of the world.

"What's going on, Nolee?"

Nolee tries to smile while answering Zelka. "Keet's not sure it's a good idea to have Marissa come to dinner."

Zelka looks out the window. "I get that."

"You do?" Nolee looks behind her as she backs out of the parking space.

"Talk about awkward. Having to pretend to not have met someone, when they only knew you as an orca. And you relied on them for friendship."

Nolee nods. "I get that, too. And…"

"And what?"

"I thought he'd moved past that."

"Maybe he's upset because he thought he'd moved past it, too."

Nolee signals and turns out of the parking lot. After passing the airport close to Osprey Bay, she looks at Zelka, who has been worried about saying the wrong thing. Even after a year of being human, she's still unsure of how to behave.

Nolee says, "I hadn't thought of that, Zee. You're very wise."

Relieved, Zelka grins. She says, "Thanks."

# CHAPTER FOURTEEN

Keet turns in a slow circle, admiring the space that Nolee and Ava have transformed into their store. The argument about Marissa is still sharp between them, but he won't ruin the grand opening by asking Nolee if Marissa's going to be here. It's become obvious that Zelka and Marissa are at the stage in their relationship where they're inseparable.

He hasn't yet touched the small glass of Scotch he carries with him. Its faint waft of peat and cinnamon mix with the fresh paint and wood smells. He catches Nolee's eye across the crowd of people who've streamed into the store. She smiles and he returns it, raising his glass and mouthing the words, "Good job." Even if he'd said the words out loud, he wouldn't have been heard over the din.

He's jostled from behind, and a nasal voice apologizes as he recovers his balance.

"Sorry, pal."

A large hand descends on Keet's shoulder, the weight of the man whose hand it is clear by the push downward. He may be apologizing with his words, but Keet also knows he's been picked out as one of the few men in the room. Turning his head, he sees a sunburned pink face and a Camas Island Golf Club hat, which give him away as either a tourist or someone who has a second home here. His black polo shirt is unbuttoned, and he has a thin gold chain around a thick neck.

Keet shifts away from the weight of the hand and its owner's beer-laden breath. Before he can reply, the guy says, "You from around here?" Keet nods as the man thrusts a meaty hand toward him. "Berkley Thoms. My friends call me Berk."

Keet shakes hands, resisting the urge to wipe his own on his jeans to get rid of the clammy sweat against his skin. "Keet Noland."

"Hey. You're that whale watching guy, right?"

"Yes, I—"

"A friend of mine went out on a sailboat ride with you. Said he saw more killer whales with you than any other time he's summered out here."

*Not local*, Keet thinks.

"I'm glad he had a good—"

"You live here?"

"Yes." Keet keeps his answers short and his steps small, hoping these movements will trigger Berk to go somewhere else. But the big man leans toward him as though sharing a secret, filling Keet's head with the scents of sweat, beer, and stale cigar smoke.

"Heard two ladies opened this place. Think they'll make it?"

"Yes."

Finally, Berk straightens out of Keet's space, and he uses the opportunity to turn his head and take a large slug of Scotch and an equally large in-breath. Peat and cinnamon replace the smell of Berk.

"Why're you here?"

Keet finds Nolee in the middle of a different crowd of people. "I'm here with my—"

Berk watches as Keet's gaze lands on Nolee. "Is your wife one of the women who own this place?"

Keet braces as Berk thumps him hard between his shoulder blades. A series of thoughts go through his head. The first is that Nolee isn't his wife, but she's more than his girlfriend. He takes a larger step away from Berk, who's tipping a beer bottle up to his mouth, index finger hooked around the neck, bottle resting on his knuckles. Keet remembers seeing college guys drinking beer like this, and frowns. It was a complicated time in his life, and he doesn't want to lump Berk with the crowd he tried, and failed, to hang out with back then.

"She's my partner, and yes, she and her friend Ava are co-owners."

Berk barks a laugh. "Ha! Partner." To Keet's horror, Berk leans closer and gives him a slow-motion wink. "Keeping your options open, then? Partner, not wife." Stifling a belch behind his fist, Berk says, "Need another one of these," and turns and lumbers away.

For the second time, Keet turns his head and takes a deep breath, enjoying air free from the warm waft of undigested beer. He looks for Zelka and sees Marissa beside her. They've got their heads together—one a halo of tight curls and the other, a black inverted bob with purple stripes.

He runs a hand through his own hair, happy it's long again; he missed its warmth. Watching as the two young women laugh together, he wonders if Zelka realizes Marissa wants to be more than friends. As though his sister feels him thinking about her, she glances up and waves to Keet, then takes Marissa's hand and pulls her behind in her eagerness to introduce them.

Wanting to get ahead of any awkwardness, he says, "Hi, Zee, Marissa." He hopes his smile doesn't come across as fake as it feels.

"I forgot—you two already met," says Zelka, beaming at Marissa. Keet throws his sister a warning glance, but she's focused only on Marissa.

"Good to see you again, Keet." Unlike Keet's, her expression is relaxed and warm.

A riptide of feeling swirls in Keet's chest: gratitude, wariness, anger. Keet knows that the last one makes little sense and is more about his months swimming in slow circles in a concrete tank, his fading memories of being human, his hunger, and the heat he could never escape. His only ally, Marissa, was the single bright spot in a torturous existence. He snaps himself out of his contemplations when Marissa's smile fades.

"Zelka says you like cars."

Her smile returns. "Yeah, I'm a bit of a motor head. Got it from my parents."

"Do you have siblings?"

Marissa shakes her head. "Nope. I'm an only child. I hear your grandmother has an amazing truck."

"She does. You should come over and talk with her about it. We can plan on dinner afterward."

"I'd like that, Keet."

Zelka beams, and Keet notices that she and Marissa are still holding hands.

The room seems to tilt, and Keet feels his chest constrict. He takes a deep breath, mumbles something about getting some air, and leaves. His sister's smile and Marissa's cool charm, Berk's smells, and the chaos of talking people—it's too much. He shoulders through the door, hearing the electronic chime as it shuts behind him.

In some remote part of his mind, he watches himself, noting the shallow breathing, the heartbeat that's too fast, the inability to focus. He knocks back the rest of the Scotch and closes his eyes. It's not as though this hasn't happened before; he's familiar with panic attacks. He knows that crowds and loud, small rooms aren't the easiest places for him to be. But this goes beyond nervousness or discomfort.

The only explanation is Marissa—her presence, her voice. He knows details about her that few others do. He can still picture the shape of the bones inside her foot, which he saw in his head when she fell in the tank and he lifted her to safety. He didn't realize she was tall; he had only seen her kneeling at the edge of his too-small pool, feeding him when he was hungriest. Despite being taken advantage of by others, Marissa showed him unwavering kindness, treating him with compassion and respect.

He hears the chime of bells again and steels himself. A hand on his arm interrupts his turn, and Nolee appears.

"Are you—"

He envelops her in an embrace, burying his face in her hair, taking refuge in the warmth of her body against his.

"I'm good now."

She gives a muffled laugh and squeezes him tighter.

Zelka and Marissa watch Keet and Nolee hold each other. Marissa, her forehead wrinkling, says, "Was it something I said?"

Zelka pauses, unsure, then decides on something neutral. "I don't think so. He doesn't like crowds."

"It's sweet, though," Marissa smiles as she continues to watch Keet and Nolee.

"What's that?"

"How into each other they are."

"It is." Zelka glances at Marissa, noticing that her expression mirrors the longing Zelka herself feels.

"How'd they meet, anyway?"

"Nolee moved in next door."

"That easy?"

Zelka shrugs. "I haven't asked them much about that time. They're perfect for each other." Now the longing becomes a full-blown ache. Her heart is calling for something, and Zelka realizes that something is *some-one*, and she's holding that someone's hand. As if Marissa senses a change in Zelka, she turns toward her, their eyes locking.

"Do you want to get out of here?"

When Zelka nods, Marissa, still holding her hand, pushes through the door. Calling out "goodbye" and "congratulations" to Keet and Nolee, they hop in Marissa's car.

"Where are we going?" Zelka laughs.

"It's a surprise." Marissa pulls out of the spot she'd reversed into, guiding her car through the parking lot and out onto the small winding road.

"I'd say our grand opening was an enormous success!" Ava exclaims as she hugs me. Turning back to the till, she rubber-bands the bills together and stashes them in the bank bag to deposit.

"Keet, thanks for being here." Ava pulls him down to her height for another hug.

Keet smiles. "I wouldn't have missed it."

"Ava, I'll close the store." I pull out a small keyring, shiny new silver keys to the door dangling from it.

"You remember the alarm code?"

I nod. "I just want to do one more circuit, then we'll go home."

The bell chimes as it shuts, and I flip the wooden sign from "open" to "closed." A sleeping dog is carved into the wood, small ZZ's floating above the dog's head. I'd asked the artist to model the dog after Fae, and even though I've seen this sign numerous times, it never fails to make me smile. Below the word "Open," a stretching cat is carved in the corner.

"Good job, Lia."

I turn and wrap my arms around Keet's narrow waist. "It's a great store, isn't it?"

He nods against the top of my head. "It is."

Both of our phones ping with a text. I tilt my head up and kiss Keet, then reach into my back pocket.

"Looks like Marissa and Zee have gone to dinner. She'll be back later."

Keet, reading the same message, scowls.

"What is it?"

Keet says, "I know it makes zero sense, but every time I see Marissa, I get mad." He shakes his head.

"I thought you have good memories of her."

"Yes. Maybe I'm getting her mixed up with my feelings about Ocean-Magic."

I glance at my phone and reply. *Have a great time!*

Keet's phone pings. He glances at it. "Do I have to say something?"

"Not unless you want to."

He grunts, shoving his phone into a jacket pocket.

"Let me double-check everything and then we can go home." I walk away, running my eyes over the floor and shelves, catching sight of a stray glass abandoned on its side at the end of an aisle. I pick it up, welcoming its cold smoothness. Keet's anger comes across as heat to me, like standing too close to a fire. We haven't talked about Marissa coming to dinner since our phone conversation a couple of weeks ago.

Breaking my train of thought, Keet says from behind me, "I invited Marissa to dinner sometime."

I turn toward him, my grip tightening around the glass.

"When?"

"When I talked with her and Zee tonight."

"No, I mean, when do you want to have her over?"

He shakes his head. A long strand of black hair falls against his face. He pushes it behind his ear and shrugs. "Maybe next week?"

"That soon?"

"What do you mean, 'that soon?'"

The anger simmers in his voice as I remind myself that this happens when a minor argument is allowed to fester.

"I mean, it seems like you're still having a hard time with Marissa. She's not blind."

Keet removes the glass from my hand and takes it to the small kitchen. I see the stiffness in his back as he washes it and sets in on the drainboard. When he comes back out, he says, "I don't want to talk about Marissa anymore tonight. It's your celebration. Why don't we end on a good note."

"Okay." I stand on tiptoe and kiss his cheek.

But even after we settle down in bed, and despite his lingering kiss, I can tell that a "good note" for Keet might well be a long time coming.

A week later, Keet and Nolee are in the kitchen preparing dinner for Marissa, Zelka, and Sylvie. A slamming door announces Zelka's arrival.

"Where's Marissa?" Keet asks.

Zelka, who was looking out of the window, turns to Keet. "What did you say?"

"I asked where Marissa is." Keet notices the smile on his sister's face, her distraction.

Nolee asks, "Zee, you okay?"

Zelka turns toward them both, smiling more broadly, and says, "She kissed me!"

She strides over to them, wrapping them in her arms as they laugh.

"Zee, that's wonderful," Nolee says.

Zelka looks out the window again. Keet joins her, seeing Marissa snug the top back on her convertible. He walks outside.

"Need any help?"

Marissa gives him a quick smile. "Sure. Can you grab that section by your left hand and give it a tug? It always hangs up there."

Keet pulls the fabric forward as Marissa pushes the button that closes the roof over the interior.

"That's slick," Keet says.

"I like it. It's a 2011, but it's all-wheel drive, has heated seats, and I can fit three more people in it."

"Zelka mentioned how much fun you two were having driving around."

"And she told me that your grandmother has a sweet truck."

Keet watches as Sylvie descends the cabin steps sideways, one by one. A shadow of worry further darkens his mood, but he turns to Marissa and tries to smile.

"She's on her way over right now. I'll introduce you, and if she's in a good mood, she might let you look at it. Don't try and touch it, though."

Marissa laughs, then, seeing Keet's face, she says, "You're serious."

"Very."

"Message received."

"Grandmother, this is Zelka's friend, Marissa. Marissa, this is our grandmother, Sylvie."

"Ma'am." Marissa holds out her hand. Sylvie takes it in both of hers.

"It is such a treat to meet you, Marissa. Zelka has talked about you nonstop for weeks."

"Oh?"

"Grandmother!" Zelka rushes toward them, blushing.

"You've been talking about me nonstop, Zee?"

Keet wonders how long it will take for them to go from friends to girlfriends after the kiss Zelka mentioned.

"I'm going to check on dinner," he says, needing to remove himself before he loses control of his brewing irritation. As he walks through the door, he hears the garage open and Marissa's exclamations as she admires Sylvie's truck. He closes the door.

Nolee looks up from the tomatoes she's cutting for the salad.

"Everything all right?"

"Sure. They're looking at Grandmother's truck."

Nolee tips the cutting board over the bowl and drops in the tomatoes, then moves to the sink to wash the dishes they've already used. Keet joins her, hoping he can let go of his anger if he's distracted by something else. Instead of helping, he puts his arms around her and bends to rest his face in her hair. She smells of citrus shampoo and dogs. She stops washing dishes, leaning toward him. "Better now," he says.

She kisses him, hands still submerged in soapy water.

"Me, too. You sure you're ready for this?"

He nods. "I'll get over myself at some point. She and Zelka seem happy together."

"They do. But?" She leans back against his body, waiting.

"But nothing."

"Keet. You're so agitated I can feel it."

"That's not saying much, since you can feel a lot of things."

"Ha ha. What's going on?"

He takes a breath, then reaches for a soapy plate and rinses it off.

"I'm still angry at Marissa, and I don't know why."

"And?"

"And, under the anger, I'm grateful and scared and confused."

Nolee laughs.

"What? Why are you laughing?"

"I'm laughing with you, Keet, not at you. If I told you how often six emotions hit me at once, I think you'd laugh, too."

"I could use it." He grabs two knives from the Japanese set Nolee gave him when she moved in, running them under a stream of hot water. "I'm worried they'll get so close that Zee will want to tell Marissa about us being Keykwin."

Nolee hands him a bowl. He takes it, his hands caressing the smooth curves as the water flows over it. His heartbeat slows, the calmness he always feels around water—even water from a faucet—returning to his unsettled mind.

"That's valid," Nolee says. "How about we deal with that if Zee finds she needs to share that part of herself with Marissa."

Nodding, Keet says, "That would be easier than being mad at Marissa in advance."

"Why mad?"

"Before she showed up, our life was the way I wanted it. We're together, Grandmother is next door, Zelka's returned from the Water Canyon House, the dogs are great, our jobs are rewarding…" His voice trails off as he taps the spigot closed. As he listens to himself, he becomes aware that his human nature has taken over, as though he's not also Blackfish. He says this to Nolee, adding, "Sometimes I forget that life is change."

"Sometimes we all do. Especially when things are going well."

The door opens, letting laughter into the house. Nolee hugs everyone, asking what they'd like to drink and offering them chairs at the table filling with food. Keet pours a Scotch for Nolee and Sylvie, a glass of wine for Marissa, and water for himself and Zelka. He's determined to be happy for his sister and welcoming to Marissa. The future will have to take care of itself.

# CHAPTER FIFTEEN

"I thought dinner last night went great." We're passing under the concrete arch that welcomes visitors to Mt. Pelorus.

Keet glances at me before looking back at the road, watching for a left-hand turn that's easy to miss. "Thank you for talking me down off the ledge."

"You're welcome, but all I did was listen. You came off that ledge yourself." I pick up the hand resting on my thigh and kiss his palm.

"I'm less worried about Marissa. I remember how kind she was to me during my captivity, and it's easy to see that she's kind to everyone."

We turn left, hugging the right side of the narrow road that winds up the mountain. Keet slows as he steers around a sharp curve.

"Keet?"

"Yes?"

"I'll always listen to you, you know that, right?"

He gives me a slow smile, then kisses my palm. "Yes. I promise I'll always listen to you, too."

After we park in a lot near the top, I shrug into my backpack, then open the rear door to clip the dogs' leashes to their harnesses. They're all wiggling bodies and panting, white-toothed smiles. "I love hiking, but I think the dogs are more excited than we are."

He puts a water bottle in his pack and looks at me as he slips the padded straps onto his shoulders. I smile at the memories of our time together here and he steps closer, leaning down until only our lips are touching. After a kiss that leaves me breathless, he says, "I doubt that."

We follow the trail up Mt. Pelorus, just as we had the first time we hiked together. I hear Keet behind me, his breathing even, and wonder if he experiences time the same way I do: both long and short, a lifetime in a day, or years in moments. My thoughts are interrupted when Keet says, "Take that little trail that branches to the left."

The dogs bounce ahead of me, noses to the ground as we walk. The vibrations of what they're smelling dance in my head, though exactly what those things are, it's hard to tell. Feeling things in my body that others experience isn't nearly as confusing as it used to be. This part of me feels familiar, and I treasure it.

"Where does this go?"

"To the same picnic table we sat at the first time we hiked here."

I look back at him. "Do you realize that it's been more than two years ago?" I stop on the trail, the next question bursting to come out. "What's time like for you, Keet? Is it different?"

He runs a hand across his head and down the ponytail that flows past the collar of his fleece jacket. The white at his temples is a stark contrast to the ponytail's deep black.

"Different from what? When I'm human, my guess is that time is much like it is for anyone else. Quick, then slow, then quick. Some time you want to get back and can't. Some you want to give away but have to go through instead."

I nod, and begin walking, breathing a little harder as the slope of the land steepens. His voice, close behind me, continues.

"But when I'm orca, time is invisible. I recognize the sun and moon, the tides, and my brothers and sisters around me, the sounds of the fish and sea lions…" his voice drifts away. I stop, as much from the burn in my legs as to look at him while he talks.

"There's no such thing as time, then. There's the turn of cycles that we all share: life and death, being born and birthing, being young, growing old, being hungry, feeling full. Our lives are always turning in that cycle, and there's no need to question or fight it."

A gust of wind whispers through the trees. Behind Keet, I see a squirrel flick its tail before it bursts up the trunk to a higher branch. I look down and see that Fae and Wallace are watching it as well, tails wagging.

"We fight a lot of things as humans, don't we?" I want to say more, but the warmth of the spring breeze and Keet's observations create a point of stillness in me, a respite from the gerbil wheel of my mind—tracking business loan numbers, my departure from the shelter, remodeling ideas for the new store, and the grocery list on my phone that keeps getting longer. I take a breath and close my eyes, letting the lists fall away as I inhale the damp earth and the scent of the man who now stands beside me, holding my hand. I rest my head on his shoulder.

"We do." His simple declaration stills me again, allowing me to accept my own messy nature, to understand that it's not unique to me. But in between heartbeats, I also feel a longing arise, one that's familiar and bittersweet because I know it will never happen: I want to enter Keet's world as orca and experience this timelessness, this bigger view of life.

As if he's read my mind, he says, "I wish I could show you my orca world, Lia. If only for one day. Or even one hour." I nod against his shoulder and whisper, "Me, too," then wrap my arms around his ribcage. He holds me closer, lays his cheek against the top of my head, then says, "Let's get moving. I'm hungry."

I laugh. "This may be a shortcut, but my thighs are telling me it's steeper."

"Not for long. And there's a picnic at the other end."

After setting our packs on the picnic table, I tie Fae and Wallace in the shade of a nearby tree, water bowls within reach. Their eyes half-closed, they gnaw on thick strips of jerky. Keet and I empty our backpacks, unfolding an orange-and-white tablecloth across the scarred wood and holding it down with stones we found scattered nearby. Between us, we've carried a miniature feast.

Keet pauses, one hand in his pack.

"What is it? Did we forget something?"

He looks at me across the table and smiles. "Not a thing." Zipping the pack shut, he sets it on the ground.

The table is loaded with bottles of sweet tea and water, tuna sandwiches, cut and sliced vegetables next to a container of ranch dip, three different cheeses and two different types of crackers, a bowl of fruit salad, and a small chocolate cake. Keet moves around the table to sit next to me. Placing his warm hand against my neck, he leans. As our foreheads meet, our mingled breath is cradled within the silence of the day. I give him a quick kiss, and say, "I've worked up an appetite since breakfast. Let's eat."

"I thought we got rid of that appetite this morning."

Laughing, I kiss him again, then sit up straight. The cry of a gull brings me back to earth, but my mind remains in the clouds.

"Here." Keet hands me a bottle. "Drink some sweet tea first."

I sip at the tea, then sigh again in pleasure. "Pass me one of those sandwiches, Keet."

We eat in silence, the only sounds are of the wind and the distant blue-green Salish Sea. The dogs have found a patch of sunlight and lay on their sides, eyes closed, mouths open, panting. I take another drink of the tea, gathering the courage to reopen what feels to me like a tricky topic.

My voice shakes. "Remember our conversation last year, about getting married?"

Keet stops chewing, looks slantwise at me, then swallows. "Yes."

All the words I had planned disappear. Keet turns toward me, wipes his hands on his jeans, then takes my hands in his.

I clear my throat, willing myself to not shy away from his gaze. "I'm ready to talk about it again."

"Okay." I can see the wariness in his eyes, hope fighting with the memory of our conversation a year ago, and how I'd told him—with a bluntness that still makes me cringe—I wasn't interested in marriage. Especially after hearing his reason: he'd never been married and wanted to "try it." I take a breath, knowing my next words will either rekindle his hope or extinguish it.

Before I can speak, he says, "I only used the word marriage because I thought it would be easiest to understand. It was thoughtless of me, Lia. I didn't stop to think about what it would mean for you, after being married to Nathan."

I nod, the weight of responsibility for our hearts lifting as I realize he's carrying the same burden.

"You're right. The one bright spot is Abbie. I'll never regret I had her, and if that's what I had to go through to have Abbie, then I can make my peace with Nathan."

Keet nods and his shoulders relax. Before he can reply, I speak the words that have caught in my throat, that I almost said as we made love early this morning, both of us still half asleep.

"I want to give the rest of my life to you, Keet Noland."

His smile begins in his sun-illuminated brown eyes, then spreads across his face. He releases my hands and puts a gentle palm on each side of my face. "I want the same, Magnolia Clark Burnett."

Perched on a mountain with only the sun, gulls, and sea as witnesses, we burst into nervous laughter as we lay our old lives to rest. We kiss again, slow this time, before he gathers me into his arms, and I move away from his mouth, taking shelter in the closeness of his body.

"What—"

"When—"

We laugh again, having interrupted each other. "You first," he says.

"What do we do next?"

"I was going to say, when would you like to do this?"

"Maybe we can decide when after we figure out what?" I move out of his embrace, taking his hands in mine. "It's obvious to me that my first marriage experience isn't something that's important anymore."

"Before we talk about that…" He gets up from the table and fetches his backpack. "I want to give you something."

"What is it?" I lean closer to him, peering into the depths of the pack. Reaching in, he closes his hand around something small.

"Close your eyes, Lia."

I close them, then feel the dry warmth of his hand opening mine. He places a small object with corners on it. Opening my eyes, I see a white box. My stomach flip-flops. Keet, catching the emotions running across my face, laughs. "It's not what you think."

I open the box. A pair of silver earrings in the shape of thick Celtic knots nestle in the tissue paper. I take one out, dangling it from my fingertips, catching the sun.

"Keet! They're beautiful!"

"I saw them at a local shop and thought of you."

One hand holding the box and the other holding the earring, I lean over and kiss him. He pulls away and touches my ear. "May I?" I nod.

His touch is deft and careful as he removes the earrings I'm wearing. I watch as he takes one of the new earrings and flips open the catch. His fingers slide the cool silver through the hole in my ear. I close my eyes again as he puts the second earring in. When I open them, he's smiling at me.

"They're more beautiful when you're wearing them."

"Thank you, sweetheart." I give him another kiss.

We finish our lunch in comfortable silence, watching as the dogs reposition themselves in the shade.

"Can you tell me about the Keykwin traditions around a ceremony that joins two people?"

He repositions himself on the bench, looking out over the islands and sea, at mountains still capped with snow under a pale blue sky.

"We begin by honoring the land and the sea and the air, recognizing that we carry them within us, just as our ancestors did. When two people wish to make a home with each other, their first ceremony is between only them. It's private."

"I like the sound of this. What else?"

"When you got married, you made marriage vows?"

I nod.

"We give promises."

"What's the difference?"

"A vow is about taking something on. A promise is something you give. And I want to give you the rest of my life."

My skin prickles, a flutter of nervousness caught underneath. "In my culture, Keet, we say that promises are made to be broken."

"What do they say about vows?"

I pause, then shake my head. "I can't think of anything, other than vows attached to being married."

"Did you and Nathan say vows when you were married?"

"Lots of them."

"Did you keep them?"

A flame of anger flares up, then dies down. "No, we didn't."

"So, people can break vows, too?"

"I get it."

"Get what, Lia?"

"What you said about vows being something we take and a promise something we give. Truth is, we can break anything, just as we can keep anything together. I guess between a vow and a promise, I'm more inclined to give you a promise. It seems more personal to me than a vow."

"That's how we see it too. A promise is held between two people, each knowing what the other gives freely."

"And risks."

Keet nods.

I turn when I hear the dogs moving and check to be sure they have enough water. When I turn back toward Keet, he's opening the container with the cake, and hands me a fork.

"Why slice it?" he grins.

I take the fork from him, spear a sizable chunk, and close my eyes as the flavor fills my mouth. A memory floats on the tide of pleasure generated by the cake's sweetness. "When Abbie was born, I made her a promise."

Keet pauses in his search for more icing.

"Everyone had left the room. It was the first time she and I had been alone since her birth. She was pink and tiny, everything about her was beautiful. My heart broke wide open, and I was so entranced by her I didn't notice if Nathan was with me or not." I wipe my mouth and set down my fork.

"I put my lips against her fuzzy head and promised I would always love her, no matter what. I promised to be the best mom I could to her, always."

"And you haven't forgotten your promise or broken it."

I shake my head. "And I won't. That was a promise my heart gave."

"In Keykwin tradition, those are the only kind of promises we make."

The dogs jumble around our legs as we carry our packs into the house. We'd held hands in silence as we drove back to Osprey Bay, but now a question occurs to me. "Keet, do we exchange rings?"

He sets his pack on the floor, leans over to give Wallace a back scratch, then says, "Only if you want to. The commitment we make with our hearts is more important than showing anything on the outside. Besides," he laughs, "I don't think a ring would be a good idea for me."

I nod in agreement. "That's good. I don't need either of us to wear one. And I have no desire to change my name."

"I don't need you to. We come to this life as individuals, each making our own choices."

"I'm getting the idea that we can design this any way we'd like?" Keet nods. "So that brings us back to where and when we'd like to do this."

"Anywhere. I'd like to include water, earth, and air in our ceremony."

"We could do that here."

"We could. Or we could have a gathering here afterward with friends and family."

"Let's have a celebration. Abbie would be furious if we didn't invite her."

"Does she get her temper from you?" When I look at Keet and the mischievous glint in his eye, I wrap my arms around him and yell, "What temper?" He breaks my embrace, picks me up and we land on the couch together, laughing.

"Now that we're talking about this, I'd like to have this ceremony… what do you call it?"

"The Promising Ceremony."

"Let's do this sooner rather than later."

He smiles and holds me as we sink into the sofa. "Yes."

# CHAPTER SIXTEEN

The next day before we open the shop, Ava and I sit at the L- shaped counter, taking a break from rearranging shelving. I open the calendar app and review the notes for each day as I sip a latte from the coffee shop next door.

"Keet and I'd like to go camping and I'm thinking about these two days." I point to May eighth and ninth, the following Thursday and Friday, on the calendar.

Ava puts her finger next to mine on the screen, peering through her glasses.

"They're installing the dog-washing stations those days, so there shouldn't be much for us to do. We've got more inventory coming in on the following Tuesday."

"I'll be back by then. Can you manage this place while I'm gone?"

She smiles. "With my eyes closed. Where are you going?"

"Keet said something about some hot springs."

"That sounds relaxing. Pete hasn't taken me anywhere in ages."

"I'll let you know how this one is, then maybe y'all can give it a try."

"Pete's idea of camping is a hotel without a bar attached. Is this a special occasion?" she asks.

The heat of my blush creeps up my neck before I can stop it.

"It is!" Ava leans over and hugs me.

I return her squeeze, still smiling. "I'll tell you more after we get back."

"Making me wait for the good news?"

I nod. "I promised Keet I would."

"Good for you. Are you taking your dogs?"

"Sylvie and Zelka are watching them for us. They spent their first year in that cabin so it should be just like home."

Keet and I set our packs on a flat rock warmed by the late-afternoon sun. I drop to the ground, grateful to sit after what seems like hours of hiking. Keet pulls out a water bottle and drinks, but I've caught a flash of turquoise through the green undergrowth. Getting up, I make my way along the stone path and down the wooden stairs, gazing in wonder at the shaded pool that lies at their base. The sun sends its rays into the crystalline depths and steam rises from the surface like ghostly orca breath pushed upward.

"How did you find this place, Keet?" I turn, taking in the forest and three other pools dotted on the hillside, all steaming. Steam also seeps from a cave, looking like smoke or wisps of dragon's breath. Memories of my obsession with dragons the year I turned ten make me smile. But the warmth of those memories turns cold when I think of my current, not-very-well-hidden obsession with becoming an orca. I refocus on Keet as he answers my question.

"During my very brief time in college, some friends convinced me to come on a hike to these springs. I was lonely enough that it seemed like a good idea. But not so lonely that watching them get high was fun."

Keet strips off his t-shirt and shorts and sinks into the pale turquoise water with a sigh. "But it wasn't all bad," he says, his eyes closing. "I didn't know these hot springs existed until they showed me."

I'd worn my bathing suit underneath my shorts and shirt, but looking at Keet, eyes closed, the steam rising around him, I think that being naked in the hot springs will feel better. I undress and sink in opposite him, closing my eyes and sighing, listening to the birdsong and the silences between. The warmth of the water reaches deep into my bones, calming the continuous tremor that I've felt since Keet and I talked about our Promise Ceremony and the upcoming summer reception.

"We can camp on that flat spot right there." Keet gestures to a space behind me. I stand up to get a better look, water sliding down my body. The cool air raises goosebumps and sends me back into the water, this time beside him, both of us perching on a smooth rock ledge.

"Looks good to me." I lean over and kiss his smooth cheek. "You shaved this morning?" Keet rarely bothers with shaving more than twice a week. When he does, it's for a purpose.

His brown eyes soften as he looks at me. "I did."

I clear my throat, then rest my head on his shoulder, letting my gaze go unfocused on the water's surface, feeling the warm, amniotic float of my limbs.

"You shave when there's something special coming up. Like new clients on your boat or …"

"Or?"

I listen to the silence of the surrounding forest. The birds are quiet.

"Or you'd like to talk about our Promise Ceremony." I keep my head on his shoulder, too nervous to look at him. He shifts toward me, putting an arm around my waist and resting his head on top of mine.

"I don't have new clients until next month."

I laugh, a small, skittish sound that evaporates as quickly as the thin vapor from our pool.

"Nolee?"

"Yes?"

"We don't have to go through with the Promise Ceremony while we're here. This can be a great camping trip with or without that. But when we talked about it, remember I told you that the first one is between two people, and then there's a gathering later?"

I nod.

"It's only us here. I talked to the ranger and no one else is staying overnight."

As though he conjured them out of the soft spring air, I hear voices in the distance.

"Sounds like we have company now, though." I sit up, eyeing my bathing suit at the edge of the pool.

"It's a good idea to put that on. I don't think the park is clothing optional." As I wrestle my wet body into my black-and-white one-piece, Keet hops out with a splash and shimmies into his shorts. As he sits back in the pool, the first of the hikers arrive, wave hello, and make their way to the pool next to ours. I smile at Keet. "Let's talk more later." He kisses the tip of my nose and smiles back.

We soak in the springs until we're wrinkled, then set up camp. Even though the sun is still up, I suggest dinner when I hear Keet's stomach rumble. He builds a fire in the firepit while I rummage in his pack for the small cooler with our meal in foil-wrapped packages.

The sounds of laughter and loud talking move away as the other visitors take the trail to the parking lot. Keet places the large foil packets on the grill above the flames. My thoughts are moving at a leisurely pace, and neither of us feel a need to make conversation. When the food is ready, we eat in silence.

I crumble the foil between my hands, then lick my fingers. Keet pulls on thick fireproof gloves and sets the small grate in a nearby patch of dirt.

"I didn't know camp food could be that amazing," I say. "I was picturing you pulling out a couple of MREs and calling it good."

"Anytime an acronym is used for food, it can't be anything worth eating."

The taste of the Cajun-spiced shrimp still vibrating in my mouth, I search my brain for the words to the acronym. "Meals Ready to Eat. The military uses them."

He cuts his eyes at me, a wry grin on his face. "You think I'd feed you something like that? On a trip like this?"

I laugh. "You're right. I should know better. You were prepping this last night, but I didn't realize it was going to be so good." I put the foil in a bag and stand up, noticing a sign for the outhouse. "Be right back."

Keet nods, stirring the embers in the firepit in front of our tent. When I get back, he says, "My turn."

As I wait for him to return, I pull graham crackers, chocolate bars, and marshmallows from my pack, then fish around for the skewers.

"What are you making?" he asks as he sits in the fire's warm circle of light.

"S'mores. Ever had them?"

He shakes his head, doubt flickering across his face. "That's not another acronym, is it?"

Laughing, I say, "It's not chocolate cake with raspberry syrup—"

"Coulis." He returns my laugh.

"The trick is to cook the marshmallows so they're gooey without burning the outside."

"I'd say they're about done," he points to one browning near the flame.

I hand him the skewer. "Hold on to it for just a minute." After assembling the chocolate and graham crackers, I slide the marshmallow he's holding onto one graham cracker, then mash two together and hand it to him.

"This will be the best S'more you'll ever eat," I assure his doubtful look.

"Why is that?"

"Because the first time discovering anything you like is always the best."

He takes a giant bite, cheeks billowing out like a chipmunk's. I pull the second marshmallow away from the fire and begin assembling my dessert.

"You're right," he says after several minutes during which the only sounds are the fire, chewing, and the nighttime breeze.

"I am?"

He nods. "I didn't think this would be any good, but I need another one."

Later that night, Nolee's back against his, Keet listens to the small sounds of the nighttime forest. Although his limbs are heavy and relaxed, his mind races. Ready to promise his life to the woman sleeping beside him, he wonders if he needs to be clearer with her, so she knows the depth of his feelings. Or maybe he needs to look at other ways a Promise Ceremony would assure her that without her, his life no longer makes sense.

He rolls on his back and scoots closer until his shoulder touches the base of Nolee's neck. She's curled in a tight ball. Keet looks up through the tent, seeing only the shadowy outlines of trees. Getting up, he tucks the covers around Nolee and returns to the spring, its steam rising in the scant light of a waxing crescent moon. He undresses and slides into its warmth. Tilting his head back, he shuts his eyes, his racing thought gradually calming. He's almost asleep when the glide of Nolee's thigh next to his brings him to alertness. Keet admires her milky skin, the curve of her hips and breasts, the water rippling as she lowers herself beside him.

Under the water, she takes his hands in her own and says, "Keet Noland, you arrived in my life when I thought I'd be alone forever. You've given me your trust and your body, and I've given you my trust and body in return. On this night, I promise you my heart and I promise you my honesty."

Keet, mind focused but heart beating in racing thumps, turns toward her. Only the sound of her voice, husky and soft with sleep, matters to him as she continues.

"I will be yours in plenty and in want, in sickness and in health, in failure and in success. I belong to myself, but while we both wish it, I promise you what is mine to give. I give you my living and my dying, each in your care."

Leaning toward him and placing her cheek against his, he feels their heartbeats merge like the hands clasped between them. His heart steadies as she speaks, the small puffs of air tickling against his ear.

"I promise to honor you and to remember our love all my days, and to allow that love to grow so that nothing can divide us. I promise loving words, and a heart open to giving forgiveness as well as receiving it. I place my heart within yours, that we may live in the flames of love between us. I promise to be the keeper of that flame, and never let it die."

Releasing her hands, he drops his own to her soft waist, then moves down to her hips, resting there. He cups her curves with his hands as though she was shaped for him.

"Magnolia Clark Burnett. Lia." At the sound of her nickname she smiles, the moonlight shimmering on the steamy water reflected to him through her eyes. Vapor curls around their bodies, encasing them in warmth.

"I was lonely and in despair when you found me. Your love inspired me to bravery when I wanted to shrink away from the world. You've inspired me to tenderness when I wanted to build walls. You mean more to me than all the stars in the sky, or the diamonds on the water at sunrise."

Tears spill from his eyes, and he sees her smile through her own. He cradles her face in his hands, wiping her cheeks with his thumbs.

"You are my heart's friend, my fire-bright warmth, my cool winter earth, the air that keeps life in my body, and the water I swim in. On this night, I promise you my life and my death, that I will shield you in both. I promise to honor you above all others, your joys becoming my joys, your sorrows ones we will carry together. I have listened to my heart, and it now beats with yours."

Keet places his hand above Nolee's heart, its beating echoed in the soft flesh over her ribcage. He repeats the words she spoke to him.

"I promise to honor you, and remember our love all my days, and to allow that love to grow so that nothing can divide us. I promise loving words, and a heart open to giving forgiveness as well as to receiving it. I place my heart within yours, that we may live in the flames of love between us. I promise to be the keeper of that flame, and never let it die."

Nolee puts her hands on his before their mouths meet in a kiss that's both new and familiar. Under the starlight, their bodies meld as the hot spring's vapor encloses them in a misty globe.

The next morning, I'm following Keet up the trail as we hike back to the car. Contemplating the contrasting emotions of committing ourselves to one another compared to the superficiality of my conventional wedding to Nate distracts me from the effort it's taking me to breathe.

"Maybe it's because I'm older now," I say, puffing on the uphill climb.

"Maybe what's because you're older?"

"Our Promising Ceremony. It was different when I married Nate in a church in front of everyone."

"Oh?"

"Stop a minute—I've got to catch my breath." I put my hand against the rain-softened bark of a nearby tree, cool against my palm. While I'm waiting for my lungs to take in more air, Keet says, "I wouldn't know, because I've nothing to compare it with."

"I was thinking that the morning after Nate and I were married, I looked at this ring on my finger and my new name on the marriage certificate, and all I could think was…" I pause, surprised by the emotion surging through me. "It was this giant disappointment. Like, 'now what?'"

"That's a low bar to get over," Keet says, taking my hand from the tree and holding it.

"After last night, I'm more connected to you than I ever was to Nate."

Keet pulls me into an embrace and rests his chin on the top of my head. "Honoring each other this way is different than the ways we thought we had to perform."

"That's it. We did this for us, in our own way, with our own words. Which took me weeks to put together."

Keet's laugh rumbles through his chest. "Our Promising Ceremony was perfect, and I won't ever forget your words."

"I wrote them down."

Keet holds me at arm's length, looking into my eyes.

"Part of my process. I wanted to be clear what I was offering to you. And to myself."

He leans down and kisses me, the encircling sense of our oneness surrounding us as intimately as birdsong.

His forehead against mine, he says, "What is mine to give is yours to have, Lia. Always."

# CHAPTER SEVENTEEN

When they get home that afternoon, they're welcomed by a chorus of yips and whines from Fae, and Wallace leans against Nolee as she scratches his back. Keet hugs Sylvie and Zelka, then watches as his grandmother and sister embrace Nolee.

"You have promised yourselves to one another?" Sylvie asks.

Nolee beams, taking Keet's hand in hers. "Yes."

"We can continue with your celebration plans?"

When Nolee looks at him, he returns her smile.

"Yes," he says.

"We're thinking after the July fourth holiday."

Happiness moves through all four as they gather in a giant hug. Keet is the last to step back.

"I've designed postcards. Once we settle on a date, I'll send them out. It's not much notice for people." Nolee says.

"People will show up if they can. The important part is between you and my grandson."


Keet leaves the tangle of sheets and comforter, switching on the gas fireplace facing their bed on his way to the closet. July mornings can be chilly. Besides, he likes the look of the flames, even if they are gas-powered. Extending his arm deep into his collection of pullovers and sweaters, his fingers locate the corners of the black square box he stashed away, biding his time for the perfect occasion to give it to Nolee. The pile of sweaters was a safe bet; when did he last wear a sweater?

Nolee is sitting up in bed, wearing one of his old black t-shirts. She also has a box, but this one is wooden. Keet sees water stains on one side, and faint writing on the top, which looks as though the top slides open.

Sliding back into bed, he offers his box to her with both hands. She takes it, kisses him, and hands him the box she's holding. Its weight surprises him.

"Open yours first, Keet Noland. I'm 'bout coming out of my skin with excitement."

"What's the story with this box?"

Nolee shakes her head, pushing the stray hair away from her face. She hasn't had it cut for months, and it's now down to her shoulders. He would love her if she were bald, but he also likes the thick weight of her auburn hair in his hands.

"I'll tell you once you open it. Here—"

She reaches to slide open the top, but Keet raises the box above his head, laughing.

"Nope. I get to do this part."

Lowering his arms, he sets the box on the comforter in front of him. It warms beneath his touch, and he wonders how many other hands have held this box, how much water from how many seas and oceans has splashed onto its surface. He pushes back the lid. Inside, cushioned in white tissue paper, is an object he has never seen, only heard about.

"It's—"

"A storm glass."

He removes it from its paper nest and runs his hands over the cool, dark metal encasing a liquid-filled glass tube with a cloudy layer of white sediment.

"Lia!" He leans over and kisses her. "This is beautiful. Where did you find it?"

"At an antique shop in Seattle. The owner said they're not accurate, but I like how it looks."

"It would be fun to mount this on *The Salish See*." As Keet inspects the storm glass more closely, he recalls the surprise he'd given Nolee last summer. On an overnight outing to a distant island, he'd transformed to orca and spangled the night with trails of swirling blue and green bioluminescence, to Nolee's delight.

She wraps her arms around him and closes her eyes. A picture of his sailboat flashes through his mind. "I have wonderful memories on that boat." Her head rests on his shoulder. "Remember our first date, which we didn't want to call a date?"

Keet laughs. "It was a date in my mind. I think you were still too cautious to see me that way."

She lifts her head, smiling. "I was scared, but deep down, I knew what it was. Who you were going to be to me. The glass may not be practical, but it's a piece of nautical history I thought you'd like."

"I do like it. Very much." Keet offers the box containing her gift. "Your turn."

A sparkly turquoise string is tied around the box. Pulling it loose, she starts to pry open the box. When she glances at Keet, his smile is so broad she can't help but smile back.

"Go on," he nudges her. "Open it."

Nolee pops off the lid. Inside, nestled in black paper confetti, is a necklace, a circle of sea glass in blues and greens interspersed with small abalone shell disks. She holds it up to the morning sun and twirls it, sending tiny points of refracted light around their bedroom.

"Here, let me put it on you."

She hands the necklace to Keet and holds up her hair so he can clasp it around her pale neck. Then, sliding out of the t-shirt, she turns to face him. "What do you think?"

"I think you're the most beautiful woman I've ever seen." He pulls her closer, and Nolee laughs as he rolls her on top of him, the sheets tangling around their bodies.

We get up to take care of the dogs and eat a late breakfast. As we eat, I ask Keet for the story behind the necklace.

"I have a family friend in Alaska who's a jeweler. I called her, gave her some ideas, texted her a photo of you, and she did the rest."

Beneath my pullover, the necklace has warmed to the temperature of my skin. "How did it get here without my knowing?"

Keet smiles. "I had it shipped to Ava's address."

"Ava!" I laugh. "She's going to catch hell for keeping a secret from me!" My words are bluster, though. I'd spent my life invisible to those who should have seen me. My father. My ex-husband. My family. Since moving to Camas Island, I'd discovered how to be visible. First, to see myself. Once Keet and I were together, we also saw ourselves through one another's eyes. Though our beginning was tumultuous, during this last year, turbulence seems to have moved around us, as water moves around obstacles in its path. There's nothing else in this life I want or need.

As he holds me, a black oblong shape shimmers into being behind my closed eyes, like Texas summer heat coming off an asphalt road. I push the remnants of the nightmare away, willing myself to focus on the here and now.


Later that morning leaving the post office, I check the list on my phone to make sure I've mailed all the invitations to our Promising Celebration. It's a thrill mixed with unease. Exhilaration, from inviting familiar individuals who will join in the celebration. Unease, from the chance my family will be there.

I'd felt obligated to invite my dad and siblings, though there's a snowflake's chance in hell that they'll join us. None of my friends from my old neighborhood in Texas are on the list, and neither are my ex-husband, Nate, and Carlos, his new husband. More than a week ago, I sent him a text to confirm our daughter's visit in July and tell him that Keet and I would be having a small celebration of our commitment ceremony. I'd chickened out before writing that I didn't want him and Carlos there.

Shoving the phone in my pocket, I get in the car. The ping of a text sounds as I click the seatbelt into place. I sigh at the sight of Nate's name.

*Congrats, Nolee. I'm overjoyed for you. May you and Keet have many long and wonderful years together.* I read and re-read the text, wondering if Carlos had anything to do with its conciliatory tone. My thumbs hover over the screen as I consider how to reply.

*Thanks, Nate! I hope you and Carlos are doing great!* I tap in, then erase with a huff of impatience. I find the use of rhymes irritating. And what's with all the exclamation marks?

*Thank you, Nate. I hope you and Carlos are having your own wonderful years together.*

Hitting send, I toss the phone on the passenger seat and head for home. It occurs to me that Nate and I may finally have reached a truce. Although this gives me some small hope that we can maintain it, the feeling of nervousness about who will show up at our celebration is just as strong.

I'm practically floating in the clouds, a mix of elation and melancholy swirling within me. As I drive, I ask myself what's going on, but aside from the maelstrom of emotions, there's no clarity.

Then my phone rings and I see Keet's name on the screen. "Hi sweetie."

"Where are you?"

Taken aback by his clipped tone, I pause before answering.

"On my way home."

"Can you meet me at the trailhead west of The Point?"

"Sure. What's it called again?"

"Madrone Trail."

"I'll be there in ten."

He hangs up without saying goodbye. As I drop the phone back on the seat, my knuckles turn white on the steering wheel. I release my death grip, shake my shoulders, and say out loud, "He's probably distracted by something and needs my feedback."

The tangle of emotions that I've carried for the past week distills into one clear-as-crystal sensation. Fear.

# CHAPTER EIGHTEEN

Keet paces in front of his 4Runner, looking at the road leading to the trailhead every few seconds, willing ten minutes to have passed. Trying to calm down, he takes some deep breaths; he's almost ready to call Nolee again when he hears the faint whine of her car's engine and the telltale rattle of its loose muffler. He restrains himself from rushing her, watching as she locks the car and puts her phone and her keys in a pocket. When she looks at him, her smile disappears.

"Keet, what's wrong?"

"Follow me and I'll show you."

Keet knows he's causing Nolee worry. He knows he should offer her a hug first, reassuring her that his anger isn't about her. Instead, he turns without waiting for her to follow and, almost running, starts down the trail leading to a small bluff with a view of the sea.

"Keet Noland."

It's not his name that stops his feet. It's the tone of her voice; one he knows means she's dealing with an emotional storm of her own. He turns, stepping backward to put more distance between them.

"Tell me, right now, what's going on."

"The male orca from the Water Canyon House is back."

Nolee's shoulders drop. "When?"

"I spotted him right before I called you."

He takes a step closer to her and holds out his hand. "I'm sorry."

She takes his hand, nodding. "Okay."

"I want to get to the trailhead to show you. If he's still there, I need you to tell me if it's the same one."

She lets go of his hand and they jog down the narrow dirt path.

In half the time it took them the first time they hiked here together, they stand on a weathered wooden platform, leaning on the rail and trying to catch their breath. The Salish Sea stretches before them, bright blue in the noon sun's blast. Small whitecaps rise from the rippling silk of the water, the islands a hazy green. But nowhere do they catch sight of a tall black dorsal fin.

"Where did you first see him?"

Keet stands, pointing toward the nearest island to the north.

"There. He was swimming toward me but staying on this side of The Point."

Nolee looks over her shoulder at the cliff rising above the sea.

"I bet he's trying to stay on this side, so we don't see him from Osprey Bay," she says.

Keet considers this, the anger in his heart dropping to dread in his stomach. He nods. "I bet you're right." He moves closer, putting his arm around her shoulders. She leans into him. When she speaks, it's forced humor. He knows she's trying to lighten their moods.

"I can't say I've ever been stalked by an orca before."

She wraps her arms around his waist and buries her face in his chest. As he closes his eyes and leans his cheek against the top of her head, he feels his heart rate slowing. A quiet puff of air returns their attention to the sea. Even before registering his shape visually, they know the male orca has returned. As they watch, he swims in slow arcs, never crossing beyond The Point, never putting himself in the sightline of Osprey Bay.

"Wait here, Nolee."

Before she can ask why, he's left the platform and is making his way to the beach. He hears his name and knows she's following him, but keeps his focus on pushing through bushes, stepping over downed trees. As he crosses the uneven ground, he hopes Nolee understands why he isn't waiting for her. He needs to find out who's watching them; he hopes that knowledge will extinguish his anger, that the cold water will soothe the heat that beats through him.

He reaches the beach—a sandbar, really—rocks and logs thrown across it like a child's pickup sticks. Shedding his shirt and shorts, he jogs into the water, eyes following the dorsal fin. The ground drops away as he plunges in and starts to swim. He dives, spinning, all his thoughts centered on finding out who's watching Nolee.

Now orca, Keet emits a series of staccato clicks, scanning for the other male. The picture in his head shows the orca surfacing for a quick breath before diving, rostrum angled toward the base of an island. Doubling his efforts, Keet also rises for a breath, then dives and pushes through the murky water. He keeps sending out clicks, not caring if the other orca knows he's being followed. Finally, he sees the male orca level out near the sea floor, then disappear. Swimming harder, determined to uncover Nolee's stalker's identity and motive, he reaches the spot at the base of the island. Scanning now with louder clicks, he cannot find the male orca. What he does see is the faint outline of oblong blackness that doesn't match its surroundings.

I wait on the shore, watching as Keet speeds away from me, his dorsal fin throwing out sunbursts before he submerges. Pacing, anger and worry swirling inside my chest, I close my eyes and reach out through my mind, trying to picture Keet and the threatening male orca. The space behind my eyes remains black. When I open my eyes, the day is still sunny and Keet is still submerged. Moments later, however, he rises in a loud exhalation of air and water and swims toward me. Submerging once again, he reappears as a man swimming toward the beach, where I stand holding his clothes. I'm eager to hear what he's found, but, judging by his expression, I'd say not a lot.

"Nothing," he says as he pulls on his shorts.

"You didn't find him?"

He bends over, shaking his head, spattering the rocks with seawater.

"I found him, then he disappeared right in front of me." He pulls on his t-shirt.

"How can that happen, Keet?"

"I saw the outline of a door at the base of that island, but I need Zelka to confirm that."

But when we get home, Zelka isn't in the cabin.

I send a text to Zee.

*Hey there … Grandmother said you and Marissa are hanging out. Can you text or call when you're home? We have a question for you.*

Keet, reading over my shoulder, says, "Can you make it sound more urgent? I need to ask her right now."

"It's not an emergency. We can wait."

Keet huffs his impatience, then turns and walks out of the cabin, muttering about going home and taking a shower.

"What happened, Granddaughter?"

A flush of warmth flares in my anxiety-chilled body, loving that my relationship with Sylvie has become so close. I sit with her at the table, describing the sighting of the unknown male orca and how Keet observed him on the other side of The Point. Once Keet had transformed into orca, the other male disappeared.

"Hmm." Sylvie stares out of the window. "Are you sure it's one of the Water Canyon House Keykwin?"

I nod.

"Is that what you need to ask Zelka?"

"Not quite. We need to know who it is."

"Could be any of the men who live down there."

"Yes. But Keet and I suspect it's a man she's met. Keet also thinks there's another door, at the base of an uninhabited island close to us."

"That's more likely than a Keykwin evaporating. We have unique abilities, but disappearing isn't one of them."

I catch her sparkling eyes, realizing she's trying to lighten the mood. I laugh. "That's good."

My phone pings with a text from Zelka.

*be home soon Em will drop me off before she gets to work love you*

I smile at her lack of punctuation. She writes like she must speak when she's orca, in a long stream of sounds. I'm also smiling at the short version of Marissa's name. An endearment. Whether Zelka realizes it, it seems she's found someone. I wonder if Marissa feels the same, worried about what will happen if it backfires.

Shelving that worry for another day, I hug Sylvie and walk back to our house. Fae and Wallace burst out, bouncing with excitement, then dash across the rocks and plunge into the cove. Keet stands in the doorway, wet hair combed back, a thunderstorm of emotions rolling across his face. I square my shoulders before I say, "She'll be home soon."

Keet nods, then goes into the kitchen and starts pulling out food from the refrigerator.

"Are we having an early dinner?"

He nods, then puts his hand on the countertop and hangs his head. When he turns toward me, the thunderstorm is gone, and in its place is the worry he's carrying. I rush to him, holding his body against mine. "We'll figure it out, Keet."

He exhales a long breath before squeezing me tighter, then trying to turn away. I keep holding him. "Right now, in this moment, you and I are safe. We're together. Nothing will change that."

He wraps his arms around me again until I let go. "Can I help you make dinner?"

He shakes his head. "No, I want to keep busy."

"In that case, I'm going outside with the dogs." I stand on tiptoe to kiss him, then grab two tennis balls and let myself focus on the joy of Fae and Wallace doing what they love in the place they call home.

As I straighten up, a sopping ball in my hand, flashes of red flicker through the trees: Marissa and Zee coming down the road to our driveway. The bass beat of a song they're singing is punctuated by their laughter. Anyone who has been in love would recognize that sound anywhere. I wonder if they do?

Marissa rolls to a stop by the cabin. Sylvie stands by the open door, watching the red sports car and the two women emerging from it. Zee takes Marissa by the hand and leads her onto the porch. Zee is incandescent and Marissa's face has the same glow. The rocks rattle behind me as Keet follows me to Sylvie's cabin, the dogs trailing behind us.

"I've asked Em to stay for dinner," Zelka says, but she has to go to work."

Marissa shrugs. "Science never sleeps."

Fae and Wallace finish sniffing Marissa's legs and her offered hand, then sit down beside her.

"Maybe another time," I say. Zee walks Marissa to her car. I look away as their hug goes on much longer than I would expect between friends.

After the rumble of Marissa's car fades, Zelka turns to face us. "What did you want to ask me?" Her smile and eyes are still bright from her time with Marissa.

I steel myself for a stern response from Keet.

"Dinner's almost ready, Zee. Why don't you and Grandmother join us?"

Zelka looks toward Sylvie. Sylvie nods, then closes the door behind her.

As we walk toward our house, the dogs trotting in front of us, my curiosity about Zelka's reply is pinging around the inside my head.

It's unusual for Keet to talk before he's filled his plate, but as they sit down, he looks at Zelka and asks, "Is there a doorway in the base of the small island to the west of here? Almost behind The Point?"

Zelka drops the salad she's scooping onto her plate. Her face closes, the brightness from her time with Marissa dimming. "Why do you want to know?"

Keet looks at her, disbelieving. "There is."

Zelka shrugs, shifting in her seat. "I made a promise, Keet. If I answer your question, I break it."

"If you don't answer my question, Nolee is in danger."

"How?"

Keet tells her about the encounter they had, and the male orca that swims where he can't be seen from Osprey Bay.

"I think it's the same male orca who tried to lure Nolee into the sea this past winter."

Zelka frowns. "When did that happen?"

"One night, while you were still in the Water Canyon House."

"You didn't tell me about this." Sylvie looks at Keet and Nolee, waiting for their response.

"Very early one morning, I woke up in a sweat," Nolee begins. "All I wanted was to cool off in the cove, then go back to bed."

"What time was this?" Zelka asks, foreboding settling in her belly.

"Three-ish in the morning," Nolee answers. "I took the dogs with me and was standing in the water when a male orca appeared outside the buoys. Before I realized what I was doing, I found myself waist-deep in high tide. Keet pulled me out."

Keet adds, "It was one of the Water Canyon House Keykwin. He didn't have any markings behind his dorsal fin."

"I didn't even notice that," Nolee says. "I didn't think of anything until Keet grabbed me and hauled me back to land."

Zelka replays her nights in the Water Canyon House, flipping through memories. The hunters went out, but she had no way of knowing if it was day or night. Then the foreboding she's been experiencing intensifies into certainty. Arogem, and their conversation, where he had answered her question about hunting with a smirk and a reply of "you could say that."

Zelka decides. "I can't tell you anything, Keet, but I can swim out and see if I can talk with the Water Canyon House People."

"I'll join you."

Zelka shakes her head, alarm growing in her chest. She must keep Keet away; she knows he'll ask her questions she can't answer, secrets that aren't meant for anyone who isn't a part of her Water Canyon House family.

"You can't. You haven't been initiated into their family like I have. Let me try first."

Keet holds her gaze for so long her eyes water. She blinks. He nods.

"We'll try it your way first, Zee." His use of her shortened name soothes her. As she reaches for food, she tells herself her way will work. She'll coax Arogem out of hiding and ask him. If he's the one bothering Nolee, she'll put a stop to it.

# CHAPTER NINETEEN

As Keet mows a long stretch of grass under the trees so we can set up tables and the dance floor, I'm on the phone confirming our choices with the caterer, Jason. Half-listening as he rattles off the food Keet and I chose for our Promising Celebration, I take the sheets out of the dryer. We're picking up Jerry and his girlfriend, Saila, at the Camas Island ferry this evening; they'll be staying with Sylvie.

"That all sounds amazing, Jason. Thanks for double-checking."

"No probs. Later!" He hangs up without saying goodbye, and I wonder if these small pleasantries will die with the coming generation. And then I wonder if that makes me officially old, thinking about younger generations. Arms full of warm sheets and towels, I slide the farm door open with my foot and dump everything on the guest bed.

It's been four days since Zelka said she would find the lone male orca who was hanging around Camas. Each evening, she swims back to the dock, frustration written in the stoop of her shoulders and the heaviness of her limbs as she boosts herself on to the platform. Last night, she mentioned swimming by the door at night to catch him while he hunts. When Keet asked why she didn't go inside, she avoids answering directly, instead mumbling about her plans for the following day. She's in the living room, talking on the phone with Marissa in a low voice. I catch the words "helping" and "family" and "I wish I could see you more, too." I hope Marissa's patient, and that Zelka finds out who the threatening presence is soon. It would be ideal if our celebration could be free of worry. But like many things in life, what I'd like and what will happen are most likely different.

I make the bed, letting the activity take the place of the worry whirling in my head. It's as though all that I've learned about myself on Camas

Island is warring with the woman I used to be in Texas. I shake the pillows into their cases and smooth the ocean quilt across the bed, hoping it will help Abbie feel at home in a strange place.

The drone of the mower cuts out. I look through the window and see Keet stretch, reaching for the sky, eyes closed, long hair loose. I leave the bedroom and fill a glass with sweet tea, a drink he asks for even in the winter. I'd left a lot of things behind when I drove out of Texas; good thing my granny's recipe for sweet tea wasn't one of them.

He's wiping the sweat from his face with his forearm when I hold out the glass.

"I think you need one of these."

He takes it with a smile and drinks half the glass in one long swallow. "Thanks. Zelka gone yet?"

"No. She's talking to Marissa."

Keet grunts, looking at the area he's mowed.

"The yard looks good. I don't think I've ever seen it all trimmed up."

"It'll do. I enjoy seeing it wild, though; I miss the dandelions and grasses."

"The rosemary's happy."

Keet nods. Unused to tiptoeing across the minefield of a recent argument, I'm at a loss for what my next comment should safely be.

Keet drinks the rest of the tea, then breaks the awkward silence between us. "When we promised ourselves to each other, you said you would be honest."

"Yes, I did." I take the glass from him.

"I promised I'd be a shield for you."

"You did."

"So why won't you help me encourage Zelka to take me with her? I'm trying to be your shield, Nolee, and neither of you will let me. What aren't you telling me?"

I've become familiar with the anger and frustration in Keet's eyes, but the intense sorrow he's holding onto is almost too difficult to witness. My phone pings with a text. I ignore it, but as I ponder my reply, a new text appears. Keet's eyes shift away from me. "Sounds like someone needs your attention."

"You need my attention, too." I move closer, smelling the cut grass, not a smell I associate with Keet.

"I still have a lot of mowing to do." He starts the engine, leaving me in a cloud of gas fumes.

I pull the phone out of my hip pocket and see that the texts are from my sister Lily. She hardly ever contacts me. I don't know whether to be alarmed or excited. Reading her message, I walk into the house.

*Dad's in the hospital. They think he's going to be fine, but none of us wants to leave him. We hope you have a nice day with Keet.*

Even after three years, none of my family can acknowledge my relationship with Keet. My unease changes to frustration. It's the same old shit, dug up from a different hole. Lily and my brothers Frank and Manny have all conformed to the life our father chose for them. Ranchers and mothers and fathers. They belong in the Burnett clan. Me, not so much.

I tilt my head back and close my eyes as the familiar sensation of being on the outside assails me like wind before a storm. When I look out the window, I see Keet bouncing along on the mower, one of my turquoise bandanas now tied around his head. The storm winds continue to gust through me, but this time, they change course. I'm flooded with love for this man I promised my life to. My present and my future, he's alive and healthy, as is our life together. My family in Texas needs to stay in the past.

I pick up my phone and dial Lily's number. About the time I expect to be sent to voicemail, she answers.

"Hey, Nolee."

"I got your text. Thanks for telling me about Dad. Is there anything I can do?"

"No, we've got it under control here."

"Lily, I wanted to call to let you know that Keet and I aren't just having a nice day together."

"Here we go." She sighs against the phone. The clank of silverware being slung into the drawer is so loud I move the phone away from my ear.

"We had a private ceremony in which we promised our lives to one another. It's an Indigenous tradition that's right for both of us."

"Glad to hear it." Her voice sounds anything but glad.

"Next week, Keet and I will be celebrating that choice with our friends and family, announcing ourselves as part of a larger community here on Camas Island. It isn't a traditional marriage and reception, but it's just as important to me. Keet's my life now, Lily, and I hope y'all will meet him one day."

I hear Lily stack plates, then close cabinet drawers. A dog barks before she answers me. "Congratulations."

I pause, waiting to see if what she said is a joke. Then, clear that it's not, I say goodbye and hang up. When I turn around, Keet's standing in the doorway.

"Did you catch all of that?" I ask.

"Most of it," he says, walking toward me.

"I thought it was time my family hears how important you are to me."

He pulls me into an embrace, our bodies melding top to bottom. He whispers, "Thank you for being honest."

I smile, my face warming as I press it against his chest. "I'm a woman of my word, Keet."

# CHAPTER TWENTY

When Zelka returns the next morning, the shine in her eyes tells Keet she has news.

"The Water Canyon House orca swam out of the door last night," she says. "He knew I was there right away, so I asked him to meet me on the beach where you and Nolee saw him."

"And?" Keet asks, not able to wait for her to explain. "Who is he? What did he say?"

Zelka glances at Keet as though unsure how to reply. Breaking through the tension, Nolee asks, "Zee, do you want something to eat? Some tea?"

"Do you have coffee? Eggs and toast would be great, too."

Nolee puts water on to boil for coffee while Keet assembles what he needs to make omelets. To steady his shaking hands, he focuses on cooking, trying to rein in emotions that threaten to bolt.

"It's Arogem."

Nolee looks at Keet, then Zelka. "Who is Arogem?"

Brother and sister exchange a glance, the memory of their conversations about Arogem passing between them. Zelka says, "He's a man who wanted me to be with him, but I didn't want the same thing."

"So he's stalking you by showing up here and trying to get me to swim with him?"

"He said he wanted my attention, which is why he showed up here the first time and tried to lure you into the sea. He wouldn't do anything."

Keet huffs a laugh. "Right."

"Keet, I believe him. He looked so sad when I told him I still wasn't interested, and that in fact, I have a girlfriend."

"A girlfriend!"

"Marissa?"

She nods, smiling. Keet hugs his sister; the knot in his belly is still there, but he's able to smile through his uncertainty and offer his congratulations, hugging his sister again before turning back to the meal prep.

"Arogem's not going to bother Nolee anymore?"

"He said he wouldn't."

Keet wants to trust Arogem's word, but his sister is an innocent, and he's not confident about her ability to detect Arogem's lies. The threat to Nolee gnaws at him. "I want to talk with him."

"Keet—" Zelka protests.

The kettle whistles. Nolee pours boiling water into a French Press. As she waits for the coffee to steep, she says, "Zee, Keet's right. We need to hear Arogem's assurances ourselves. The last thing we want is him showing up here on the day of our party."

"He told me he won't come back here again. I was very clear that I'd chosen someone, and it isn't him."

"Did he try to change your mind?"

Zelka looks away. "He did, but it didn't work. I like Marissa. She's the one I want to be with." She pours a cup of coffee and takes it to the table.

Keet finishes chopping the vegetables, scrapes them into the bowl with the eggs, and begins mixing.

"He's not coming back," Zelka repeats. But to Keet's ears, it sounds as though she's trying to convince them of something she doesn't believe herself.

"Did you tell him that if he comes back, he's dealing with me?" Keet asks.

Nodding, Zelka says, "Yes, I shared your message. He laughed and said you don't scare him."

"It's not a tactic, Zee. It's a truth."

"He won't come back, Keet. He gave me his word."

"What happened after this talk on the beach?" As Keet whips the contents of the bowl, he realizes he needs to slow down—in his agitation, he's causing the eggs to froth.

"It wasn't a talk on the beach."

"I thought you said—"

"He was on the beach. I stayed in the water."

Nolee says, "Why did you stay in the water—" then answers her own question. "No clothes."

Zelka nods. "I didn't want him to see me naked again."

"Again?" Keet asks, pausing before pouring the eggs into the skillet.

Zelka takes a sip of coffee, looking away from her brother's eyes. "I tried to leave Water Canyon House three times. Two of those times, I took my robe off, as is customary when the People go hunting. Arogem was there both times." She takes another large gulp of coffee, still not looking at Keet.

"You don't think that Arogem could've interpreted your nakedness as you saying you don't want to be with him, but you did want him looking at you?"

"I didn't want him looking at me, Keet!"

"How was he supposed to know that? Did you ask him to cover his eyes?"

"I didn't! Who cares! It's just a body!"

"You should care, Zelka. Because to Arogem, it isn't 'just' a body. It's your body, and he wants it."

Zelka stands up and tries to leave, but Nolee steps in front of her. "Zee, please, sit down. We can talk about this after we eat."

But the tension increases as they share the meal. Conversation is minimal, the silence punctuated by "pass the salt" or "this is great." Keet hears Nolee invite Zelka to join her on a beach walk, and then the sound of their footsteps as they leave the house. Only after they're gone does he allow his head to drop, to experience the dread that the threat of Arogem become more real, not less.

"What happened out there, Zee?"

Her gaze shifts from me to the channel, toward a small piece of land between The Point and the uninhabited island of Waldron.

"What I told you happened."

"I believe you, but there's a gap between you finding him as he swam out of the door as orca, and him on the beach by The Point." As Zelka increases her pace, the wet rocks slide and rattle under her bare feet. I put my hand on her arm. "We need to slow down—my legs aren't as long as yours. Shall we sit somewhere?"

Seeing a dry log above the waterline, we sit down. Zelka stares at the island. When I touch her arm, the shame radiates off her skin, but over what, I can't tell. "What's bothering you?"

She looks down at her hands, then says, "When I was in the Water Canyon House, Arogem tried to attract me with his words, and…"

"And?" I know where this is going and try to hide my smile of recognition because this is Zelka's first experience as a human woman, and the workings of attraction.

"He kissed me a lot. I liked it at first, but then I didn't."

"He knew this?"

Zelka nods.

"Did he threaten you?" My smile disappears, thinking he may have done more than kiss her without her consent.

"No. But he wouldn't leave me alone. He was always touching me or finding ways to be alone with me. He gave me some small stones he'd carved. They were pretty."

"Did you keep them?"

"No. Yiskal braided them into the hair that I left at the Water Canyon House. She runs her hands over the back of her head and frowns.

"Just because someone wants to be with you, doesn't mean you have to be with them."

"I've figured that out. How I feel with Em is so different than how I felt with Arogem."

I watch as a boat speeds by in the channel, engine buzzing like an impatient mosquito.

Zelka says, "I called him 'cousin,' which in the People's tradition, means I view him as family, not a lover or a beloved."

"It sounds like you were as clear with him as you could be."

"I thought I was. But he won't give up this idea of us being together."

"What happened last night?"

A sudden breeze fills the channel with whitecaps. When the waves strike the shore, they boom rather than their usual quiet rattle and hiss.

"When he came through the door, I touched his tail as he swam by me. I knew it was Arogem." She watches the waves beating the rocks on the shore. "I asked him to meet me on the beach, both of us as human," she continues.

She looks at me, worry creasing her forehead. I put my hand on hers.

"He got to the beach first. He walked up on the shore and then turned toward me. I was still in the water up to my shoulders. There was no way I was going to be naked with him."

"Good call."

She's encouraged by my words, but the rest of the story comes tumbling out in a rush. "He stood there, like I was supposed to be impressed or something, and asked me to come up on the beach with him. I asked him if he was the orca swimming around Osprey Bay. He said yes. He was *proud* of it, Nolee! I told him what Keet said, and he laughed. Once he realized I wasn't going to come to him, he started walking toward me. I told him I needed his word that he'd leave you alone."

"What did he say?"

"He said, 'Sure. I'll leave your friend Nolee alone.' I told him I liked Marissa and was with her. He looked like he was sad, but I think he was making fun of me. By that time, I was backing up because he was in the water up to his knees. I didn't want to find out what would happen if he reached me when I was still human, so I swam out and dove, almost got stuck on a sandbar when I changed to orca, then swim back here. He didn't follow me."

"That's why you were so rattled."

"I pity him, but I'm also afraid of him. How can that be possible?"

"It's possible because you're kind, Zee. Maybe a little innocent, too."

"Keet said that. What does it mean?"

"It means that you're learning about the darker parts of human nature. We lie, we manipulate, we use what's available to get what we want."

"That doesn't tell me what innocent is, just what it's not."

I smile. Although she's only been human for a year, she's catching on.

"Innocence is a state of wonder, Zee. It's choosing to see the world with fresh eyes, which you can't help but do since you spent the first thirty years of your life as Blackfish."

"So innocent isn't a bad thing?"

My head tilts sideways. "Depends on the context I guess."

"Are you saying it's only safe to be innocent with people you trust?"

"That's one way of looking at it."

She huffs in exasperation. "The only thing I want to be with Arogem is as far away as possible."


The next morning, I shrug the orange life vest over my jacket, smiling at the memory of the first time Keet took me sailing during one of his whale-watching charters. He called life jackets "personal flotation devices." It still seems like too much of a mouthful, something you'd say to satisfy an insurance company.

I drag the kayak Keet gave me after I moved in, sliding the bow into the waves.  After all the activity for our Promising Celebration, I wanted to be out on the water and soak in the quiet of a warm summer day. It might be my last chance for peace before Osprey Bay was overrun with people. Keet went to the marina, and Jerry and Saila ran to town for groceries.

As I roll up my pants above my water shoes, the water hits my feet, and I gasp at how cold it is. Taking a few quick steps, I swing into the kayak and use my paddle to push into deeper water. Behind me, I hear Fae whining in the front yard and in front of me, I see a dark splotch of cormorants bobbing on the waves.

The next thing I hear is an explosive exhale.  As I turn to look, a large dorsal fin rises beside me, without any gray or white saddle patch on his back. The orca grabs my paddle in his teeth. I notice his lavender-ringed eye.

We both pull against the paddle, then I open my hands, hoping to catch him off guard, but he's too big and too quick to fall for it. He sinks with the paddle, then swims farther into the channel and releases it on an outgoing current. I scan the area for other boaters, but they're too far away to see me. The orca flips around and swims toward me, plowing a large V in the water with his rostrum. I hold on to the sides of the kayak. Rage and helplessness run through me in equal measure. This must be Arogem.

He sinks beneath the surface, the ripples disappearing in the waves. I risk a look over the side of the kayak, but I can't see him through the green and turbulent murk. The kayak faces into the channel. I grit my teeth as I watch the bobbing orange paddle drift away from me. A small splash behind me, then the kayak tilts on its side, and I hear a laugh. I throw my weight the opposite way. Arogem won't have the satisfaction of seeing my fear, so I curse him instead.

"Dammit, Arogem, get your sorry ass off my kayak."

"Temper, Nolee. I'm not putting you in the water. Even I know you'd freeze to death before we got where we're going."

"You're not taking me anywhere." I glance over my shoulder in time to see him swim toward the bow.

"You and I are going to visit the Water Canyon House together."

"Don't be a damn idiot. You can't push this kayak and me through the channel without anyone noticing." But in a small part of my mind, I wonder if I'd become Keykwin if this happens.

Arogem interrupts my thoughts. "I don't care about being noticed. There's a doorway underneath that island you see in front of you. No one has used it in a very long time, but I've been watching you for months. I'll take you through it and then you and I can have a long visit in your new home, the Water Canyon House."

"I know about the door. I won't go."

"You will." Arogem's voice registers his surprise, but he recovers. "You want to. I can sense it." Swimming to the front of the kayak, he drapes a muscular arm over the prow. "You don't have a choice. Once I'm Blackfish and you're in the water with me, I can make you go to sleep. I'll just tuck you beside me like I'm holding your kayak right now, and you won't know anything until we're inside."

"My family will come looking for me. When they find me, you won't like what happens."

Arogem's face creases into a grin. "Those land Keykwin don't scare me. But it's not you I want. I want Zelka." The bravado gone, I see longing flit through his eyes. "She stays, you go. An easy trade. Plus, you become Keykwin. Everyone wins."

Focusing on Zelka, I say, "She's made it more than clear that she doesn't want *you*, Arogem."

"She doesn't know me well enough to make that decision. Our time together in the Water Canyon House was brief. I was passive, always backing off too soon."

"That's what's supposed to happen, asshole."

Arogem laughs again. "Your anger is impressive. But it won't change my decision. And you can't deny your own desire, can you?"

As he dives beneath the surface, I plunge my hand into the freezing water, pushing against it, trying to turn back toward Osprey Bay. It's a fruitless attempt. My best chance is staying in the kayak as long as possible.

In the distance, the dogs are barking, Wallace's deep bay joining Fae's high-pitched howls. Behind me, another a loud expulsion of air, followed by a head-snapping shove that pushes the kayak farther from shore. My mind whirs as the kayak lurches through the water. I need a stronger attachment, something more secure than a bungee cord. In the bottom of the kayak is the extra marine line and a water bottle; my thigh's resting against a block, and the padded seat has an extra line for adjustment but lacks hardware. Everything within my reach is the solid plastic of the kayak, or the much-too-flimsy bungee cord and marine line.

Running my fingers over the line, an idea forms. I wrap the extra line around my waist under my life vest, then tie each end to the tail of the black rope that attaches the seat to the kayak. My fingers shake as I tie a knot once, and then again. Pulling against the line around my torso, testing the knots, I feel the thin rope biting into my waist through my sweater. When he was teaching me to kayak, Keet stressed numerous safety techniques, with the highest priority being "never tie yourself in." Now, all other choices taken from me, I decide there's a time and place for every rule to be broken.

The kayak's forward momentum slows, and it bobs to a stop. Arogem, almost as big as Keet when he's orca, glides alongside, then spyhops, looking me over. Passing boats are still too far away for me to motion or yell for help. I put my hands in my lap, not wanting to risk touching Arogem, afraid I might fall into some enchanted sleep and wake up where I don't want to be. My desire to be Keykwin and join Keet in his world is far overshadowed by the terrifying way it could come true. I don't want Arogem to be the one to change me. I don't want to be changed at all, not on the cusp of a life where I have more than I could ever ask for.

"Arogem, I've tied myself in. Good luck trying to swim underwater with a kayak attached."

I hear a distant splash. The dogs are still barking. Arogem disappears, his dorsal fin dropping beneath the waves. The quiet that follows is heavy, the silence of a gathering of portents, lining up like ravens on a dead tree branch. I look in the water on both sides of the kayak. No flash of white, no Arogem. I reach down and splash, hoping to draw him out if he's there. Nothing. The gulls screech overhead, flying toward The Point. Water laps against the hull. I tuck my hands under my arms, squeezing myself, hoping to calm the shaking. After minutes of nothing happening, and no sight of Arogem nearby, I think it might be safe to try again to turn the kayak.

The silence is rended by a flurry of high-pitched wails. On the shore is a woman, hair loose and billowing around her. My heart leaps when I recognize Saila; she and Jerry are back from town. I wave my arms in the air, hoping she sees me. But she's not looking at me, and I turn to see what she's watching.

Two male orcas are fighting. One is much bigger than Arogem, his saddle patch a jagged whorl of white, skin shiny and taut over his ample flesh. His unmarked dorsal fin sways back and forth as he charges Arogem, mouth open. Watching him reminds me of a child learning to walk; stops and starts, missteps, flailing.

He throws himself on top of Arogem, and that's when the pictures flow in my head. I shut my eyes, sensing the pressure of bodies coming together as Arogem tries to keep the other male orca submerged until he inhales water. The larger orca dives deeper, flipping around to ram Arogem's belly with his rostrum. Water froths, revealing a lone male orca, ink-like blood seeping into the sea from gashes on his side. I open my eyes, looking for Arogem, hoping he doesn't choose to capsize me in the kayak. The new male orca surfaces and takes several breaths, then dives; the next thing I see is his dorsal fin heading toward the paddle bobbing in the distance.

Not wanting to take any chances, I check the water beneath me again and paddle with my hands. The breathing of the unknown male orca drifts back to me; his breaths are deeper, more regular. I focus again on Saila on the shoreline, wondering where Jerry is. Did he go into the house?

The orca's breath sounds are coming closer. I glance behind me. He has my paddle in his mouth, bringing it back to me like Wallace does with a stick. I'm not even tempted to smile at this image, though. Now I know where Jerry is, and what he's done to save me.

# CHAPTER TWENTY-ONE

When Jerry and Saila reach Keet's house, he stops the car. He hears dogs barking and howling, the shrill notes not unlike a human's frantic scream. Tightening his grip on Saila's hand, he scans the bay and sees Nolee in a kayak, and an unfamiliar man in the water, one arm over the front of the kayak. Then he sees the man let go of the kayak, slip into the water, and resurface as Blackfish, pushing the kayak farther out into deep water. Saila rests a gentle hand on his arm. "What is it, Jerry?"

He looks at his girlfriend, then back out to the bay at Nolee's paddle floating loose. Leaning over, he takes Saila's face in his hands and gives her a quick kiss. "Wait here for me. Nolee's in trouble."

He runs into the water as the waves push him back to shore. He takes a breath, puts his head down, and flails against the surface with his arms and legs. Throwing his head up to the sky, he gasps a breath, then, keeping his eyes open, looks down at the sea floor beneath him. It's too close. As he swims out, he feels increasingly coordinated, turning his head and taking a breath as the water buoys him on the surface. Jerry remembers his mother telling him that changing to Blackfish was natural. He remembers his sister Hazel taunting him while she swam outside their cabin in Sitka, changing to orca and back to human again, laughing because he fumed on the shore. As he looks at the sea floor again, he wonders if he has enough room.

Hearing Nolee's voice drift back to him on the wind, defiance and fear wrapped together, Jerry pauses for only an instant, remembering his buddies in 'Nam, screaming the same way as they went into battle. A tremor runs through him, but as he turns his head and gulps air, he clears his mind of the echo of war, focusing on his mother's quiet voice: "It's easy, son. You swim, then dive, holding the spirit of the Blackfish close inside you." The love in his mother's voice, as close as though she was swimming beside him, quiets his heartbeat. He sees her as Blackfish, the fluid black-and-white lines of her body as she surfaces.

One last breath, and he kicks as hard as he can, pointing his head down, forcing his body through the water with every muscle. Sensing his mother's voice inside his chest, he spins, envisioning the beauty of the orca. The spin slows and then stops, and he hangs in the water, the bottom of the sea brushing against his arms, which are now huge pectoral fins. He opens his eyes, seeing grains of sand and dull gray kelp he'd stirred up from the sea floor. What was once bone-chilling cold water now seems like a pleasant bath. His body feels enormous.

What hasn't enlarged is his supply of air. He tilts his body upward, seeing sunlight undulating through water that's a lighter shade of gray. The rough scrape of sand rasps against his tail as he aims for the surface. Once there, he takes a breath, surprised at the way the air moves into his lungs. Staying on the surface, he moves his tail and thrashes his oversized pectoral fins until he figures out how to glide. Finally, he dives, admiring the strength coursing through his body.

He feels as though he can hear from his head to the tips of his giant tail: the motors of boats buzzing through the water, the splash of gulls and cormorants as they land on the surface, the zing of fish swimming to the east, the metronome waves as they run to land.

He can also hear Nolee's heart pounding, but the orca who is pushing her out to sea is silent. Jerry rises again, taking a breath. His eyes no longer sting, and through the pale murk, he sees the other male orca bump the kayak with his head.

The other orca has turned and now glides underneath him. Jerry loses sight of the other orca before feeling the sudden impact of being rammed. He lets the push pitch him toward the surface, where he takes a quick breath, then dives and yells. What comes out are high-pitched squeals. Jerry opens his mouth, meaning to grab the other orca and pull him away. He misses, but not before a stinging heat slashes down his ribcage.

Another push down, away from the air. Jerry cries again, the sound vibrating against the soft structures beneath his blowhole. Rolling into a dark cloud of his own blood, he sees the other Blackfish in front of him and knows he means to force him deeper. Jerry rams his head into the black-and-white belly as hard as he can, opening his mouth to grab anything within reach. The other orca rolls over and swims away.

Jerry propels himself to the surface and takes several breaths. He hears the slap of water against the kayak and Nolee's ragged breathing. He wonders if he can find her missing paddle. Diving once again, he tries to send out the clicks he heard his mother talk about. One click shows a strand of kelp in front of him. With two clicks, he can see through the transparent jellyfish in front of the kelp. As he gets the hang of making the sound, he sends out a slow stream of clicks, and there, black against the gray waves, the paddle appears. As he swims toward it, he closes his eyes; he can see the pictures in his head more clearly. When he reaches the paddle, he takes it in his mouth and swims back to Nolee. As he nudges it toward her, he hears her heart racing. As she reaches for the paddle, he sees the tremor in her hands.

Nolee stares at him, wide-eyed. He lets himself drift closer, head bobbing in time with the kayak she's in. She rests her hand on his rostrum. He closes his eyes; her hand is colder than the water he's in, and fear radiates through her touch. Jerry's anger and disorientation are ebbing, and her touch relaxes him. He adjusts his position so his head rests against the kayak.

"Jerry?" she says.

He clicks in response. The thud of her heart slows, her breathing eases. In the distance, the dogs are quiet. He feels an outpouring of gratitude, but can't tell if it's from his heart, or hers. He hears her say "thank you," but isn't sure if she whispered it or if it blossomed from her mind to his. Disoriented by the lack of separation, he pulls his head away, dives, and turns toward shore, hearing the splash of the paddle as Nolee follows. He wants to be human again.

Unable to wait, he dives and spins, picturing himself as the man he knows. By the time he's wading through the water, Nolee is dragging her kayak up the beach toward the house. He brushes his hand over his face, wiping the water away, then gazes, unblinking, at the vast blue above. A warm rivulet of blood seeps down his side, but—mesmerized by the colors of the trees and sky and sea—he doesn't notice.

I stand on shaking legs, unbuckling the life vest and tossing it into the kayak next to the paddle. When I turn, Jerry is standing in the sea up to his waist, staring at the sky. Saila jogs to the cabin. When I get closer, I can see the red slashes across Jerry's broad chest. He catches my eye and yells, "Saltwater stings like a sonofabitch."

"It's the best thing for those cuts."

Jerry looks down, shrugs, and says, "I've had worse."

I'm closer now and see what he means. Four old, round scars run along his upper arm, the flesh puckered and pale against his brown skin. Under one collarbone is a long and jagged gash. Saila returns with a bundle of towels in her arms.

"Saila, I'll meet you both at the house."

She nods, her eyes still on Jerry. And why wouldn't they be? She just saw her boyfriend become a giant killer whale. As I turn my back on the sounds of Jerry making his way to shore—the click of the rocks, the susurrations of the sea—I wonder if Saila knows about Jerry and his family. *If she didn't before, she does now. It's a good sign she didn't get in her car and drive away.* My legs quiver as I strain to drag the kayak farther up the beach.

When I get to the cabin, Keet's sitting on the sofa next to Jerry. Wearing jeans but no shirt, he has a towel around his neck to catch the water dripping from his hair. Before they see me, I notice that the gashes on his chest extend across his ribcage, and his sternum is bruised. They stop talking when I close the door. I put the first aid bag on the coffee table.

"First aid service here." My voice shakes as Arogem's face and the poison in his words replay in my head.

Hearing the tremor in my voice, Keet enfolds me against his body, and the tears I'd been doing my best to hold back start to flow. "Nolee and I will be back in a little bit."

We walk to our favorite driftwood log and sit down. Keet pulls me close. "I thought he was gone, Nolee. I would never have left if I'd known he was still around." He smiles into my tear-washed eyes, then wipes my face with the end of his shirt sleeve.

"It's not your fault Arogem's a liar."

"No, but it *is* my fault for believing him when he told Zee he'd leave you alone."

I can't argue this time, but my body speaks for me, quaking like a leaf in a storm, teeth chattering. Keet stands and pulls me up with him. "Come on. Let's walk this out."

A burst of surprised laughter escapes me. "You sound like me."

"Learned from the best."

Letting go of Keet's hand, I wrap my arm around his lean torso; eyes closed, I hold him close, soothed by his body heat. Navigating the beach's rocky surface brings me back to the present.

"How about we let the dogs out of the yard?" he says.

I pace the shoreline while he walks back to the house and opens the gate. In an instant, I'm being bowled over by Wallace and Fae, a furry hurricane of joyful yips and snuffles and wagging tails. I wrap my arms around both, burying my face in Fae's red coat, inhaling her corn-chip scent as Wallace presses his bulk against me. Keet sits with us, and we become a living blanket against the dark events of this day. Closing my eyes again, I feel the flow of comfort from all directions, with me in the middle, a light where a black cloud lingered.

The dogs are the first to move away, nosing the ground. Keet shifts me onto his lap, and I curl into his body, his heartbeat in one ear and island wind in the other. "What do you need now?"

I shake my head. "Nothing." But my rumbling stomach says otherwise. Keet laughs.

"Your stomach says you need to eat."

"True, but I think it would help to walk a little more." We stand, interlock our fingers, and follow the dogs.

After finishing up some reheated leftovers, Keet and Nolee go to Sylvie's cabin. The door is open, and Keet sees his uncle and Saila sitting on the sofa; Jerry's dressed and seems comfortable. Keet feels Nolee's hand tremble in his and wonders if this is another wave of shock. Catching her eye, he smiles at her, and she smiles back. The trembling stops.

"How are you, Uncle?"

"Saila's as good a medic as most of those guys in 'Nam." Saila smiles as she gathers the bandage wrappings and empty packets of antibiotic ointment. She kisses his cheek. "You're just saying that because we sleep together."

Jerry chuckles and nods. When Saila moves toward the kitchen, Nolee follows her. Sylvie's at the stove with Zelka beside her. The smell of frying dough fills the air. Despite having just eaten, Keet's mouth waters at the thought of warm bread drizzled with honey.

Keet sits next to Jerry. "Thank you." When Jerry looks at him, Keet can tell that his uncle doesn't understand why Keet is thanking him. "For saving Nolee."

Jerry shrugs, then looks for Saila, who's talking with Nolee and his mother. "I hope Mom remembers the honey for the fry bread," he says.

Since seeing the scars on his uncle's body that afternoon, Keet realizes he doesn't know much about Jerry's time in Vietnam. He wonders what other wounds he carries, the invisible ones that lie in ambush. Putting his hand on Jerry's arm, Keet thanks him again.

"You don't have to keep thanking me. You would've done the same."

Keet nods. "But I wasn't here."

"I was," Jerry says.

Keet asks his next question, even though he's sure of the answer. He wants to find a way behind the wall that Jerry keeps up.

"Have you ever been Blackfish before?"

Jerry's eyes darken and he lifts his chin. Shaking his head, he says, "And I don't plan on doing it again, so don't get any ideas."

Keet nods, "I understand."

"Do you, Nephew?"

Keet shifts away from Jerry's bulk and turns to face him. Jerry's eyes are angry, and his fists are clenched. Before Keet can apologize for stepping on an emotional landmine, Jerry says in a voice barely above a whisper, "Did you have a sister who went crazy, who swam as Blackfish more than walking as a human? Did you watch your whole family hide who they were for decades? Have you been so far inland that you couldn't remember the sound of the ocean? Have you seen friends blown apart, shot, and tortured? Have you had wounds that caused your body to give up before your spirit?"

"No."

"Then you don't understand."

# CHAPTER TWENTY-TWO

Without appearing to, Sylvie listens to her son's clipped words to her grandson. Fry bread done, she turns down the heat under the thick chili, then watches as Keet sits, holding Jerry's eyes, not turning away from the scars of anger. Finally, she looks away, tunes instead to the conversation between Nolee and Saila.

"Saila, it didn't scare you? Jerry being Blackfish?"

Saila gives Nolee a small smile and Sylvie can see why Jerry likes her; she's thoughtful when she speaks, and her round cheeks dimple when she smiles.

"I learned from my parents and grandparents that all life—the wind, the waves, the forest, land creatures, sea creatures—are our relations. I've known about Blackfish since I was little."

Sylvie thinks Nolee looks wistful, her eyes a cloudy green as she considers what Saila's saying. "I wish I'd grown up with that knowledge," Nolee says.

"You have it now." Zelka puts her arm around Nolee and gives her a squeeze.

Saila adds, "Jerry told me before we got here that he belonged to a People called Keykwin, but that he'd never changed from man to Blackfish before."

"Did he tell you about me?" Zelka asks.

Saila dimples a smile at her. "Yes, and about your grandmother Sylvie, Keet, and Nolee."

Nolee smiles, then looks at Sylvie. "Do you want me to get some bowls out, Grandmother?"

Sylvie nods, turning the burner off. "Give Jerry and Keet a few more moments, then we'll eat."

Keet looks at his uncle's flushed face, the truth of his words sinking into his mind. There's much Keet doesn't understand, and fighting a war in a foreign country is one of them. But he *does* understand fighting for your life and being helpless against an outcome. He's survived starvation and loneliness, both overlaid with fear. He's been shot and has a scar to show for it. As the moments pass, Keet sees that his uncle's outburst is left over from what must've been a terrifying experience.

"I haven't been through what you have in your life. But that doesn't mean I haven't had similar experiences," he tells his uncle.

Jerry looks down at his hands and shakes his head. Still looking down, he grunts, then says, "Nolee needed help. But never again."

Keet nods and rests his hand on Jerry's shoulder. "Thank you."

As the aroma of Sylvie's chili drifts into the room, both men stand and Jerry pulls Keet into a brief hug, thumping his back. They head to the kitchen. "I know there's fry bread around here somewhere," he says.

After finishing their early supper, Keet and Jerry wash the dishes. Keet wonders if Arogem is gone for good, or if he'll try again to abduct Nolee, to use her as a bargaining piece in return for Zelka. Following close behind is a question: Is Nolee being honest with herself? Maybe part of her still wants to be Keykwin. Why would she go out on the sea when he wasn't there?

"Keet." Jerry's gruff voice pulls Keet from his thoughts, and he sees that Jerry's waiting for him to hand him a plate.

"Sorry."

"Where were you?"

Keet drains the water from the sink and dries his hands. "I don't like what happened this afternoon."

Jerry leans against the counter, the wood creaking as his weight settles against it. "I don't either."

"I'm going to swim back out to the Water Canyon House and stop this before something happens to Nolee that we can't undo."

"Good idea."

Keet waits to see if his uncle will offer to swim with him, but Jerry shakes his head as if reading his mind. "I'm not going. I'm never changing into Blackfish again. Once was plenty." Jerry taps Keet's shoulder. "Good luck."

Keet nods. When he turns, he almost trips over Zelka.

"Did I hear you're swimming to the Water Canyon House?"

"Yes. The more I think about Arogem, the angrier I get."

As Keet looks out the window at the soft evening light falling around the island, Zelka shifts her weight from side to side, then folds her arms across her chest.

"Are you going with me?" Keet asks.

She shakes her head. "I can't."

"Why not?"

"Because I'm afraid if I go inside the Water Canyon House again, it won't let me leave."

Keet notices that his sister won't look him in the eye. Then she says, "Keet, I need to tell you something, but you can't tell Nolee."

"What?" Too late, he realizes that he's unleashing the anger he feels at Arogem on Zelka; the surprise on her face tells him that his tone was too severe. Glancing over Zelka's shoulder, he sees Nolee with her hand on Jerry's forearm, thanking him again.

"You can't tell her, Keet. I'm not even supposed to tell you."

Struggling to control his anger and pay attention, he asks again, "What is it?"

"My family in the Water Canyon House showed me a second door." Zelka pauses, then leans closer to Keet so the others won't overhear.

"Where's this other door?"

Zelka hesitates again. "I'm not supposed to tell anyone outside of the family."

"Zee," Keet takes a deep breath, "tell me. One of those family members endangered both Nolee and Jerry. I think that voids any promise you made."

Zelka searches his face, nodding as she decides. "Come outside with me."

Keet goes to Nolee and gives her arm a squeeze and says, "I'll be right back," then turns away before she can question him.

Once outside, Keet and his sister walk along the rocky beach exposed by low tide. Zelka points to a small island between two larger ones.

"There."

Keet says, "I already found that door."

"The one hidden under a ledge on the eastern side, down near the seabed?"

Keet nods, then asks, "Why? Is there another door besides the two we know about?"

Zelka shakes her head. "I can't tell you. I've broken my promise already."

"Tell Nolee I'll be back later tonight."

"Keet—"

"This obsession of Arogem's has to end, and it's going to end today."

Keet pulls off his t-shirt and tosses it on the rocks, then steps out of his shorts and he wades into the water. He hears Nolee call his name, then Zelka as she clatters over the rocks to deliver Keet's message. Once past the buoys, he takes a breath and dives through green water with its schools of small fish and waving kelp. When he opens his eyes, the world is monochrome. Sending out pulses and clicks, he knifes through the water to an unnamed island with a door at its base.

"Zee, where is Keet going, and why aren't you with him?" I ask, watching Keet's dorsal fin disappear into the night sea.

Zelka wrinkles her brow and frowns, then switches on a smile that doesn't reassure me. "He's going to find Arogem."

"Does that mean he's swimming all the way to the Pacific again?"

Zelka shakes her head. "I don't think so."

"You 'don't think so'?" My disbelief is clear in my voice. "I would be less worried if you joined him."

Jerry breaks into our conversation. "Let him go. There's something he needs to do, then he'll be back."

I walk down to the shoreline, shielding my eyes with my hand, and Zelka follows me. The water's pattern changes, then a tall black dorsal fin with a notch at the top rises from the waves.

"Zee, we've never had secrets from each other. What's going on?"

"I can't tell you, Nolee. I promised my Water Canyon House family I wouldn't."

"We're your family too. We don't keep secrets from one another." I turn back toward the sea in time to see Keet surface; even at this distance, I can hear the forceful expulsion of air from his lungs. He points his rostrum away from us and dives.

"That's not true, Nolee. You and Keet don't want me to share our secret with Marissa. The more time we spend together, the more I like her. She likes me, too. But what if she finds out about me, about my family? Then I've lied to her."

Zee clatters over the rocks and jogs into the water. As she submerges, I shiver, hoping it's only the cold air, not my anxious thoughts, that's affecting me. Seconds later, I see her clothes floating on the quiet sea. Past the buoys, her dorsal fin rises as she swims after her brother. Jerry stands beside me; I look up at him, hoping he can answer my unspoken question.

"They'll be okay, Nolee," he says, putting his arm across my shoulders. In the distance, two dorsal fins move into the last rays of the setting sun.

I wake up to a watercolor morning. A sky washed in soft blues and pinks, and in the east, dark green islands are framed by snowcapped peaks. Near a mooring buoy out in the cove, a seal pokes her shiny nose above the water. A second nose appears next to hers, then both drop back. Waves sluice the shoreline in curls of blue and white, and overhead, a pair of geese honk. The swallows darting in the cool morning air are black brush-strokes against the puffy white clouds. On this island morning, nature is in harmony with herself. I wish I could say the same.

The geese return, close enough that I can see the ring of white feathers around their necks and hear the air move through their wings. Calls bounce between them as they fly side by side, reminding me of the way my life and Keet's now echo one another.

Some relationships force you to keep parts of yourself hidden, some inflict damage. More rarely, you find one that not only allows you to grow into who you're meant to be, but also, challenges you in ways you can't predict. Meeting Keet began with him being my neighbor. From that, we've created a life far different than I'd imagined possible a few years earlier.

Yet here I sit on a sun- and saltwater-bleached log, looking out into the Salish Sea with a heart full of storm clouds. Seeking to calm down, I take a quick inventory, running through the good things in my life: a blossoming new business with my friend Ava; teaching classes at a local pet shelter, sharing how to listen to and care for dogs in need, preparing them for new homes—work that satisfies a deep need to share kindness in a world that all too often feels capricious and cruel.

The only missing piece is Keet. I wonder if he and Zelka have found Arogem yet. But Keet's not the reason I'm sitting on this log, questioning my life choices. My inner compass, which once aligned with my goals, is now spinning. What I thought I wanted most feels predictable and small.

It wasn't always like this. Do we realize our true selves when our desired life clashes with our necessary life? When we make a choice, other options close off; pick door number one and the other doors vanish, like the last rays of sun over a dark horizon.

Despite living my dream life on Camas Island, an insatiable hunger drives me to become something more. When I arrived here after a long drive from my native state of Texas, the setting sun gilded everything with a bright yellow glow. Ending my marriage with Nate was the best decision I could've made. Healing meant discovering myself without others defining me, but shedding the stories I had been led to believe about myself was painful, and so was the choice to leave my only child as she began her university career.

A cold nose on my hand draws me out of my contemplation and brings a smile to my face. I tell Fae hi and give her a scratch behind the ears. She closes her amber eyes and tilts her head into my hand. Tail wagging, Wallace joins us, coat dripping after his swim. As I stroke his broad head, I know he's missing Zelka, his other favorite human.

"They'll be back soon, Wallace."

As I stand up and stretch into the new day, I hope my words are true.

Back home that evening, feeling a little calmer after working at the store with Ava, I gather up a stack of towels and two robes and put them on the dock, hoping that Zelka and Keet will soon be home to use them. The wind through the fir trees, the murmur of the undulating water, the creak of the dock: the sounds give me a comforting soundtrack to my life, a balance to the discomfort I faced this morning.

With the dogs beside me, I look at the distant lights of the city of Vancouver and the dark masses of islands between Camas and the mainland. The moon hides behind the clouds, outlining them in a soft silver glow.

How many hours have I spent on this dock in the last three years, waiting for someone I love to swim home? Now it's not only Keet, but Zelka as well. A lightning bolt of anger strikes again, fueling a need to lash out. But at what? The moon, the sea, the wind, the stars? They're unaffected by my emotions. I close my eyes, giving my anger to the wind, asking it to clear my mind so I can rest.

"C'mon dogs. Looks like we're on our own again tonight."

After a hot bath, I curl up in bed with a book from the stack that's so tall, I've had to move it from my nightstand onto the floor. After I've read the same paragraph four times, I shut it, turn off the light, then open the curtains so I can see the night sky. Staring at the stars, I fall asleep.

# CHAPTER TWENTY-THREE

Zelka opens the door—Nolee might not be awake yet. The dogs are, though. Wallace wiggles over to her, and Fae gives a soft "whuff" of recognition as she stretches, chin to floor and butt in the air, then joins them.

As she steps into the house, she hears the shower running. Hungry, she takes a banana from the bowl on the counter, sits at the table, and eats it. When the water shuts off, she calls Nolee's name.

"Be right out, Zee."

Nolee comes into the kitchen, towel wrapped around her head and dressed in shorts and a blue Austin University t-shirt. She hugs Zelka then glances into the living room. "Where's Keet?"

"He tried all night to get through the door in that little island. This morning, he decided to swim through the strait to find the door we went through the first time, the main Water Canyon House entrance."

Nolee's eyes drop, then she looks at Zelka again. "You couldn't have stopped him?"

"I tried. He was so mad maybe he'll make it."

"'Maybe' isn't good enough. He told me that when he entered the Water Canyon, he was blacking out from lack of oxygen. That if you hadn't been there to guide him, he wouldn't have made it on his own."

Zelka steps back, hoping to get out of range of Nolee's tone, and the hardness in her eyes.

"Why did you let him go alone?"

Zelka hears the sadness underneath Nolee's words and wants desperately to give her a reason that makes sense. She loves both Keet and Nolee, but she's torn by the promises she made to her family in the Water Canyon House. The real reason, the one that causes her the most discomfort, is that she's afraid of the Water Canyon House. She's not sure it will let her out if she returns to it.

"My hair is gone," she blurts, unable to keep her fear in check.

Nolee pulls out two chairs. "Let's sit down and you can tell me what your hair has to do with letting Keet go by himself."

Zelka pulls her hair into a stubby ponytail. She's kept the purple streaks and is letting it grow, hoping it will be long again. "The Water Canyon House wouldn't let me out until I'd sacrificed something that meant a lot to me. If I go back without my hair, what will I have to give to be released again?"

"I thought you said you also had to make peace with Arogem, and that you offered your blood as well?"

Zelka nods. "I'm not sure if it wanted all three or only my hair. Nolee, I can't go back. I can't live there, with no sunlight and no moon or stars. Without you and Keet and Grandmother."

Nolee says, "I understand. We'll wait here for Keet. If he's not back in a couple of days, we can drive out to Neah Bay and look for him."

Later that night, as Sylvie, Nolee, and Zelka sit at Sylvie's table, the dogs jump up, wagging their tails and tilting their heads at the door. Zelka's stomach clenches as Nolee opens the door to a dripping Keet, wearing the robe Nolee left for him on the dock.  He gives her a quick peck on the cheek, walks over to the table, and drops into a chair. Sylvie gets up to reheat their dinner.

"I couldn't do it," Keet says, putting his head in his hands. Zelka feels sorry for her brother, who looks as defeated as she feels.

"How close did you get?" Nolee asks.

"By the time I passed Ediz Hook, my anger was gone, and I realized how foolish it was to attempt the Water Canyon alone. Dodging container ships for two days focused my thinking."

He reaches for Zelka's hand. "I'm sorry. I know you were trying to protect me." Zelka gives him a small smile. "No problem, bro." They laugh, the tension evaporating.

Sylvie sets a bowl of cheese soup and a slice of sourdough bread in front of him. Touching his shoulder, she says, "Eat, Grandson. Tomorrow is another day. We will figure this out together."

Despite her grandmother's words, Zelka's mind continues to spin, wondering what she must do to make Arogem give up. She eats a second helping without tasting, consumed by the fear that she has somehow made the biggest mistake of her life. She watches as Nolee laughs, watches as Keet, his bowl empty, pulls Nolee toward him and kisses the top of her head. *What have I done?* Zelka thinks. *Will it destroy my family?*

# CHAPTER TWENTY-FOUR

Abbie leans against the ferry's railing, long auburn hair blowing behind her. She has her father's straight nose and blue eyes, my hair and round cheeks. The wind is cool and I'm glad I didn't agree with her request to come over from Anacortes by herself. She drove Nathan's truck, boxes of my books from Texas in the back seat. I've missed my daughter.

After our initial hug, she's been avoiding my eyes. It doesn't take empathic skills to sense she needs to say something. Knowing my daughter, and her directness, she'll say it soon.

"Mom?"

I link my arm through hers and look up, since she is now taller than me by several inches. "Yes?"

"You have Keet. Dad has Carlos. I feel like I've disappeared from both of your lives!" Her words come out in a rush, a sirocco of emotion. "I mean, one minute you're dating Keet and the next you're marrying him."

Startled, I bite back a quick reply. I want to tell her that finding someone in later adulthood is a gift. That love is much different in midlife than when you're first experiencing it as a young person. But I doubt that will make her feel better.

Seeing Abbie's eyes fill with tears starts an ache in my chest. My daughter, an only child, had known parents who put her at the center of their world. Now those parents are asking her to share that world with others.

"Abbie..."

She leans against me, back heaving under my hand, tears dampening my shoulder. When she asks for a tissue, I dig around in my backpack and hand her one.

"You'll always be my daughter. Your dad loves you, too. But I suspect our divorce, and my move happened so fast that it was disorienting for you."

Looking down at her hands, she nods.

"Your dad and I were busy dissolving our marriage, and you've always been self-sufficient. I shouldn't have assumed you were handling everything, and I'm sorry for that."

"Thanks, Mom."

Before I can catch myself, I say, "I can feel everything you feel. It's a lot."

Abbie steps away, removing her arm from mine. "What? What do you mean, you feel everything I feel?"

"I mean…" Hoping something sensible will come to me, I lean against the rail and look out into the setting sun. I see the splash and shine of a harbor porpoise. It doesn't surface again. I tell myself to speak the truth, trusting that she will sort it out for herself. While I will always be her mother, she is also transitioning into my peer.

"You know I've always been good with dogs?"

"So? Lots of people are good with animals."

I laugh, hoping it dissipates my nervousness. "The reason I'm good with animals is because I can sense what they're feeling. In my body. I can help them calm down by sharing what being calm feels like."

"I don't understand."

"Even though I'm not scared, my chest contracts when one of our dogs, Wallace, is scared. When he's happy, I'm like a balloon filled with glitter—"

Abbie shakes her head again, then holds up her hand to stop me. Confusion radiates from her.

"I understand this might be hard to take in—"

"Mom. Just stop."

My chest aches with her sadness, which is mixed with rolling waves of anger. She keeps her eyes on the pastel sky. I gaze at the same view, not seeing the sparkling ocean or the gulls that swoop above it.

"Have you been hiding this from me for my whole life?"

In the chaotic days leading up to her visit, I'd been practicing different ways of telling Abbie about what I could do, and how I've made peace with myself. I thought we would walk on the beach at Osprey Bay, and it would be the conversation I planned. How could I have forgotten that Abbie didn't tolerate subtext or hiding? Why did I think she'd wait for me to start a difficult conversation?

"No. But I have been hiding it from myself. I don't want any secrets between us, Abbie, which is why I'm telling you now."

With a bitter laugh, she shakes her head. "What other secrets do you have, Mom? Let's get everything out in the open." Her blue gaze is like a spotlight, singling me out against the darkness. A flash of pictures blazes in my head: Keet becoming orca. The family pod he swims with. Zelka's arrival on our beach, long black hair covering her nakedness like a cloak.

"Any other secrets aren't mine to share."

"Then who do I need to go after next?" Abbie crosses her arms over her chest. "Why didn't you tell me all this before I drove thousands of miles to see you?" She paces in front of me. "I've been trying to work out how to tell you how alone I feel, and now I find out you can somehow magically feel what I'm feeling." She swipes at her eyes with the back of her hand.

"Abbie—"

"It's not right! You have this whole new life and I'm nowhere in it."

"Abbie—"

"And now you tell me you're some kind of… of… Dr. Dolittle."

Despite the heat of her anger boiling inside of my head, I smile. Dr. Dolittle was one of her favorite characters, and I spent many nights reading those books to her as we made our way through the series.

"Why are you smiling?!" Her voice ricochets through me.

"Those were some of your favorite books."

Her face bunches in anger, which brings another wave of memories: a tantrum before bed, a favorite toy missing, a fight with her father that left her so angry she was speechless.

"I'm spilling my guts and you're talking about my favorite books?"

Abbie stalks to the ferry's glass door and storms inside. I follow at a distance, wondering where she's going to land, wondering if it would be better to share everything about my life with Keet during another, less emotionally charged, visit. But doling out the truth in pieces is something the old Nolee would've done. I owe it to my daughter to give her as much information as I can and let her decide.

She stops by the vending machine, taps her card against the reader, and grabs the can of soda that pops out. Moving to the neighboring machine, she repeats the process, this time selecting a bag of cheese crackers. When she turns toward me, she frowns.

"Let's sit on one of these benches. It's too windy on the deck to eat."

Once we're seated on the faded wooden benches, I say, "I was smiling because your comment reminded me of the Dr. Dolittle books I read to you." I put my hand on her leg and try again. "There are things I needed to say to you in person. My life has transformed in this place, and I've gained a self-awareness that would've been impossible if I'd stayed married to your father, if I'd stayed in Texas." Under my hand, her leg jigs with nervousness, then stops. She takes a large gulp of soda.

"I finally like who I am. I hope, at some point, you can accept it, too."

Abbie's face mirrors the many emotions that knot inside my chest.

"What's going on inside me right now, Mom? Because even I don't know."

"I don't know either. What I do know is that I will always be your mother, and I will always be honest with you. Even when it may be hard to hear."

Her face softens and she hugs me. Where there was the tightness of anger, there's now a flood of relief.

"I love you, Mom. I'm sorry I get so mad sometimes."

"You come by it honestly."

She sniffs, then laughs, then finishes her snack. "Who else has secrets?" Her smile wobbles.

"Chat with Keet. I'm happy to be there with you, if you'd like."

"So, he has a secret, and you're okay with it?"

"I promised him the rest of my life. I wouldn't have done that if I'd had doubts."

She looks at me, uncertainty flashing across her face before being erased by the determination I've watched her develop since she was a toddler. "Okay, then. I'll talk to Keet."


I drive Nate's pickup from the ferry landing so Abbie can enjoy the scenery. As we bounce down the hill that ends at our driveway, Abbie says, "No way! Are you kidding me?!"

I brake and pull over so she can watch the orcas swimming outside our bay. It's Keet's family. George leaps, flips onto his back, and crashes into the water. Abbie's entranced by the small cluster of shiny dorsal fins rising and falling out in the bay.

"You didn't tell me killer whales hang out here!" I have a moment of trepidation, wondering if this will lead us back into the disagreement that I "haven't told her everything." But I see the curve of her smiling cheek as she watches the dorsal fins disappear.

We pull up to our house and I shut off the engine, turning to Abbie.

"Let me talk to Keet first and give him the chance to approach you and share when he's ready."

"Okay. I'll practice being patient."

It's my turn to laugh, knowing that when it comes to patience, we both tend to race the clock but trip over the seconds.

I show Abbie into the guest room, where she sets her suitcase on the floor and drops her backpack on the bed. When she looks at me again, she's trying to smile, then leans in to give me a hug. "It's not that I don't like Keet, or Carlos. It's just weird to have you and Dad with other people."

"I hope it won't be weird for too long, Abbs."

I hear Keet's 4Runner pull into the gravel driveway. "Sounds like Keet and Zee are back from the store."

At the front door, Abbie takes one of the canvas grocery bags from Keet, and I start putting away the food as they finish unloading. When I glance out the window, I see Abbie and Zelka shake hands, then Zelka taking her shopping bags to the cabin. Abbie speaks to Keet, putting her hand on his arm. He smiles, asks her a question, and when she nods, hugs her.

Bounding inside, Abbie kisses me on the cheek. "I'm going to catch up on some extra credit schoolwork. See you around dinner time." The guest bedroom door slides shut.

"What was that about?" I ask Keet.

He smiles. "She thanked me for making you happy."

"And then you asked her a question."

"I asked if I could hug her, and she said I could."

I prop a hip against the counter. "I told her how I communicate with animals."

He looks up from the grocery receipt. "How'd that go?"

"She was angry."

"I get that. I get her temper, too." He smiles, leaning down to give me a quick kiss.

"You're funny." But I collapse against him, my forehead against his chest.

"Did you tell her about me?"

This time I push away from him, shaking my head. "That's your story to tell."

Keet nods. "How likely is it she'll get angry again?"

"I'd say there's a fifty-fifty chance. She's studying engineering; she's always been more comfortable with things she can measure and touch."

"So… my being a person who can change into orca might be a stretch for her?"

"I hope not as much, since she and I talked about what I can do."

He nods, then turns his gaze towards the open door.

"I'm going to talk with Grandmother and Zee." He holds out his hand. "Want to come with me?"

I take his hand as we walk out the door.

# CHAPTER TWENTY-FIVE

Keet, Nolee, and the dogs follow the sounds of laughter coming from the cabin's living room—Zelka's, high and bright; Sylvie's, low and punctuated with coughing. The laughter is a respite from the anger at Arogem that still burns in Keet's belly.

"What's funny?" he asks, as he and Nolee sit on the sofa.

"I was telling Grandmother about the guy who asked me to go to coffee with him last year."

"Oh yeah, Eric." Keet smiles.

Nolee asks, "Why is that funny?"

"Because he asked me again, and when I told him I had a girlfriend, he stared at me and then stared at Keet."

"I told him I was her brother. He acted like he's never seen a guy with long hair, and I didn't want him thinking I was Zee's girlfriend."

"Then Eric said…" Zelka giggles, and she and Keet say in unison, "Dude!"

After they settle down, Keet says, "Grandmother, Nolee would like to involve her daughter in our Keykwin culture."

Sylvie nods. "I've been thinking about that, too."

"Does this mean I can tell Marissa?" Zelka, on the edge of her seat, seems to bubble over with excitement.

Sylvie smiles at her. "In time, Zee. Nolee's daughter is of more immediate concern."

"I haven't told her anything," Nolee says, her hand resting on Keet's. "Just about myself, and how I can share what animals are feeling."

"How did she respond to that?"

"She got angry. But," Nolee rushes to give Sylvie a fuller impression, "she's also confused about her dad and I having new partners and what that means for her."

Sylvie nods again. "She's an only child?"

"Yes. My marriage to Nate started falling apart not long after she was born."

"She seems to have a good head on her shoulders," Keet adds.

"She was thrilled to see the orcas in the bay when we got home," Nolee says, smiling.

Keet isn't sure if he'd rather Sylvie said their secret can be shared or must be kept. His own nervousness, his concern that Nolee's daughter may fear him, are heavy in his chest.

"Please tell her if you wish," Sylvie says.

Keet expresses his worry that he doesn't know Abbie well enough and the fear he has of scaring her. Sylvie listens, nodding. When Keet is done talking, Sylvie says, "Those are real concerns. I don't know Abbie well either, but I think she's stronger than you or I know."

Next to Nolee, Fae flops to the floor with a sigh. Keet sighs, too, the small hope Sylvie would say "no" now gone. Their party is in two days, which doesn't give him much time to become closer to Abbie, to figure out a way to include her in their family rather than scaring her out of it. That night, he falls into bed exhausted. But the worries about Abbie are still there, small creatures nibbling at his mind.

The next day, Keet, Nolee, and Abbie run into town, picking up last-minute supplies. As they walk down Northsound's Main Street, a radiant Nolee links arms between Abbie and Keet. "We should've done this sooner!" Her joy is contagious, and Keet smiles back, kissing her before it occurs to him that Abbie might object.

"Y'all are too cute," Abbie says, but removes her arm and turns to a window filled with books.

Later that day, errands accomplished, Keet decides there's nothing to be gained from procrastinating. Truth is a funny thing, he thinks. Once it takes flight, it's easier to deal with than when it's sitting on your head, talons digging into your scalp.

Throughout dinner, Keet struggles to maintain the extra attention he's giving Abbie. Finally, he knows the moment has come. Pushing his empty plate away, he asks Abbie if he can share his culture with her.

"Sure," she says. "Mom's told me that you're from Alaska, part of an Indigenous people called Keykwin."

"You see me as a human man, right?"

Abbie looks at Nolee, then back at Keet. "Is this a trick question?"

He shakes his head. "No tricks."

"Yes, Keet, you're a human man."

Before he can second-guess himself, Keet says, "I'm also orca. Or as my people call them, Blackfish."

"Wait. What?"

She looks between Keet and Nolee as though watching a tennis match, warring emotions crossing her face. She shakes her head. "Mom, you're telling me that not only can you hear animals, but you can talk to them. Keet, you're telling me you can also be a killer whale?"

Her voice goes up on the last two words.

Nolee reaches across the table to touch her hand. Abbie pulls away with a hard laugh. "I guess it's better than a sparkly vampire…"

Keet looks at Nolee, questioning what this last statement means. She shakes her head.

"Abbie, I can show you." He sees the anger in her eyes and adds, "If you want."

She stands. Her chair tilts, almost falling on the floor. "Yeah, I want. Go on, Keet, right now. Show me."

"I can't show you in the house. I need to swim."

She laughs. "Right. Of course. You need to be in the water, where all those killer whales that keep showing up are."

"Abbie," Nolee says.

"No, Mom. I can't believe you're buying this, and that you're okay with it."

"Of course I'm okay with it. It's a part of who Keet is. I love all of him." Shaking her head again, Abbie flings open the door and strides outside. Keet gives Nolee a quick kiss and follows Abbie.

By the time I join Abbie on the rocky beach, the evening sun is setting. Keet, on the dock, looks at the horizon, then jumps in. His shorts float to the surface, a bright orange dot on the waves.

I can hear Abbie's breathing coming in sharp gasps. When I look past the buoys, a towering black dorsal fin, a large notch at the top the only flaw, breaks through the mist of his exhale. I look at Abbie again, but her face is still closed, taut with anger.

The dorsal fin disappears, and a moment later, Keet rises, treading water, flinging his hair out of his eyes, and waves. Abbie huffs, a derisive sound she picked up from her father. Cupping her hand around her mouth, she shouts, "Great trick!" then turns and stomps back into the house as Keet swims to the dock.

The sun is lower, and the water is changing from blue-green to gunmetal grays and blacks. On the dock, his back to our house, Keet slips into his shorts.

"What now?" he asks.

"Give her time."

He nods, his face heavy with sadness.

"Keet."

He looks at me, water still running down his face. I reach up to his jaw, holding its warmth in the palm of my hand.

"She'll figure it out. It'll be okay."

"How can you be certain of that?"

I smile. "From a lifetime of raising her. She doesn't respond well to things she can't understand, and she gets scared, which makes her angry."

Keet nods. "Sounds familiar," he says. As we turn and walk back toward the house, he says, "What are sparkly vampires?"

I laugh, and with the sunset at our backs, explain the books and movies that were part of Abbie's obsession for a while.

Once inside, Keet tells me he's going to take a shower.

I knock on the guest room door. "Abbie? Can I come in?"

She slides open the door and nods, then sits on the edge of the bed, on the ocean quilt, the quilt under which I'd had so many vivid dreams after leaving Texas. I trace the outline of a white gull set against a brilliant blue background. The cloth is soft under my fingertips.

"What does it mean?" Crying has made her voice raspy.

"Did I tell you Ava gave me this quilt when Keet and I moved in together?"

She shakes her head. "Yet another thing I didn't know."

I ignore her comment, knowing how vulnerable she's feeling.

"Ava made it. She wanted me to feel at home…" I trail off, wiping the tears spilling from my eyes.

"Mom?"

"She understood I'd moved away from everything that was familiar, so she put this quilt on the bed as a welcome gift. When I moved from the cabin where Sylvie and Zelka are now, she gave it to Keet and me."

"That was nice of her."

"It was kind, Abbie, which is more thoughtful than nice. There's a big difference between the two."

Abbie shakes her head and closes her eyes. When she opens them again, questions swirl in their depths.

"Nice is lying to you about who Keet is. Kind is telling you the truth. It wouldn't have been a kindness for me to hide who Keet is. It's not kind for me to let you stew in the guest room because you don't understand what happened."

"It was a trick—"

"What you saw was real."

"Is this you being kind, Mom? Is it kind to upset me?"

I put my hand on her knee. "It's kind to show you the truth. You can draw your own conclusions. Life is sometimes upsetting, Abbie. And we can't always fight it."

"Is that why it took you so long to leave Dad?"

That dart hit home. Standing, I walk to the door, clasping my elbows. When I turn, Abbie's face has softened.

"Sorry."

I sit beside her again, formulating my thoughts. "There's something I want to share with you, woman to woman."

"It's not another secret, is it?"

"I doubt it." A laugh escapes me, and more tears.

Abbie says, "What's so funny?"

"You can do whatever you want with your life, but no one can live it for you."

"That's it?"

I nod. "The reason it took me so long to create a life of my choosing is because for most of it, I was everything to everyone else, and nothing to myself."

Abbie stays silent.

"The thing is, Abbs …" She takes my hand when I use her childhood nickname. "The thing is, I thought that being a wife and a mother were it for me. Before I say anything else, you are the greatest gift of my life, and I wouldn't change one thing. Not one."

Abbie nods. "I know, Mom. You've always been good about telling me you love me."

"What I haven't been good about telling you is that *you* don't owe anyone anything. Not a boyfriend or lover or a girlfriend or your parents. You understand?"

"I think so…" she trails off, worry lines crinkling her forehead.

"What are you thinking?" I ask.

"I haven't told you about Max?"

I shake my head.

"He's this guy I've been hooking up with."

I keep my face as neutral as possible.

She watches my expression as she says, "He wants us to only date each other. He wants to be my boyfriend."

"Is that what you want?"

Abbie shrugs. "I like him. But he's always talking about getting married and having kids."

"Is that what you want?" I repeat.

She looks at me, sighs. "Maybe someday. Maybe not. I want to be an engineer, and that's taking all my focus."

"So let it take all your focus."

"Really?"

"You don't owe Max just because he wants something from you, Abbie."

"He's been pressuring me. He texts all the time. The more he texts, the less I want to see him."

"Call him and break it off."

"Just like that?"

"Just like that."

"I can say I want to focus on getting my degree and being an engineer?"

"You don't have to explain your choices, Abbie. Not unless you want to." She picks up her phone and looks at the screen, then lays it back down beside her.

I say, "For a long time, I defaulted to my roles as a wife, mother, chauffeur, cook, maid, and personal assistant. Later, I was a dog trainer and then a business owner."

She sits up straighter. "What does that mean?"

"It means I grew up in a family where I was expected to do as I was told, where my feelings didn't matter. My mother was so worn out raising the four of us and helping run the ranch that it was easier for her to be compliant than to stand up for herself. I wanted something different, so I married a businessman, moved to the suburbs, and had you."

I kiss her on the cheek.

"Did dad want you to be compliant?"

"No. But I was so wrapped up in what I thought I 'should' be doing as a wife and mother that for a long time I didn't realize I was repeating my mother's patterns."

"He told me at his and Carlos' wedding that he wished he'd been better to you."

"Well, that goes both ways. I wish I'd been better to him, too. I was angry a lot. When expressing that anger didn't work, I used silence, as he did with me."

In the dining room, I hear Keet setting the table, the soft clatter of dishes returning a little peace to my overheated emotions. How many meals have we shared now?

"Abbie, what I'm trying to say is that you're in a position in your life to decide what to do with it. As a woman, you will find that many people want to tell you what you should do—"

"Mom, it's not like that anymore. A ton of women in my dorm are studying to be engineers, doctors, lawyers…"

"Really? I just read that your current university president has slithered out of four accusations of sexual harassment. A woman at your university was fired because of unfounded allegations that she had sex with a male student."

"There's way more to that—"

I put my hand on her arm. "My point is, this imbalance of power still exists. Now's the time for you to open your eyes to your world."

"This is important to you, isn't it?"

"You're important to me. I could say I was a victim of my life. The argument could also be made that your dad and Carlos gave me a gift when they fell in love. I don't like the way I found out, but from this distance, I appreciate that your dad's bravery to go after what he needed set me free."

"Did you go after what you needed, mom?"

I nod as I warm her chilly hand with my mine. "I did. My life is good now. But the most significant benefit of sharing my life with Keet is that I've gained a deeper understanding of myself. It took a long time. It's important to belong to yourself first."

Abbie removes her hand and reaches for her phone.

"I'm calling Max."

I stand up, kiss the top of her head, and close the door behind me. Lingering beneath the words I said to Abbie is the shimmering mirage of a black door, my aging body pressed against it, and the whispers that it could've been different had I not been afraid to take Arogem's offer to change me to Keykwin. I don't know whether this is the next dream my heart wishes to fulfill, or a nightmare waiting to happen if I do. What I do know is that I feel like an imposter after my conversation with Abbie.

# CHAPTER TWENTY-SIX

Keet's stirring a pot of black beans, adding spices. He watches as Nolee walks into the kitchen.

"Did you have a good talk?" he asks.

Nolee smiles. "We did."

"Does she believe me?"

"We talked about other things. But she's calmer. Give her time, Keet."

He nods as he places the wooden spoon on a small dish.

"Smells great! Tacos for dinner?"

"I thought Abbie might appreciate food that's familiar."

"Keet Noland, have I told you how much I love your thoughtfulness?"

He smiles, takes her face between his hands, and presses the tip of his nose against hers. "You have, and you can tell me again any time."

At the sound of the guest room door sliding and banging against the hinges, they both turn around.

"How'd it go with Max?"

"He said he was seeing other women anyway."

"How's that land with you?" Keet asks.

When she looks at him, her gaze is thoughtful and sharp. Her blue eyes narrow. "As a relief."

"That's good," Nolee replies, giving her daughter a hug as Keet stirs the beans.

"Keet?"

He looks at Abbie, surprised to hear his name coming from her. "Yes?"

"Whatever happened out there, whether you can become a killer whale—Blackfish—or not, seeing my mom happy means a lot to me. Thanks for being a part of that."

Keet smiles at her. "You're welcome."

Taking a small spoon from the cutlery drawer, he scoops some beans and hands it to Abbie. "Tell me how this tastes."

She tastes them and her eyes light up. "Ohmygod, those are amazing!"

"Not too spicy?"

"Not even close."

Abbie turns to Nolee. "What are y'all wearing tomorrow for the party?"

Nolee takes Abbie's hand. "Come back here and I'll show you."

Keet reduces the heat under the beans and smiles to himself, he's happy his hair is long again. That's one decision he doesn't have to make, but trying to find something to wear for the celebration had been a challenge for he and Nolee.

The murmur of Abbie and Nolee's voices filters through to the kitchen. Nolee chose an aquamarine cotton sundress with a deep V neck; it was fitted through her waist, then the flowing material draped over her hips to her calves. He thought it was an excellent choice, not only because it flattered her curves, but also because it brought a shine to her eyes when she twirled, showing it off to him.

After dinner, while Abbie works on a school project, he and Nolee go to the cabin. Grandmother leads them up to her room and opens the ancient ceder chest. The first object she takes from it is a wooden chalice, dark with age. Carved around the outside of the cup is the Blackfish design. She hands it to Nolee.

"This is the cup we use for ceremonies. It hasn't been out of this chest since…" She pauses, caressing the wood with bent fingers. "Since Keet's mother and father wed."

Nolee puts her hands over Grandmother's. "It's an honor to include it."

"Thank you, Grandmother," Keet says, his throat suddenly tight, warmth suffusing his body.

She gives the cup to Nolee, then leans over the chest again. Keet hears the rustle of tissue paper, then Zelka's voice from downstairs. "Can I come up?"

"Yes, get on up here!  I thought you and Em would be out later than this," Nolee says. Keet hears the thump of his sister's feet on the staircase.

"I told Marissa you were picking out your celebration clothes tonight. We thought it was more important for me to be here with you."

Sylvie sets the tissue-wrapped bundle on the bed and peels away the paper to reveal another layer; dark, soft leather held together with red string. Carefully untying the strings, she unfolds the leather and the robe is revealed: a swirl of red, black, and white wool, the traditional Blackfish design stitched in thick, black thread; a red collar; and, on the front, a swath of white abalone shells sewn down its length, all the way to the floor.

"Keet!" Nolee gasps as Sylvie holds up the robe. "I'm going to need a better dress."

"Did my dad wear this for his wedding to my mom?" Keet strokes the old wool.

"We offered, but he didn't want to. Your grandfather, my husband, was the last person to wear it. You're about his size."

"Grandmother, are you sure?" Keet holds the heavy garment by the shoulders. When he moves it, the shells click against one another.

"Of course, I'm sure. This is an important event in your life. You honor your Ancestors by wearing a robe they made." She goes back to the chest, then turns, holding a belt in her hand.

"Nolee, would you wear this?"

Nolee lifts the belt from Sylvie's hands and lets it fall open. The white leather is adorned with indigo, navy, and sky-blue beads in a running pattern of half-circles. Sylvie points to the pattern. "This is our symbol for the ocean, the water that sustains our lives as Keykwin."

"Sylvie—" Nolee moves as though she might hand back the belt, but Sylvie shakes her head.

"You do not turn down the honor of a gift, Granddaughter. After your Promising Celebration is over, you can return the belt and the robe to the chest."

Nolee's eyes fill with tears as she nods, whispering, "Thank you."

"It will be beautiful with your dress," Keet says. Nolee leans against his shoulder, smiling at the belt in her hands.

# CHAPTER TWENTY-SEVEN

Sylvie stands in front of us holding the wooden cup, white hair in two braids, black-and-white blouse tucked into a red skirt. The afternoon sun shining through the branches stipples her face and warms our backs. Chairs scrape on the wooden platform and conversations trail away. Overhead, an eagle calls for its mate; I watch as the two soar west. Smiling, Keet squeezes my hand. I linger in his gaze until Sylvie's voice reminds me of our purpose this day.

"Treat yourselves and each other with kindness and remind yourselves often of what brought you together. Tenderness, gentleness, and respect are the signposts that will guide you through difficulties, through times of frustration, or anger, or sadness.

"When fear enters your relationship, as it does all relationships some-times, remember to focus on what is good between you. In this way, you can ride out the storms when the seas are rough, when the clouds are dark. Remember: Even if you lose sight of the sun, it is still there, shining."

Sylvie clears her throat. I feel friends and friends who've become family behind us, witnessing our union. The July afternoon is hot, and Keet, wearing the wool robe, is surely the warmest, even in the dappled shade of the trees. My arm through his, he returns my smile. After the misunderstandings and drama, the way he looks at me brings me the belief that our lives together will withstand everything.

"Nolee Burnett and Keet Noland, do you promise to accept each other, and stand by one another's side through all of life?"

"We promise," Keet and I say in unison.

"Do you promise to support one another in health and illness, in plenty and in want, in joy and sorrow?"

"We promise."

"Do you promise to hold each other's bodies and hearts as sacred gifts from your ancestors, and from our Mother Earth?"

"We promise."

"Do you promise to love one another for the rest of your days?"

"We promise."

Sylvie smiles as she hands us the ancient wooden cup filled with her elderberry wine.

"Then drink from the cup of plenty together, and may your own cup always be full."

Keet hands the cup to me. I take a large swallow and sputter; he wipes my lip with his thumb and drinks his share, leaving enough for Grandmother to finish.

She takes the cup in both hands and drinks, then says, "Now kiss each other!"

She didn't mention this part last night when we were talking about the Promising Ceremony. Her command provokes a surprised laugh from me, and our friends laugh with us. Still laughing, Keet kisses me, wraps his arms around my waist, and lifts me off the ground. When he sets me down, Marissa lets out a loud "whoop whoop!" To the sounds of clapping and whistling, I turn and take in the beaming faces of our friends and family.

I set my drink on the picnic table and take a moment to look around at everyone who has gathered to celebrate our special day. There are our friends Ava, Pete, and their son Alex, as well as people we know from town, Graham and Steve from the Sugar Bear Bakery. Even Keet's business manager, Trish, has joined us. And Keet's family, of course. But aside from Abbie, no one from my family is here. I refuse to dwell on it.

Andi tugs a handsome man behind her, then gives me a one-armed hug before introducing us.

"Nolee, this is Mason." He shakes my hand, saying it's wonderful to be included in our celebration. They move to the tables of food after I whisper in Andi's ear, "He's a keeper!"

Platter-laden tables draped with colorful fabric are set up underneath the trees, and lights have been strung from the branches. Each table has an old-fashioned hurricane lamp with a rusted blue patina. When it gets darker, this oasis of music and laughter and celebration will also be lit by soft globes, larger versions of fairy lights.

Afternoon is turning to evening and most of the food has been eaten.

Marissa's taken control of the bar, and people have been flocking to it, and to the dessert canoe.

When I'd asked Keet how he thought it would be best to present the Sugar Bear Bakery desserts that Graham and Steve had offered to bring, he'd showed me an old canoe propped in a corner of the garage. We hosed it off, set it on sawhorses notched to fit its bottom, and stabilized it with driftwood. Keet then brought out a long board and cut it to fit inside. Voilà—a dessert canoe!

"I knew I'd use this again."

I'd pointed to a hole the size of my fist in the hull. "Not on the water."

He'd laughed, then kissed me. "I meant the lumber."

Maneuvering through small groups around the canoe, I grab a berry tart and pop it in my mouth. Its cream filling and salty crust merge with the fruit's tang into a flavorful morsel. As I turn to snag a slice of one of the white cream cakes topped with chocolate shavings, the music changes. Abbie and Zelka huddle over Abbie's phone, choosing songs from a playlist they created with Marissa's help.

"All I ask," Keet had said to them before the ceremony started, "is not too many eighties tunes."

Marissa disagreed. "There's no way we're sticking to music made decades before we were born. There's some great music out right now. C'mon, Keet, trust me." Her sparkling smile had melted his resistance. He looked at me as he repeated, "No eighties music would be great, but I'm outnumbered." His request was met with laughing assurance, but so far, I've counted five songs from that decade, mostly rock ballads about love. Every time one plays, Abbie, Marissa, and Zelka direct their gaze at Keet and grin.

As I swallow the last bite of cake, thinking I should've chosen a slice with more chocolate on top, Keet is talking to Jerry and Saila. He turns his head and our eyes meet, and his smile broadens. There's a jolt of electricity in my own smile as I think about Keet and I alone later in our bed. He touches Saila's shoulder, then walks over to me, wraps me in his arms, and kisses me. There's laughter, but I kiss him back, not caring.

"Were you just thinking what I was thinking?" I whisper in his ear.

"About getting more dessert?"

"Keet Noland!"

He laughs and tightens his arms around me, then whispers in my ear. "We need to be alone, don't we?"

"We do. But let's dance instead."

"It's an eighties song."

"You can't tell me that the harmonies on this one are bad. And the words are sweet." I take his hand and lead him to the wooden platform that now doubles as a dance floor.

"The harmonies aren't the Eagles. Or Poco," he grumbles.

As I pull him close to me, I sing, "I'm the one who wants to be with you…"

He sighs, "Okay. This one isn't that bad."

As we hold each other, turning in place, I see six dorsal fins cut through the bay. The smallest of the orcas spyhops, lingering above the surface. I mentally reach out to George, beaming my love at him.

"Our family pod is happy, too," Keet says, his voice low and content. I bite back the comment that since I'm not Keykwin, they're *his* family pod. Ruining this perfect day is the last thing I want to do.

The next song is by Pink, which brings everyone but Trish onto the dance floor. Raising their drinks above their heads, they shout the chorus: "So raise your glass if you're all wrong, in all the right ways…"

Keet and I walk to a table set with flowers and gifts. I caress the edge of a pottery bowl with fluted edges. "It was amazing of your friends to give us this, Keet."

"I've known the owners of Camas Island Pottery as long as I've lived here. But I didn't expect this."

The bowl is off-white on the outside, but the interior is decorated with flowers defined by purple and blue glazes A green spiral swirls from the rim to its center. The bowl is big enough that I need both arms to hold it, reminding me of another bowl, this one wooden, that Keet and Zelka had returned to the Water Canyon House this past winter.

"Maybe we need to find a different bowl for the rocks?" I run my hands over the variety of colors and sizes of rocks that people brought or sent to us. Once the celebration ends, they'll go in the bowl, serving as a reminder of our connection with the community and their connection to the land.

"I don't think so," Keet says, tracing his finger over a rock that looks like petrified reptile skin.

"Which one is that?" I ask.

"It's Petoskey, from Michigan."

"Who do you know in Michigan?"

Keet turns and points to an older man and woman chatting with Sylvie. "They've been clients for more than a decade. They summer here."

"I recognize this one." I pick up a polished stone that fits in the palm of my hand. It's the light blue of a morning sky.

"This is the Texas state gemstone. Blue topaz."

"Who sent that?" Keet asks.

"My family."

Keet takes the stone from my hand and rolls it around in his fingers.

"Of course," I say, "they couldn't believe I'd only want a rock for a gift, so they pitched in and also got us a nice blender."

Keet sets the stone down. "Ours is falling apart anyway."

I pick up a dark green angular stone.

"That's jade from Alaska." I look at Jerry and Saila, smiling. They wave. I hold up the stone and mouth, "Thanks."

We examine the rest of the rocks, reading the notes that accompany them. Granite from the Rocky Mountains of Colorado; basalt from Canada; Lake Superior agate from Wisconsin; a beautiful petaled, dusky red rock called a barite rose from Oklahoma. *Marissa must've brought this,* I think. There are black rocks, white rocks, some shiny with sharp edges, others rounded by time and water. I pick up a black-and-white speckled rock, smiling.

"I think this one comes from our beach."

Keet takes it from me, his fingertips lingering against mine. "It does. We need a grounding stone, something that anchors us to home."

In a rush of emotion, I kiss him again.

There's a pause in the music, then a slow bass line and a keyboard fill the air.

"A song I actually like." Keet settles his hands around my waist. I reach up, joining my hands behind his neck. "It's *Lady*, by The Whispers."

"I've never heard it."

"It didn't get a lot of airtime back in the day."

I close my eyes as we rock to the music, bodies moving together. If I were to describe a perfect moment, it would be this one.

"Thanks." Keet raises the glass of water as a thank you to Jerry, who has taken over the bar duties from Marissa. Turning back to the dance floor, he watches Nolee, Andi, Abbie, Zelka, Ava, and Marissa move in and out of the flashing colors. Short and tall and round and slim, they streak across the dance floor like comets, hair loosened from braids and ponytails flying. Laughing, they close their eyes as they sway, sensuousness coming off them like a musky perfume. As the tempo of the music slows, they reach for one another's hands and throw their heads back in sheer joy. Marissa spins Zelka, who spins Abbie, who spins Nolee—a whirling dervish of feminine frenzy expressing itself through the bounce of breasts and the sway of round hips.

Pulled by the desire to be included in the voluptuous dance, Keet takes two long steps toward Nolee then stops, realizing he's witnessing a pure moment shared between women, the sanctity of dancing only for themselves.

After Sascha and before Nolee, when he saw women moving like this, he would choose one, put all his attention on her, take her home. He had yearned to claim that sensuousness, even if just for a few hours or a night. But once he interjected himself between a woman and her dancing, the sensuousness changed. His touch, his gaze, and his words changed her power. She narrowed it, adjusting who she was in relation to him.

Standing by their table, he continues to watch as they bounce on their toes with their arms raised, a hurricane of women caught in high winds. Three more women join the group. Young and old, they move in spirals, facing each other, turning away, bumping shoulders and hips, laughing, ages dropping away. Keet sees the men retreat to the edges, like him, either enchanted by their beauty, and the power they generate, or intimidated by it.

# CHAPTER TWENTY-EIGHT

After what seems like a thousand hugs and thanks to our friends for joining us, I watch as a parade of red lights glows down the driveway and up the hill. Andi helps Steve and Graham stack the empty dessert trays, Trish folds the tablecloths, and Jerry and Saila empty leftover food into containers for us to enjoy later. There's quiet laughter behind us. Turning, I see Zelka and Marissa returning the empty bottles to the crates, dismantling the bar in between kisses. I smile as Abbie comes toward me. Despite the soft glow of the lights, she's pale beneath her tan.

"Mom, did you get the text about Grandad?" I grab my phone from the table and open the texts, skimming. The more texts I read from my sister, the further the conversations retreat into the background, a cacophony of noise drowned by the silence enveloping me.

Keet joins us, standing next to me as Abbie and I huddle over our phones. "What's happened?"

I look at him, unable to speak.

"We need to go to Texas. Grandad is dying," Abbie says, before I can break through the glass cage of my shock. "We can take turns driving and get there in…" she taps her phone, thumbs moving over the screen. "Thirty-one hours. Easy, between the two of us. You can fly home."

I nod, her plan coalescing into reality through my silence.

Keet's arm slides around my waist, and I rest my head against his shoulder. My voice returns. "We can leave tomorrow Abbie. It's too late to catch the ferry. Can you text everyone our plans?"

She nods.

"Nolee?"

The tone of Keet's voice catches my attention. His eyes are clouded by his own emotions.

"What is it?"

"Grandmother is taking her Walk Into the Water."

I stumble to a chair and collapse into it. It feels like I'm standing on shifting sand. "When?"

"Tomorrow morning. Sunrise."

The ping of a text arrives, and I reach for my phone, holding it at arm's length. *The doctors think he only has a couple of days. The family needs to be here ASAP.*

I show Keet the text, and he nods. Abbie stares into the bay. Does she notice the six orca fins bobbing on the waves? Now that the music has stopped, I can hear their breathing, the whoosh of air leaving their bodies, the quick inhale before they sink underwater.

"Abbie, we're going to the cabin to talk with Sylvie. Are you staying here, or coming along?"

She shakes her head. "I'll stay here."

Jerry and Saila have already set up the sofa bed when Keet and I arrive at the cabin. They sit with Zelka. No one is talking or laughing; the light heartedness we shared just an hour ago is gone.

"Where's Marissa?" Keet asks.

"I told her we had a family thing."

I'm standing in front of Sylvie, speaking the only words the silence inside of me allows.

"Grandmother. Why?"

She smiles, patting the chair next to her. I sit down and take her hand in mine. When I meet her eyes, mine fill with tears.

"Because, Granddaughter, I'm old. And I'm tired. I don't want to live in this aching human body anymore."

I nod, trying to understand, but feeling a sense of misery and self-centeredness because I need her in my life. Before I can stop myself, I lean over and whisper into our clasped hands, as though I could hold on to her longer, "I don't want you to go."

Sylvie nods and then explains, "We don't bury our Keykwin ancestors in a graveyard. We can only visit them when we are orca, surrounded by the ocean and life in the sea. When we are lost or need help, our ancestors guide us. I experience a stronger connection to my ancestors when I swim as Blackfish."

Silence surrounds us, a shroud of sadness almost thick enough to drown out the sobs that escape me. She puts her arms around me, and I lean my forehead against her shoulder. Her hand is warm as she rubs my back.

"This is difficult, Granddaughter. If I could stay here, I would. You are my family, too."

"You're my family," I gasp. Then it hits me. I'm not Keykwin. I'll never be able to ask for her advice, or listen to her sing, ever again. When she makes the Walk Into the Water, a ceremony bidding farewell to humanity, she will be embracing life as Blackfish forever. This thought brings another storm of sobs.

"Nolee," she whispers. "I'll always be with you…"

"But I can't see you ever again." Bereft, I cling even more tightly to Sylvie, wanting to convince her to still return to land so I can see her, too.

Another realization crashes through me, the conversation I had with Abbie when she arrived. The promise I made when she was born was to always love her as best I could. Part of loving someone is being honest with them. As miserable as I am, the honesty that Sylvie has shown must've been more difficult.

"How long have you been thinking about this?" I ask.

She gives me a napkin, its cloth thin from many washings, and I swipe at my face.

"Since I got here."

"You've had to think about this for more than a year?"

"Yes."

The grief echoing through my aching heart is now joined by the truth that Sylvie has shared. I have to release her.

"Come with me." Letting go of my hand, Sylvie pushes herself to her feet and walks into the kitchen. "Zelka, you, too."

Once we're in the kitchen, she looks back into the living room, where the rest of the family is huddled, speaking in quiet tones. As she moves to one of the cabinets, she turns and puts her finger against her lips. "This is a secret for the two of you only," she says.

I almost laugh at her attempt at deviousness, the quirk of her mischievous smile. Zelka and I stand close as she moves cans of food, then brings out a glass jar.

"What's this, Grandmother?" Zelka asks. I take the jar from her hands, shielding it with my body so no one else can see.

"Saffron."

It dawns on me then. "This is the secret ingredient in your halibut stew, isn't it?"

Sylvie takes the jar from my hand and puts it back behind the cans.

"I won't tell Keet," I say.

"Neither will I," says Zelka.

"That's good, because Keet gets my truck. He doesn't need my secret ingredient, too." We put our arms around each other, a bittersweet rush of laughter between us. Sylvie breaks our group hug first, wiping her eyes.

"You also need to bless the stew. Bless all the food you make, that it helps those you feed to be strong."

Zelka and I reply in unison, "We will."

As we walk out of the kitchen, my arm linked through Sylvie's on one side and Zelka's on the other, I ask, "What do you need?"

Keet rests his hands on Nolee's shoulders as she leans her back against him, and Jerry, Saila, and Zelka stand with them, waiting for Sylvie's answer.

"I need all of you to be with me."

"Of course, Mom," Jerry says. Saila nods, gripping Jerry's hand.

"We'll be there," Zelka adds in a soft voice.

Sylvie looks at Keet and takes his hand.

"I've put all my clothes in bags. Take them to the thrift store," she says. "I've paid the rent on the cabin for another year, so Zelka has time to figure out what she'd like to do."

Keet glances at his sister, her face wet with tears.

Her voice stronger, Sylvie says, "Everything that is important to me is in the cedar chest. I'm leaving that to Zelka and Nolee."

Nolee tenses under Keet's hands, then draws a breath to say something, but before she can, Sylvie continues. "I've told Zelka the stories of everything in the chest. She will share them with you when you're ready, Nolee."

"But I'm not—" Nolee begins. Sylvie scoots closer to Nolee.

"You are a part of this family. You have as much right as Zelka to share in our history. Our stories are meant to be shared, not forgotten."

Keet hears the finality in his grandmother's tone and knows there will be no more discussion about the ancient ceder chest. He remembers Sylvie pulling the water clock from it last year, holding it in her lap before deciding it needed to be returned to their cousins under the waves. The same family group that Arogem is part of. *What did we set in motion?* Keet wonders. *How does doing good bring such sorrow?* He unconsciously tightens his grip on Nolee's shoulders. She looks up at him, startled. She stands and says, "Grandmother, can you please walk outside with me and Keet?"

Sylvie pushes against the edge of the chair. When she can't rise, Keet offers his hand and pulls her to her feet.

"That's a good idea. I'm getting too stiff sitting here." She pauses, looking at her family, then takes Saila's hand.

"It brings me peace to see you with my son, Saila. Thank you."

Saila nods, then hugs Sylvie. "I'll be with him for the rest of my life."

Sylvie lays her hand against her chest. "That makes me happy." She shuffles to the door, Keet and Nolee in her wake. She pauses, turns, and then says, "Everyone who is important to me is in this room," before making her slow way onto the porch, down the steps, and to the beach.

The lights still hang between the trees, but everyone has left. Keet looks at the bare picnic tables and the plastic tables folded up against the trees. The cool night air clears his head. He has a sudden urge to jump into the sea to cool his body, to escape the complexity of being human. To escape the rising tide of conflict he feels in Nolee.

Sylvie points to the dock as they walk toward it.

"I want to leave from there. To step away from the earth. To drop into the sea."

Nolee is silent. Keet senses Nolee's conflicting emotions, witnessing as she tries to control herself.

Sylvie turns to Nolee.

"Granddaughter, I need you to be content in your life."

"What do you mean?"

Keet is thrust outside of the conversation. Instead of wanting to dive into the sea to cool off, to escape, he wants to stay here and protect Nolee. *From what?* he wonders. *From whom?*

"You are a human woman, not Keykwin. You are part of our family, but we cannot change you into Blackfish."

A bubble of hope fills Keet's chest. He hopes Sylvie's words are being imprinted in Nolee's brain. But when he looks at her, he sees they've skipped off the surface entirely. On this day of their Promising Celebration, she looks sad, as though she's alone, carrying the weight of life. As though she's forgotten the promises they shared with one another. As though he doesn't walk beside her. When she talks, Keet pulls himself away from his fears to listen.

"I don't know why I'm so obsessed with being Keykwin."

"This isn't an obsession, Granddaughter. It is a decision to covet someone else's life and claim it for your own. Saying you don't know is a child's answer."

Nolee rocks back as though slapped.

"You want to be something other than you are. You want to walk a path that isn't yours, and so you ignore the power of your own way."

"Keet had to struggle to figure out who he was, too. That's all this is, Grandmother. I'm in a new chapter in my life, and I want to discover who I am. And yes, I want to share in your lives." She looks at Keet with something like pleading. To understand or to agree with her, Keet can't tell.

Sylvie says, "Keet held the illusion that he had to choose who he had to be. In his mind and heart, there was a war: human or orca. His healing happened when he accepted both sides of his nature. He did not walk a path that didn't belong to him."

Nolee nods as Keet puts his arm around her waist, drawing comfort from her familiarity. She gives him a hesitant smile.

When they return to the house, Nolee walks to Abbie's room. Keet lets the dogs out one last time, hearing the jingling of their tags as they head to the backyard. He's undressing when Nolee closes their door.

"Abbie's packed and ready to leave tomorrow."

Keet watches as Nolee drags a suitcase from the closet and begins putting clothes in it.

"We'll plan on leaving right after Sylvie…" Unable to say the words, Nolee instead flops onto the bed and puts her face in her hands. Keet sits next to her.

"This is a lot, Lia. Your father. Grandmother."

He leans across her to get the box of tissues on her nightstand. She takes one and wipes her face. He wraps his arms around her, holding her tight against his chest.

"I never liked my father," she says, her voice muffled against his chest.

Keet is silent, wondering where this conversation is going.

"I love him," she continues, "but I don't like him. He's a hard man. I always hoped we'd find some sort of peace, and now it's too late." Her sobs begin again, and Keet feels the slide of her tears down his chest.

Her phone vibrates, and she moves away from him to look at it.

"Do you want to take a shower with me?" he asks.

She shakes her head. "I need to call Lily."

When he gets out of the shower, water speckling his skin as he dries his hair, he hears the indistinct murmur of Nolee's voice, and then the sound of the phone dropping onto the table by the bed. He finishes drying off, pulls on the shorts he sleeps in, and returns to the room.

"Is there any way you can take me with you tomorrow morning…or ever?" Nolee says.

"What do you mean?"

"I mean, is there any way for me to be with you, so I can experience being orca, too?"

Muscles relaxed by the warm water of the shower tense again. "You want to swim away with Grandmother, Zelka, and me?" He sits on the bed next to her and takes her shaking hand in his.

"I thought that once you and I committed to each other…"

"What?"

Nolee shakes her head, a small, nervous laugh escaping. "I thought I could become Keykwin, too."

"That's not how it works, Lia." The softness in Keet's voice has no effect on Nolee, nor does his use of her nickname.

"Then how does it work? All I want is to be closer to you, to know you in every way."

Keet takes a breath, willing himself to remain calm.

"How it works is that we're born being both human and orca."

"Zelka changed, though. She's different from her mother because of what her mother did during her gestation."

"Yes, but her mother was Keykwin. Your parents are human. Where is this coming from, Nolee?"

She drops his hand and stands up, pacing in front of him.

"You and Zelka both told me that the Water Canyon House People used to take humans from the land and change them to Keykwin."

Keet, still sitting, stares at her. "I still don't understand what this is about, Nolee."

He sees her take a breath, closing her eyes and trying not to give into anger. When she speaks, her words snap with tension. "What it's about,

Keet, is that I thought promising myself to you would mean that I could be Keykwin, too."

As soon as the words have left her mouth, she gasps, then sits next to him. "I didn't mean—"

"You promised yourself to me, and I did the same. I thought that's what your heart wanted."

"It was! I did—"

"Now you tell me the real reason you promised yourself to me is because you hoped to become Keykwin." It's his turn to stand, and she follows, trying to take his hand. He steps away so she can't.

"What was your plan, Nolee? If I said yes? If I even *could* say yes?"

"I don't know! Keet—"

Keet's voice lowers, his eyes focusing on Nolee. "Were you going to let Abbie drive back to Texas by herself? Let your father die without seeing him for the last time?"

Nolee stands in front of him, her eyes meeting his. "I wasn't thinking, and I didn't promise myself to you to become like you. But it occurred to me when Grandmother said she was leaving…"

"This idea occurred to you then?"

Nolee lets out a deep breath, says something in a whisper that Keet can't quite hear. "What did you say?"

"I said, when I came home to an empty house, while you were still with Zelka in the Water Canyon, that's when I thought about the possibility of becoming Keykwin. I wanted to be there with you so much."

Keet scowls, walks into the bathroom, then storms back out. He slides the bedroom door shut, hoping their voices aren't carrying to Abbie.

"So that was your plan? Lure me into a Promise Ceremony so you could get what you wanted?"

"Of course not! I want you, Keet. I just didn't know whether that included being like you."

"But you hoped it would?"

"I hoped it *might.* And then…"

Keet sits on the edge of the bed, waiting for Nolee to finish what she's saying. When she remains silent, he darts a glance at her.

"And then?" he asks.

She stands up straighter. "And then Arogem tried to kidnap me. He told me he could make me Keykwin."

"You didn't tell us that."

She shakes her head. "I wanted to forget it. But I can't."

"You can't forget Arogem, or his offer." Keet hears the edge in his voice, and it cuts him.

"Keet. I only want you. I want to be with you. But me being human and you being who you are… there's only so close we can get."

Keet stares at his hands gripping one another. "If you believe that, I've nothing to offer you, Nolee." He stands. "I'm going to sleep on the sofa. We've got an important day tomorrow."

"Keet—"

He raises a hand in front of him as she tries to get closer.

"I need to be alone right now."

She nods, and steps away from the door, which he opens, then closes with a quiet click. Padding down the hallway, he takes a pillow and blankets from the hall closet and goes to the living room. Eyes half-closed, Fae and Wallace glance at him, then lower their heads and go back to sleep. Keet knows sleep will be elusive for him tonight. He knows the ache in the middle of his chest won't go away when he closes his eyes. Resisting these thoughts, he drops the pillow on the sofa, lies down on top of the blankets, and stares into the darkness.

# CHAPTER TWENTY-NINE

Keet looks as tired as I feel. I doubt either of us got any rest last night. He stands next to me, stiff and unyielding. The scissors I'm holding tremble when Sylvie asks me to join her and Zelka and Saila. Taking the scissors, then winding her hair into one hand, she stretches it taut before giving the scissors to Zelka. There are no words between them, but there's a shared understanding. Zelka's shoulder-length hair rises in the breeze, and I see her shiver, even though the day is already warming the dock under our bare feet. Opening the scissors, she places Sylvie's white hair between the blades. For centuries, members of the Keykwin clan offered their hair as a sacrifice when they chose to swim as Blackfish for the rest of their days.

"Stop!"

Sylvie's voice is sharp, urgent. It affects me like I've collided with a wall. Zelka freezes, a few long strands of white hair floating in the breeze. Sylvie releases her hair and holds out her hands for the scissors, then hands them back to me with a mischievous glint in her eye.

"I will keep my hair with me," she says, as she smiles at Zelka, "in memory of my granddaughter."

Sylvie begins to sing in a language older than any I've known, the soft sounds escaping into the dawn, clicks and glottal stops shaping the music of her voice. An elbow against my ribs reminds me that Abbie is standing on my other side.

"What's she saying, Mom?"

I take Abbie's hand, trying to smile and failing. "Close your eyes and pay attention to your emotions as you listen to her voice."

Abbie's narrowed eyes tell me that if she weren't standing as a part of this family, she would argue with that idea. She gives her head a small shake, then closes her eyes, and I see her face relax as the words and the music flow around us, Grandmother's wispy voice joining the wind brushing through the trees and the calls of gulls circling above us. In the distance is the high chittering call of an eagle. Waves lap against the dock, and I shift my gaze out to the cove as an eruption of breaths announces the arrival of Keet's family pod.

Six dorsal fins bob in a half circle. I watch the smallest dorsal fin. George no longer resembles the youngster I'd met not so long ago. The longing to join them swells inside of me again, and I squeeze my eyes shut, letting go of Abbie's hand to wipe away my tears. Keet stands silent beside me.

The singing stops and all I hear are the sounds of a new day: wind, waves, gulls flying overhead. I open my eyes, watching as Grandmother sits on the edge of the dock, head bowed. I fight the urge to run to her, to pull her away from the edge, to keep her with me.

Beside me, Keet trains his gaze on his family pod. We don't touch. I'm drowning in regret and sadness, trapped in a dark hole of loss. Keet, Grandmother, my daughter's disbelief in my new life, my father. It feels as though everything is fracturing, vanishing into different universes. The solitude is much stronger, much colder, than any I'd experienced when submerged in the Salish Sea.

Sylvie shrugs out of her robe, letting it puddle around her. Raising her hands to the sky, she speaks soft sibilant words and murmurs. She pauses, then repeats the words in English.

*It is a good day.*
*My heart is filled with gratitude for this day.*
*My heart is filled with gratitude for my ancestors.*
*It is a good day*
*To swim in these waters.*
*May I never forget*
*The good days of this life*
*And the one that now ends*
*And the one that now begins.*
*It is a good day.*
*And I give thanks.*
*I give thanks for my last Walk Into the Water.*
*I give thanks for my Walk Into the Sea.*
*I dive into the sea as woman and*
*I rise from the sea as Blackfish.*

Before the sound of Grandmother's name can leave my throat, she slips off the dock into the water. I run to the edge in time to see her long white hair disappear in spirals as she first sinks, then swims away from the land, away from us. Abbie joins me, linking her arm through mine. I lean into her warmth as my tears drop into the sea.

"Come on, Mom. Let's get ready to go."

We walk past Keet and Zelka on the dock. I try to catch Keet's eye, but he looks away. Zelka offers me a small smile and puts a hand on my shoulder. She whispers into my ear, "We'll wait until you're in the house."

I nod, numb even to the longing to change to orca and swim with them.

I glance over my shoulder at Jerry and Saila, Keet and Zelka, a tight knot of family. My heart gives a painful thump as I wonder if I'm a part of that family anymore. Jerry and Saila will be taking the same ferry as we are, but our ways will part once they turn north toward Alaska, and we head south. I glance at Abbie, her profile stern, then hear a tandem splash that tells me Zelka and Keet have gone into the sea. I glance back toward the dock before Abbie and I enter the house. Keet and Zelka's dorsal fins rise beside each other, swimming west. Jerry and Saila watch them leave.

Andi pulls into our driveway and gets out of the car.

"I can't thank you enough, Andi."

"It's no trouble at all. You have a lot going on, and I'm happy to stay here and take care of your awesome dogs." Setting down her suitcase, she kneels to greet Wallace and Fae.

When she stands, I hug her, wishing I could tell her everything that's going on instead of the manufactured story about Keet, Zelka, and Sylvie needing to take care of a family matter in Alaska while Abbie and I drive to Texas.

"We'd better go, Mom." Abbie is standing beside me, her hand on my shoulder. "Andi, it was great meeting you. I'll be back and maybe we can hang out more." She leans over and gives her a hug.

"You take care, Abbie. Next time we'll go into Seattle and dance."

Abbie grabs my suitcase and tosses it behind the seat, then goes back into the house to get her own. She has three bags to my one.

"She comes prepared, doesn't she?" Andi says. I nod, distracted by worry about Keet and self-doubt that gnaws at my stomach, filling it instead of the breakfast I should've eaten.

"Nolee?" I snap back to the present, seeing Andi's soft face wrinkled with concern.

"Sorry. Mornings aren't my best time."

"Uh-huh." The doubt in her voice tells me she's not buying it.

I blow out a breath. "Truth is, Andi, Keet and I had an argument, and now my father is dying, and I'm fretting about seeing my family in Texas."

"That's a lot. Promise me you'll take care of yourself?"

I nod.

"Promise me you'll text me any time?"

I nod again, hearing the whistle of the kettle. Abbie must be making tea to take with us.

"Nolee. When I say, 'any time,' I mean it literally."

In a rush of emotion, I hug her, unable to control the sobs rising from my chest.

She pats my back. "It'll sort itself out. You're going to be okay, and while you're not okay, you've got people who love you."

I step away from her, wiping my eyes with the end of my sleeve. "Thanks, Andi. I owe you dinner when I get back."

"You don't owe me anything. But I'll take you up on dinner." She smiles, the wrinkles fanning out from her eyes. The front door slams.

"That's everything. Let's go, Mom."

As we drive away, I watch the bay, hoping to see the rise and fall of black dorsal fins. But the only thing I see are the churning waves.


Over the next two and a half days, Abbie and I take turns driving, fueled by worry and fast food. After a rest stop in Amarillo, I tilt my head back, hoping for a bit of sleep before we get to the hospital.

"Mom, I won't say anything about Keet."

The concern in her voice rouses me from my drowsiness.

"I know that, Abbs. Of all the things to worry about, you can toss that one." The roar of the truck's engine lulls me into somnolence again, and I don't wake until it slows down. Sitting up straighter, I rub my face and run my fingers through my tousled hair. As I look out at the flat brown earth, I have a growing sense of unreality.

"Where are we? Where's the hospital?" I ask Abbie.

"Google maps is already taking us there." She points to her phone. I see the thick blue line connecting our dot to the hospital where my family waits. Every minute it grows shorter, and in a panic, I want to open the door and run away, letting the hard Texas ground swallow me whole.

When Abbie and I enter my father's hospital room, I see my two brothers, Frank and Manny; my mom's younger sister, Iris; and my sister, Lily, seated around the bed in which my withered father lies. His breath is erratic, and his skin is stretched tightly over the strong bones of his face. Their quiet conversation stops as everyone looks at me. Iris stands, opening her arms to hug Abbie, then me.

"I'm so glad you're here."

"You just missed your dad, punkin," Frank says to Abbie as he slings his arm around her shoulders.

"I'll see him soon. He needs his truck back."

They continue talking, leaving me and Iris in the room with my dying father.

Separated from the group, I'm overwhelmed by the feeling of not belonging, an old and familiar experience. Lost in my own thoughts, I don't realize I'd closed my eyes. I open them when a small hand touches my arm and see Aunt Iris.

"Thank you for being here, Nolee. It means a lot to me."

I lean over and kiss her cheek, soft with age and wrinkles, then approach the bed in a daze. I'm hesitant to touch my father's withered hand, knuckles swollen from decades of ranch work and arthritis, the skin paper thin. Iris is beside me, her gray hair pulled into a bun on top of her head, her eyes red from crying.

"Iris, why don't you take a break. I'll stay with him, and you can go down to the cafeteria." The clock on the wall says it's two in the morning—a time I've often found myself awake. This night is a yawning abyss, a dark corridor in my head with too many tunnels to navigate.

"I don't think they're open, but I could stretch my legs a bit." She touches my father's arm. "I'll be right back, John." After the door closes, I get out of the chair and stretch, then bend and touch my palms to the floor.

A distant whisper pulls me back to my dying father's bedside.

"Nolee?"

"Hi." I smile, touching his hand below the bruising from the IV needle.

"I'm dying," he whispers.

After a moment of sorting through possible replies, I find the only one that matters. "Yes, you are."

He nods, his eyes closed, breath fluttering in and out of his body.

I stand watch for another few minutes, keeping my hand on his. I'm turning to go back to the chair when he whispers my name again.

"Nolee."

"Yes?"

"I'm a piss-poor dad to you."

"Don't say that—"

"Luna's a wonderful dog. You have a way with her." He gasps again and gives a weak cough, turning his head away from me. I can see the thin skin of his scalp stretched tight over his skull. Luna's been dead for years. Pain knifes through my heart when I realize that, for my father, my past is his present.

I'm still standing beside him when Iris returns, holding a steaming Styrofoam cup.

"They didn't have tea. I brought you hot cocoa. It's from a machine, so no promises."

"Thanks." I take a sip, tasting the cardboard sweetness, glad to have something warm. "He told me I was good with Luna."

Iris sets her coffee on the table beside my father's bed and puts her arms around me. For the thousandth time, I cry.

"John's been talking about you a lot these last few months. He wanted to apologize."

I pull a tissue from the box and blow my nose. "He didn't apologize as much as said he knew he was a 'piss-poor dad.'"

"Well, that counts as something from a man who never let an apology escape his mouth."

# CHAPTER THIRTY

By six o'clock that morning, my father has died. We surround him, each of us touching part of his body. After the nurses remove the needles and detach the monitors, my sister is the first to speak. The erratic green line that showed his heartbeat is gone, as is the erratic beep as his heart failed.

"Goodbye, Dad." Lily leans over and kisses his forehead, her bleached-blond hair brushing his sunken cheek. At the end of the line, when I'm alone with the body of my father, I can't say goodbye, nor can I call him Dad. The sounds outside the room are the sounds of life continuing even as I hold his cold hand, trying to summon the last words I'll say to him.

Shoes squeak out in the hallway, followed by a burst of quiet laughter from the nurses' station.

"Go in peace." I lean down and kiss his head, then leave.

Three days later, our family gathers for his memorial service, sitting on uncomfortable chairs in the funeral home, listening as people stand up and tell stories about my father. In every memory, he is someone I never knew: kind, funny, patient. Abbie praises him as the world's greatest grandfather and mentions how she'll miss their Sunday ice cream outings.

My memories of this man are a dark cloud. I can still feel the familiar knot of resentment in my heart. Iris takes my hand and gives me a tired smile.

The last night in my hotel room, I'm worn out and stretched thin. Flopping onto the bed, I text Keet, not expecting an answer. Looking at the texts Andi has sent, I smile when I see a short video of Fae and Wallace romping on the beach. I'm flying home in the morning, and it won't be soon enough.

Before it's light outside, I tumble out of the hotel bed, throwing my phone against the sheets. Another day without a response from Keet. He's most likely still with Grandmother and his family pod, but I can't also help but wonder if he's deliberately cutting himself off from me, from my attempts to set things right between us.

It becomes clear to me how reason has been a stranger these last couple of months. I sit on the edge of the rumpled bed holding my head in my hands. From my fourth-floor room, the sunrise I see is devoid of warmth or beauty. I pick up my phone and tap on Keet's number. When I get his voicemail again, my voice trembles—with anger or panic, I'm not sure.

"You can't be gone forever, Keet Noland. I'm flying home today and we're going to figure this out. I made a promise to you, and I intend to keep it."

Each day he swims to Osprey Bay, pulled between his family and seeing if Nolee is home. He senses the familiar urge to shift into his human form, to have the ground beneath his feet. To see the bright blue sky and the white gulls moving in shifting semaphores across it.

This afternoon, he swims past the dock, tilting his head above the water and taking a breath at the same time. Andi's car is still there, but he can see her putting her bags into the trunk. He dives, kelp and jellyfish slipping along the length of his body as he clicks and listens for the water to carry the sounds of his family feeding to the south.

When the sun begins to drop behind a small rocky island, Keet nudges each of his family, touching Zelka to ask her to stay behind with them for several more sunsets. He wants time to apologize to Nolee, to mend their relationship without the rest of the family being witness to what may happen. Like their Promising Ceremony, Keet wants their words to stay between them.

Nana and Sylvie hover in the water and he nudges them last, his heart billowing through his chest like one of the *Salish See*'s white sails when it catches the wind. After many days of the others hunting for her, Grandmother is gaining weight, and her spirit is light again. She whistles his name, then flips and swims away. He sends click trains after her until her tail merges with the gray of the water, his family swimming behind her. All except George, who turns, surfaces for a breath, then races to

Keet's side. They rise together, touching. George clicks and the picture is of Nolee's face. He misses his friend. Keet senses George's longing, one he shares.

Keet nudges George, bobbing with him in the lazy current, reassuring him that Nolee is on her way home. Calling George's name in an ever-rising series of notes, he swims away before George can hear his next thought, which is that he hopes Nolee *is* coming home.

As he swims toward Camas Island, his need for resolution fuels his speed. As though Nolee has heard his yearning, he sees her parked in the driveway, Wallace and Fae dancing around her legs. Keet surfaces and blows, then dives. He turns his rostrum to the bright surface, using his tail to propel him above the water, where he flips and lands on his back, joy splashing through his body. He dives again, rockets to the sky, spinning above the sea. Before he gives his body to the water, he hears Nolee shout his name.

By the time he changes and swims to the dock, she's there, sitting cross-legged and holding a towel out to him.

"Why don't we grab some dinner at Casa Mariachi," Nolee says. She places a tentative hand on Keet's arm, looking at him to be sure it's welcome. He smiles, warming to her touch even though he feels a muddle of emotion: anger and hurt, disappointment, missing her, wanting to be together again. He stops himself from putting his hand on top of hers and instead boosts himself on to the dock, sitting at the edge, rubbing his wet hair

"Sounds great."

He watches as she walks to the house, longing and foreboding both pulling at his heart. He dries off, ties the towel around his waist, and goes inside to shower and dress.

They pile into his 4Runner, Nolee with her backpack over her shoulder. He doesn't ask about her time in Texas, but she seems lighter, unburdened by the sadness that she was carrying when they left each other.

They're passing the airport when she reaches for the volume knob, turning it up. The sounds of harmonies and an acoustic guitar fill the vehicle.

*"…but tomorrow may rain so I'll follow the sun."*

"I don't care what anyone says, I've always liked the Monkees."

Keet looks at her to see if she's joking. She looks back, an impish grin lighting up her face.

"You know this is the Beatles, right?"

She nods, laughing.

"Paul McCartney wrote this when he was sixteen."

"Really? What else?"

He reaches across the console and lays his hand on her thigh.

"Ringo isn't playing drums in this one."

"What's the sound then?"

"Him slapping his knees."

She laughs again, then picks up his hand and kisses it. The heat of her mouth runs from his hand through his body.

"I still like the Monkees. They must've been in England at the same time as the Beatles."

It's Keet's turn to laugh.

"What?" she asks.

"The Monkees are an American band, put together to make a TV show."

Nolee shrugs, smiling. "Doesn't matter." She turns and looks out the window.

Keet is ready to share more music trivia, hoping to extend a fleeting moment that resembles their previous normalcy when Nolee turns to him and says, "I'm sorry."

He glances at her, then turns the music down. Waits. He knows she's watching him for a response. "I'm sorry, too."

Nolee laughs in surprise. "For what? I'm the one who made it sound like I had ulterior motives for promising myself to you."

Keet shrugs, discomfort running down his spine. "I should've talked with you more, instead of assuming you didn't want to be with me."

"It was a complicated time for both of us. I'm sorry we couldn't get through it together."

"It won't happen again, Lia." He parks the car and turns it off.

"I want to be with you for the rest of our lives. I got scared because loss and death felt like my only reality. I don't want to lose you," Nolee says.

Keet unclicks his seatbelt, then turns to her, holding her face in his palm. "You'll never lose me." Their lips meet, the tension dissolving as she holds his head in her hands.

At the restaurant, sitting outside under a red umbrella with a margarita pitcher between them, Keet decides he'll take Nolee at her word. He'll choose to believe she's happy with her life, and with him. He takes a small sip of the chilled drink, watching as she empties her glass and pours herself another.

"I've decided that being around my family isn't good for me," she says.

"Many people feel that way about their blood family."

"You're good for me. So is your family."

"They would say they're your family, too."

Nolee sips at her drink, her eyes a dark green. She smiles. "I hope so."

"What happened in Texas?"

"Same old, same old. Lily and my brothers were distant. Aunt Iris was amazing."

"I don't think you've told me about Iris."

"She's the youngest on my mom 's side of the family. She's the only one I trust, besides Abbie."

"How's Abbie doing?"

"Sad about her grandpa. Happy we got to road trip together. Not sure about who you are, but she seems to accept you."

Keet nods. "We have time. I hope she'll get more comfortable with me."

"She will." Nolee twirls the stem of the glass between her fingers. "Do we have time, though, Keet?"

"What do you mean?"

"It's hitting me that one day, it will be you or I in a hospital bed, and we may not get out of it."

Keet stills himself, wanting to answer her question without damaging the tender new skin of intimacy between them. Taking her hand, he says, "Until that happens, don't you think it's better to focus on what we have, instead of what we might lose?"

Nolee takes a drink and then their food arrives. As they eat, Keet waits for her to respond, wondering if he's started another fight.

"I'm afraid of what we'll lose. Death is non-negotiable."

"It is. But there's a lot of life to live before that."

"Grandmother is still living hers, but for me, she may as well be gone."

Keet sets his fork on the plate, hearing the sharp edge of Nolee's words. "I miss her, too."

"You still get to be with her."

Nolee finishes her drink, pours herself another. "It's easier for me to accept that my father is gone than it is for me to be at peace with Grandmother's decision to Walk Into the Water."

Keet nods. Before he can examine whether it's right or wrong to say, he blurts, "She asked me to tell you that she loves you and carries you with her every day."

Nolee rubs her eyes. "Tell her I miss her every day and love her, too."

During their slow lovemaking that night, Keet holds Nolee's gaze, persuading himself that she has let go of the desire to be Keykwin, and would focus on life rather than thoughts of death. He allows the heat of their bodies to soothe him even as he loses all thought. It is only afterward, when he finds comfort in Nolee's embrace, that he contemplates her worry about the limited time they have together. He lets this worry go, soothed into sleep by her breathing.

# CHAPTER THIRTY-ONE

I get out of bed with the sun, leaving Keet sleeping. I'm restless, unable to ease into the day. Our fight is weeks behind us, but my heart feels leaden and agitated.

A life of apathy was behind me when I boarded the ferry for the first time, then watched the prow split the green water, white froth curling against the bow as it made its way to Camas Island. But this day, apathy seems to have found me again. I don't miss the place I was born, but this time of year, I do sometimes think about its wide blue skies and the heat that mirages from the earth, reflecting the sun in wavering columns.

I can't find a reason for this heavy mood. Keet and I have recovered from our argument, and I'm sure I wish to remain human. Indulging my curiosity wasn't nearly enough reason to sacrifice our relationship and all the promises we gave to one another. Ava and I have a smooth business partnership. I'm healthy. Abbie is busy with school. Zelka and Marissa, even if they don't admit it to themselves, are falling in love. Zelka's working part time to cover the store's extended hours, and Andi and I get together every Tuesday night at Casa Mariachi. I haven't had visions of the black door in months, not since Keet and I made up from our fight. When I think of my father, I'm relieved, but when I think of Grandmother, who Keet tells me is gaining weight, sadness anchors my heart somewhere in the middle of the planet. Shaking my head in irritation with myself, I make some green tea, follow the dogs outside, and settle on the log.

Amazement catches me sometimes, especially when I think my real life began when I moved to this small island, a life that mirrors the woman I've been waiting to be. There's no sense of amazement today, however. Just a smothering boredom, like the gray waves and gray sky and the clouds that aren't clouds but rather fog settling between me and the sun.

Beside me, Fae whines, amber eyes narrowed. Wallace sniffs along the beach, then raises his nose in the air before lying down nearby. I rest my hand on Fae's narrow head. "What's going on with me, red dog?" She wags her tail, showing me that at least one of us is content.

"You don't have to guard me all the time," I tell Keet.

I check my watch, estimating how much time I have before I need to leave to cover the final shift of the day at the store. This time of the year, it's difficult to judge by the light. The sun is setting earlier, and fog blankets the island for longer stretches.

"I thought you wanted to go hiking with us," he says, touching my arm.

I look over at Marissa and Zelka, sitting on the cabin's porch with backpacks at their feet and hands intertwined, talking and laughing.

"That hammock is looking better to me than a hike. Take Wallace and Fae, they'll love going along."

"That means you're here by yourself." I flick my eyes past Keet's gaze, knowing he still worries about Arogem.

"We haven't seen hide nor hair of Arogem for months. Jerry ran him off for good."

"We can't be sure of that."

"We don't know anything for sure, sweetheart." Softening my tone, I give him a quick kiss. "I haven't been alone in months. I'm planning on reading and taking a nap in the hammock, then going to work. It will be a day like any other day."

My smile doesn't dispel Keet's scowl. He looks at Osprey Bay, shimmering under the September sun. Along its edge, the forest is a muted green and tan, highlighted by a few splashes of yellow.

Using the word that carries weight with Keet, I say, "I promise I won't go kayaking. I won't go near the water. If I see him, I'll lock myself in the house and call you."

Keet nods, kisses me, then turns and calls the dogs to jump in the 4Runner. Marissa and Zee hug me before they get in with Keet and drive away.

I turn toward the bay again, closing my eyes and listening to the gulls, the sea, the distant chugging of a container ship, the whine of an outboard motor. When I open my eyes, the sun is still throwing bursts of light on the water, and the sky opens between the clouds, a radiant blue. I pick up my book and a glass of water and make my way to the hammock, where after five minutes of reading, I fall into an easy doze, sun warming on my face.

Waking up in time to shower and dress, I text Keet as I walk to my car. *All is well. Off to work. Love you!*

I toss the phone and my backpack on the passenger seat and lean in to put a travel mug of tea in the center console. When my back is turned and Arogem is far, far from my mind, I'm grabbed from behind, arms pinned tightly to my sides and air driven from my lungs.

"Hello, Nolee."

Despite my struggling, kicking backward at his knees and shins, Arogem easily lifts me off my feet and walks with me toward the water.

"You're crazy, Arogem! Let me go!"

When we reach the water's edge, he sets me down and his grip loosens. Dropping a shoulder, I find my pocketknife, pry it open, and stab behind me. Arogem grunts but doesn't let me go. The knife is wrenched from my hand before his arms tighten around me again and he drags me into the sea. When the water hits my feet, I gasp. By the time the waves are at my waist, terror is setting in. I try to slow down my breath as he takes us farther out into cove's frigid water "Arogem, stop! How are you going to hold onto me when you change?" Arogem's reply chills me more than the water.

"You'll be asleep soon."

Near the buoys, I feel Arogem release me. The second I'm free, I turn and put all my effort into swimming back to shore. Still no cars. No barking dogs. Behind me, I hear Arogem exhale as orca, and I take a deep breath, knowing that he will soon take me underwater. As I frantically swim, he glides on his side next to me, large pectoral fin in the air. The solid weight of his belly glides against my body. As I watch, helpless, his black fin lowers toward me. The blue sky becomes a black void, and I'm furious it may be the last thing I see while I'm human. One easy flip and I'm underwater, tucked between his fin and his body.

Shaking, I free my arms so I can grab the fin; pulling myself forward, I open my eyes to see how far away I am from the surface and almost lose what little air I've saved. The sea is a monochromatic gray and next to my head, Arogem's skin is shiny black. It's hard to keep my eyes open—sleep is descending on me. My last thought before sleep overtakes me is that when I wake up, it will be in a room of strangers, with no way home.

A steady pounding in my chest drowns out the fear, and I think of the

Japanese Taiko drummers I'd seen in Dallas forever ago. That memory fades and my next sensation is the size of my body; it seems enormous, and I'm not shaking because the water is warm and alive against my skin. The drum in my chest slows and my legs seem to have disappeared. I am no longer only human, no longer just a woman, but orca as well. Our tail powers us through the water with strength and speed. Pictures arise behind our eyes as we read the surrounding sea. We hear other orcas in the distance, their clicks also revealing pictures. Silken water caressing our skin, we glide to a rocking stop. When we stop moving, we feel a pull in our mind, a dissonance that slices through our head. We dive deeper and the pull goes away. The drum slows, the gliding stops. And the dissonance shatters us into two again, the echo of the scream blending into the clicks and whistles of an orca pod speeding toward us. George rushes to push my body out from under Arogem's fin.

But it seems he's already released me and is swimming away as George propels me to the surface. The young orca bumps my back, making me cough. He's producing arpeggios of sound, and I catch each one in my mind, almost understanding what he's saying. But their meaning fades as I chase after them.

As if yanked backward, I open my eyes to a murky green sea. Limp and lungs burning, I hack up saltwater. The pod circles me, bodies touching, gently guiding me back to the beach. I'm freezing, shaking so hard I can't swim. A nudge on the soles of my feet, then I'm astride George. His dorsal fin seems far away, but I'm able to grab it. I press my cheek to its warmth. Streams of pictures are coming from him, and I feel as though if I allowed myself, I could *be* George, just as I'd merged with Arogem. Sleep is taking me again, its embrace as smothering as Arogem's had been. My heart slows and as I fight to open my stinging eyes, I see the dock bobbing nearby. George glides to a stop, unsure what to do next. I can no longer fight the exhaustion that envelops me and slump against George's fin.

# CHAPTER THIRTY-TWO

As soon as Keet turns onto the dirt road leading to Osprey Bay, the dogs begin to whine, becoming more agitated the closer they get to home. Keet stops and lets them out, and they race down the road. Worry building, he follows them, hands tight around the steering wheel. He hears Marissa ask Zelka what's going on.

"Whatever it is, it can't be good. The dogs are frantic," Zelka replies.

When he pulls up next to the house, he sees Nolee's car, door wide open, then sees her bobbing by the dock, slumped against George's dorsal fin; she's not moving. His pod, breath steaming in the cold air, circles by the buoys, unable to swim closer.

"Nolee!" Keet races to the dock and jumps into the water. He grabs Nolee around the waist. She's not breathing.

Back on the dock, Zelka and Marissa lift Nolee by her arms and haul her out of the water. Keet boosts himself up, turns Nolee on her side, and pounds her back between her shoulder blades. She coughs and spits out water but doesn't open her eyes. Picking her up, he jogs toward the house, shouting directions to Zelka and Marissa.

"We need a fire! Warm tea, dry clothes, and lots of blankets. Hurry!"

Keet takes Nolee into the bathroom and turns on the taps, filling the tub with warm water. As he undresses her, he notices how pallid her skin is. Her chest rises and falls, and small puffs of breath leave her mouth, but the pauses between are too long. Pressing his fingers against her carotid artery, he feels a pulse, erratic and faint.

Closing the door, he strips off his sodden clothes and pulls Nolee into the tub, leaning her against his chest, wrapping his arms around her shoulders, willing her to take his warmth, to use his body heat as a door closed to death.

Only when his skin puckers does he remove them both from the tepid bath. Lifting Nolee, he props her against the tub and grabs a few towels. He can hear the fire crackling in the living room and hears the low voices of Marissa and Zee. Marissa asks, "What was going on with all these orcas? And why was Nolee on the smallest one?" He doesn't hear Zelka's reply.

When they are dry and dressed, he carries Nolee to the sofa and piles blankets over her. His sister's voice interrupts his worry.

"Keet?"

He turns toward her, silent.

"I need to fix this."

"How will you do that, when it's not your fault?"

"I need to find Arogem."

"Who is Arogem?" Marissa's voice breaks between them.

Before Keet can come up with a suitable lie, Zelka says, "Em, there's something I need to share with you, but I can't do it right now. Arogem is a distant cousin, and he's causing trouble. Nolee got caught in the middle. I'll explain everything when Nolee is better."

Marissa turns her attention back to Nolee. "Why isn't she waking up?"

Voice louder than he intended, Keet says, "She will. She's still too cold." Zelka must've put the kettle on, and he hears it whistling. Going into the kitchen, he pours hot water over a tea bag and stands there a minute, breathing in the sharp tannins billowing on the steam. Then he adds honey and gives it a quick stir.

Zelka and Marissa come into the kitchen, and Marissa touches his shoulder. "Zee has asked me to leave y'all alone for a little bit." Keet can't form the words to reply, but Marissa gives him a small smile. "I'm sure she'll be okay. Please call me if I can do anything."

Keet nods, but the rock in his belly refuses to move, despite his Sisyphean efforts to shift it. Looking down at her pale face, he fights the thoughts that tell him she may never wake up.

He hears the door click closed behind Marissa. Zelka stands beside him. "Let's see if we can get some of that tea into her," she says.

If I'm dreaming, I never want to wake up. I glide through the warm sea, the kelp, the gulls, the air, and the water a vast, pulsing kaleidoscope of life. Shifting tones of gray, black, and white are lit by the sunbeams that pierce the surface in a dance of light. When I flip my body sideways and look down at the sandy sea floor, interrupted by the bump of half-buried rocks, it glistens as though paved with diamonds. I close my eyes, and my vision extends farther: boats, humpback whales, the flashing black-and-white bodies of my orca cousins.

Then I feel warm liquid in my mouth; I cough, sputter, then swallow. Once again sensing my legs, once again confined to a body that is too small. I raise my hands to ward off the cup. Eyes half-closed, I see two faces hovering over mine, faces I should know but don't. Where am I? Why am I here? My place is in the sea.

Closing my eyes again, I turn onto my side and sink once again into the sea's warm water, letting life weave me into its vast panorama.

"Keet, maybe we need to take Nolee to a doctor?"

Keet shakes his head, not taking his eyes off Nolee. "We can't. What would we tell them?"

"They'd know how to warm her up again—"

"And once she gets warm, but doesn't wake up?" Keet takes Zelka's elbow, steering her into the kitchen.

"Zee, I can get her warm. What I can't do is leave her."

Zelka nods. "I'll go find Arogem."

Zelka heads for the dock, impatient to face Arogem. She hears Marissa call her name and turns. "Em. I thought you left?"

Marissa takes one of Zelka's hands in her own, and Zelka's anger subsides. She gazes down into Marissa's dark eyes, and, lifting a curl away from her face, kisses her. "That thing I need to tell you, but I can't yet?"

Marissa nods.

"I need you to trust me now. Get in your car and drive away. I'll text when I'm back."

"Be safe, Zee, whatever it is you have to do."

Zelka holds Marissa, wishing she could promise that, wishing she could promise that life in Osprey Bay would return to what it had been earlier in the day when they'd left to go hiking. But she's filled with a sense of dread, along with the fear that if Nolee returns to consciousness, she might not be the same woman Zelka's grown to love.

Marissa kisses Zelka's cheek, cradles her face in her soft hands, then turns to leave. Waiting until the sound of Marissa's engine has faded, Zelka walks to the dock, then turns to make sure she's alone. But she's not. Wallace—ears pointed forward, body stiff with worry—watches her from behind the fence.

"How could I forget you, buddy?" She jogs to the gate and opens it, letting Wallace out; Fae must be with Nolee. Zelka kneels and strokes Wallace's head, folding his furry bulk against her body, burying her nose in his coat and inhaling. When she walks to the dock again, Wallace trots beside her.

Checking once more that she's alone. Zelka strips out of her jeans and t-shirt, dives, spins until she's once again Blackfish. When she surfaces for air, she sees Wallace standing on the beach, a canine sentinel bathed in sunlight.

As Zelka swims, power streams through her body; despite her agitation over Nolee's attempted abduction, she still finds solace in the music of the sea. Rising again to breathe, she then sinks deeper and finds the current beneath all other currents, letting it pull her toward the island with the door in its base.

When a series of clicks reveal the door, an icy shard of fear pierces her heart. She wonders if she'll be trapped again. However, this fear is smaller than the fear that swallows her when she thinks about Nolee never waking up.

Pushing against the water with her flukes, she bursts through the door and stands upright, wiping the water from her face. The tunnel is as she remembers it, and she sees a row of robes hanging on the wall and takes one. Wrapping it around herself, she ties it at one shoulder, and cinches it closed with a dark belt. She doesn't want Arogem seeing any more of her than necessary. As she jogs toward the main chamber, she wonders what she'll say to Arogem when she finds him.

Another long hallway opens into the main room of the Water Canyon House, this one filled with familiar faces who greet her with wide eyes and smiles. Children hold her around her legs, waist, and ankles, and she murmurs to them, patting their faces. At the far end, she sees Yiskal and Byree sitting at the fire, watching her approach. Zelka hesitates, still uncertain about her words, then walks to them. All conversation around her ceases.

"Where is Arogem Stonecarver? Where is he? He abducted a human woman and tried to bring her here." Zelka clenches her trembling hands into fists. "That woman is as a mother to me, and he's harmed her."

Faces closed. No smiles greet her now. The Water Canyon House People stand, children tucked at their sides.

Byree says, "Come, sit down beside me child, and tell me what has happened."

Animated by a chaos of emotion that threatens to topple what little control she has, Zelka walks to Byree, but doesn't sit down. Yiskal rises to stand close beside her, looking into her eyes.

"Arogem tried to bring Nolee—a human woman—here, to change her to Keykwin." Zelka doesn't lower her voice. She wants every member of the Water Canyon House to hear what he'd done. "It didn't work, but now she can't wake up. I need him to fix what he did to her."

Byree pushes herself to her feet. "Arogem isn't here."

Zelka hears the truth in Byree's answer. Though she's still afraid the Water Canyon House won't let her leave, she's overcome with a need to find Arogem. As she turns to leave, Yiskal's hand on her elbow stops her.

"Let us help," she says.

"How? Have any of you ever changed a human into Keykwin?"

The fire crackles, a baby cries. Byree turns and faces the people. "We will sit together and share what we have been told about our history with humans."

Zelka watches as each person nods, whispering to those around them.

"When we have an answer," Byree says, "we will find you."

"Look for a blue house on the edge of a bay, on the big island to the south."

As Byree embraces Zelka, she whispers, "We will bring your Nolee back." Zelka lowers her forehead to Byree's shoulder, allowing herself a moment of comfort, a pause to grieve. When she straightens, she says to Byree and Yiskal, "Thank you."

As she strides toward the door that opens to the sea, she raises her chin and straightens her shoulders. After hanging her robe on the hook, she stands in front of the door, fists clenched at her sides. "Maybe you know about Arogem and Nolee, and maybe you don't." She swallows a sob. "But I need to be with my brother, and the woman we love. I need to leave."

Inhaling, Zelka pushes on the door. When she surfaces moments later, the sea is leaden, and the sky is dark. She breathes, dives, and swims toward Osprey Bay.

The woman sitting across from me on this twilit beach smiles. She seems familiar, as though I've seen her face before. Her auburn hair has the beginnings of silver at the temples. The wind lifts it, creating a nimbus of dark and light around her face. Why is she so familiar? Is it her pale skin? Her green eyes that shift between green and blue, like the color of the sea?

It's her eyes. They're mine.

Where exactly am I? I feel as though I'm made of smoke. When I look down, I see rocks and sand through my crossed legs. I touch my thighs, but my vaporous hand plunges through and disappears.

There's no fear. There's nothing. Across from me, a woman stands, extending her hand, beckoning. Turning away from her offer, I lower my head into the mist and disappear.

*Nolee is a zombie*, Keet thinks, *thanks to Arogem.* Hours pass as he battles his anger while spooning soup and broth and fruit smoothies into her mouth. Helping her drink warm tea. Walking her to the bathroom. Tucking her in bed. Her eyes lack light and her face lacks emotion. She is a body with no spirit. He wishes Grandmother were here. He wishes Zelka could stay with Nolee so he could swim and find Grandmother. For the first time in years, he and Nolee are the only ones in Osprey Bay.

As he stokes the fire, he wonders how he was able to live such a solitary existence for so many years. While he no longer remembers why being alone appealed to him, he does remember when that appeal vanished: when Nolee arrived. Her brightness and spark ignited his own guttering flame, making him realize that being alone wasn't good for him, but it felt better than the heartbreak of being different.

He throws a chunk of wood on the fire and listens to its crackle. Nolee, on the sofa, stares vacantly into space. He leaves the fire and kneels in front her, brushes a strand of hair away from her eyes. Feeling helpless, he moves to sit beside her, cradling her body next to his. Her head lolls back on his shoulder, eyes open but unseeing. Keet shivers; if not for the rise and fall of her chest, he'd swear she was dead.

*But she's as good as dead, isn't she?* He closes his eyes, holding her as tightly as he dares, hoping that his heartbeat and breath and the warmth of his body will transfer to her. Invoking an ancient rhythm, he prays, reminding himself of who he is and of all those from whom Nolee is descended. From whom he is descended.

He is made up of his ancestors. Like the woman in his arms, he is a blend of those who came before him and also unique. As he continues his melodic prayer, he notices that Nolee's breathing has deepened, and her eyes are closed. He eases her onto her back and stands up. After covering her with blankets and giving the fire a stir, he lets the dogs in. Fae is the only one at the door; she trots to Nolee, sniffs her face, and extends a tentative tongue toward her nose. When Keet looks for Wallace, he sees him sitting on the beach, looking out at the gray waves. Fae, watching Keet with worried amber eyes, places a paw on the sofa.

"Go ahead, Fae. She'd want you there."

Fae jumps up and curls herself into a shiny red circle at Nolee's feet.

Keet hears Wallace bark, the higher pitch telling him it's someone he knows. Going to the window, he sees Zelka on the dock with her back toward him, wrapping a towel around her head. Waiting a few moments, he kisses Nolee's cheek. "I'll be right back, Lia."

When he reaches the dock, Zelka is dressed and sitting cross-legged, stroking Wallace. When she looks into Keet's eyes, he feels her despair.

"What happened, Zee?"

"I went into the Water Canyon House, but Arogem wasn't there. Byree and Yiskal have called a Council with every member of their family. They'll find out if anyone remembers anything about their history with humans."

"How long will that take?" Keet fast-forwards the routine of the last few hours, wondering how long he can keep Nolee alive.

Zelka shrugs. "I don't know, and neither do they."

"What do we do about Arogem?"

"Keet, I don't have any answers. I wish I did."

He paces the dock, the worn wood soft under his feet. As clouds shift across his vision, he thinks, then turns to Zelka.

"Stay with Nolee, please. She's sleeping. I gave her some food, but she might get thirsty."

"Where are you going?"

"I need to find Grandmother. She can help."

Not waiting for Zelka to answer, Keet jumps into the water and spins, the tatters of his clothes floating away from his body. Surfacing for air, he dives, singing Grandmother's name, scanning the images in his head for Arogem, hoping for respite from the weight of his grief. The longer he swims and the farther he gets from Nolee, the more it feels like broken glass is flowing through his veins. He speeds through a channel, surfacing long enough to catch the air, then submerges, scanning for his family pod. It's almost nightfall before he finds them feeding farther north than he's ever known them to go.

The ache in his chest softens as they swim over and under and beside him. Here in these nighttime waters with his family, the weight of his grief is lighter. He takes comfort in the touch of their pectoral fins as he swims between Nana and his grandmother. As he shares the images of Arogem and Nolee, they feel his distress, and turn as one, swimming south. George stays close by Keet's side, steady as the black-and-white bodies flowing through the water in front of them.

With his family pod swimming outside the bay listening for Arogem, Keet climbs onto the dock. The night air bites at his skin, but he ignores it. When he looks down, he sees that Zee's left a towel and robe for him. He rubs his head with the towel, then slips into the robe's worn softness. He'd hoped to return with something useful, but the dispiriting fact was that Grandmother knows nothing about the history of changing humans to Keykwin, or if something like this has happened before. He pauses at the front door to gather the remnants of his hope, tattered as the clothes he burst out of earlier. He goes inside.

"Did she wake up?" he asks his sister. He can tell from her face and Nolee's curled form under the blankets that nothing has changed.

"No, and I couldn't get her to drink any tea. She spat it out." Zelka pulls her damp t-shirt away from her body.

"Why don't you call it a night? I'll stay here with her."

Zelka kisses Nolee's head and whispers in her ear. Keet does his best to not listen. Zelka hugs him as she walks by.

"Thanks for putting a towel and robe out on the dock."

"You're welcome. Good night."

The door shuts behind her. Keet peers out the window, but against the black night and sea, he's unable to tell if his family pod is still nearby.

# CHAPTER THIRTY-THREE

Four days have passed since Arogem tried to change Nolee. Each day she eats less, drinks less, and doesn't open her eyes. Nolee's phone pings with a text from Abbie. *Hi Mom! Haven't heard from you in a couple of days. You okay? I've got midterms, but text me back. xoxox*

When Zelka walks in, she sees the text message and picks up Nolee's phone. "Do you want me to text her back?" she asks.

"Yes."

"What should I say?"

"Tell her that her mom is ill, but it's nothing to worry about and she'll text her as soon as she's better."

Zelka taps in the message then sets the phone back on the table.

"Can you stay with her while I get a bath ready?"

"Sure. Do you want me to offer her some water?"

Keet shakes his head. "I just tried. No luck."

Another text pings on Nolee's phone. Zelka reads it to Keet. *Do I need to fly up there and help y'all take care of her??*

Keet's jaw hardens. He's treading very close to the edge of deception, but what's he supposed to tell Abbie? A love-sick Keykwin cousin abducted her mother, then let her go, and now she won't wake up? He takes the phone from Zelka's hand. *I don't think it's that serious. I'll keep you posted. We're taking good care of her.*

As soon as he sends it, the phone rings. Keet looks at his sister, wondering if his face mirrors the dread in hers. He answers it as he walks to the bedroom, Abbie's worry speeding through the air into his ear.

Once they disconnect, Zelka asks him, "Is she coming?"

"No. I talked her out of that and told her we'd update as often as we could."

"We can call her when we have good news," Zelka says, as she opens the refrigerator. She takes out the pineapple Keet sliced into chunks that morning and pops several into her mouth.

Wallace barks, a deep bellow that tells Keet strangers are nearby. When he and Zelka look out at the dock, they see three bobbing heads: two with black hair, and one with white.

"That's Byree, Yiskal, and—"

"Arogem." Keet says the name in a low growl. He watches Arogem hang onto the dock. He registers Zelka grabbing another pile of towels and robes, arms full as she walks by him to the front door. When he turns to follow her, she blocks him.

"Keet, stay here with Nolee."

He looks at her, fury igniting inside of him. He tries to step around Zelka, but she blocks him again.

"I'm serious, Keet. Stay here. Let me find out what they want."

Keet turns and walks stiffly back to Nolee. Taking her in his arms, he rolls her onto her back and settles her against the pillows, then checks to make sure she's not too warm. Leaning his forehead against hers, he whispers. "Creator, I need help. Nolee needs help." His heart wants to break open, but he can't let it, not with Arogem in his front yard.

He hears the front door open. It's his sister, and she's alone.

"They want to come in and share their information with you."

"Arogem can wait outside."

"He's part of this, Keet. He seems to be sorry for—"

"It's too late for sorry, Zee!"

She pauses, looking at the floor. When she looks at him again, her jaw is set, and her eyes are burning. "Don't you *dare* say it's too late. Don't you dare give up, not when Nolee needs us the most."

"I'm not giving up—"

"You are if you're not willing to try everything to bring her back. Even if that means Arogem is part of it."

Keet glances at the dock, where the three Keykwin stand, arms crossed, looking up at the sky. Keet takes a breath, willing himself to control the panic that's had him in its jaws for four days.

"You're right, Zee. Invite them in."

As Zelka goes back outside, Keet puts a shirt on Nolee then lets the dogs in. Fae jumps onto the couch, curling at Nolee's feet as she has for the past four days and nights. Wallace sits by the couch at Nolee's head, ears erect, body stiff. Keet pats his back. "It's okay, Wallace. It's going to be okay."

But Keet realizes he's lying again, this time to himself.

When the door opens, Wallace stands, tail straight up, every muscle tensed; a low growl rumbles in his throat. Keet puts his hand on the dog's head, Wallace's fur soft against his palm. "Easy, buddy. It's okay."

The growling stops, but Wallace doesn't relax.

Zelka sits at the kitchen table, while Byree and Yiskal stand in the doorway, Arogem hovering behind them. Keet invites them in, and they choose chairs closest to the wall.

As Yiskal and Byree braid their wet hair, Keet hears the drone of a plane taking off, and closer, Nolee's erratic breathing. His heartbeat thumps in his ears.

"We've come to tell you what we have discovered," Byree says.

"I'm listening."

"May we have some water first, Cousin?"

Keet bristles at the word, which implies they're closer than he wants to be. Still, he and Zelka fill three glasses and pass them around. It's not lost on Keet that Arogem can't take his eyes off his sister.

"What've you found out?" he asks, trying to distract himself from the fury that threatens to consume him.

But it isn't Byree who answers him. Arogem speaks instead.

"When I swam with her, she didn't go to sleep. She became me, got into my head and my body somehow. I didn't expect that, and I panicked. When your Blackfish family found us, I dropped Nolee. I thought she'd wake up once I let her go."

Keet bunches his hands into fists and sits down, reining in the desire to beat Arogem senseless. He's taller than Keet, and broader, but Keet has anger on his side. He wants revenge, and he wants it paid with Arogem's blood.

"I tried to get back into the Water Canyon House using the door at the base of the island north of here. It wouldn't let me in. Then I swam out to the ocean and tried to get in that way, but I still wasn't allowed. I've been by myself for four days—"

"If you think I have sympathy for you, I don't. You got us into this mess. Get us out."

Arogem shakes his head. "You won't like the solution."

Byree speaks next. "When a Keykwin from our Clan changes a

human, the process must not be interrupted. From the time they go to sleep tucked against our bodies to the time we deliver them to the Water Canyon House, they must stay in constant contact with us for the change to complete itself."

Byree takes a sip of water. Yiskal continues, holding the end of her braid as if for comfort.

"Arogem let go of Nolee before she could finish her change. We think her spirit is stuck in the halfway lands: an earth with no horizon, a sea with no bottom."

Byree says, "No one can force her spirit back into her body, Keet. Not even you, or your love for her." Yiskal looks at the floor, running her bare brown toes across the wooden surface.

"Arogem did this to her. He needs to bring her back," Keet says, anger lending volume to his voice.

"Arogem made mistakes—"

"I don't think we can talk about his choice to abduct my beloved as a 'mistake.' He's tried this before—"

"From a misguided place of wanting to secure Zelka's heart." Byree looks him in the eye. Keet shifts his gaze from her to his sister. The misery on her face mirrors his own. He bites back the words he was going to say, knowing that under his anger is despair, and under the despair is fear for Nolee.

"You can't make me love you, Arogem." Zelka's clear voice slices through the silence. "And I now hesitate to even call you 'Cousin.' What you've done…" She trails away, moving over to the sofa where Nolee lies, eyes closed, face turned away from the fire. Wallace sits next to Zelka, leaning against her leg, and she rests her hand on his broad head.

Keet turns to Byree, tearing his eyes from the two people he loves to the distant family members in front of him.

"Well, Arogem? How will you bring Nolee back?"

Arogem throws out his chest and raises his chin, teeth clenched so hard that the muscles in his jaw stand out. "You won't like it."

As much as Keet wants to punish Arogem, he knows he needs to give him space to calm down, to allow answers to come without feeling the need to defend himself. Getting up from the table, Keet stands by Nolee, waiting to hear what else they may have to say.

Byree says, "My daughter and I," she nods to Yiskal, "have an idea. We need you to let Arogem swim with her again."

All thought evaporates inside Keet's head. He stands, stunned into silence, staring at the two women in front of him. Yiskal looks away but Byree holds his gaze, her face unyielding.

Keet's words come out fast and loud. "You want to give her to the same person who took her away from me? Who put her in this condition?" He points at Arogem. "Now?"

Byree nods. "Since Nolee cannot consent, you must be her voice."

A red dog sits by the woman with green eyes. The dog's eyes are burnished yellow, like leaves in the fall. I look down again. The mist that is my body is darker and moves like oil across water. When I try to touch it, my fingers fuse, and I see a small black pectoral fin.

The dog's sharp bark breaks my attention. The green-eyed woman i s frowning, one hand on the dog's shoulder. I can almost remember the warmth and soft fur. What *is* that dog's name?

A breeze whips around us, and both the woman and the dog stare through me. The breeze becomes wings beating the air against my liquid gray body. Between the frantic wingbeats, I hear voices. One is male, and angry. The other sounds like an older woman. Another voice, this one a young female…

"Keet, this might be our only chance. Nolee's fading."

Keet knows his sister's words are true.

Byree has moved from the chair and now sits cross-legged on the floor, Arogem and Yiskal beside her.

"If your idea is wrong, Byree, Nolee could die."

"Or be remade as one of us."

"Which she doesn't want!"

"If she doesn't want it, why hasn't her spirit returned to her body? Would you rather she was dead than one of us?"

Keet stops, the words he was going to say slipping away.

Yiskal steps closer, raising her hand as though to touch him. His look stops her.

Instead, she says, "It's her choice, Keet. Stay human and be with you or become Keykwin and a member of the Water Canyon House family."

"She can make that choice without risking her life." But even as Keet speaks, he knows what he says isn't true. His courage, like his hope, is in tatters around his feet.

"Those words are wasting time, Keet. Time we no longer have," Byree reminds him.

Keet lets out a long breath, then joins Zelka and the dogs on the sofa. Propping Nolee's head on his lap, he touches her face, trying to quieten his heart, to hear what it says. Hoping Nolee's heart will speak back.

The fire chunters in small hisses and pops. Zelka and the dogs sit in front of them. They are a circle, and Nolee, silent and walking in places Keet cannot follow, is its center. He sees days stretching before him, the routine of forcing Nolee to walk and eat an endless treadmill of despair. The choice Byree offers him is not a choice, since turning it down will no doubt doom Nolee to being trapped in a half-life.

Zelka takes his hand in hers and says, "We can go with Arogem and Nolee, Brother. She won't be alone with him."

Keet motions to the three Keykwin to join them. Arogem gets too close to Zelka and Wallace growls; Yiskal grabs Arogem's elbow and pulls him back. Arogem steps toward Nolee and this time, Keet puts himself in the way, putting his hands on Arogem's chest and shoving him.

"You've done enough damage. Stay away from her."

Arogem recovers from a stumble and draws himself up to his full height, trying to stare Keet down. Keet hears the dogs' rising whining, and out of the corner of his eye, sees Byree put a restraining hand on Yiskal's arm.

"I think you realize by now that I'm the only one who can bring her back." Arogem raises his chin, arms folded across his chest.

Yiskal interrupts, "We've told Arogem of his responsibilities if Nolee is changed into Keykwin."

Keet drags his gaze from Arogem and steps back. "What responsibilities?"

Arogem answers. "If I change Nolee and make her one of the Water Canyon House People, I am responsible for her safety. Not just the six moons she stays in our House, but when she comes back here, I must follow. To live with you both."

Keet sees his own distaste mirrored in Arogem's frown. "That won't happen."

"You have no say in this, Keet. If I'm not with her, she dies."

"Did you know this before you abducted her?"

He shakes his head. "I was only told after your sister…" he pauses, sneaking a glance at Zelka, an old misery deep in his eyes. "After your sister told our people what I'd done."

"He would not have done this, Cousin," says Byree, "if he'd talked to us first. He knew he had the power to change her, but not what that change meant."

"Is this supposed to make me trust him?"

Silent, Byree holds his gaze.

Suddenly, Nolee's breathing changes to gasps; her unseeing eyes are open, their brilliant green obscured by a milky film. Keet feels as though time has stopped, as though the floor has dropped from under his feet.

"What's happening to her?"

Byree answers. "If we don't get her into the water with Arogem right now, we're going to find out."

# CHAPTER THIRTY-FOUR

Byree, Yiskal, and Arogem return to the water and change to Blackfish, waiting as Keet undresses Nolee, wraps her in a robe, and brings her onto the dock. Sunlight flickers, diluted by the low clouds that cover Camas Island in a silver cloak. He hears his sister's soft steps behind him, and Wallace and Fae's heartbroken howling. Gently, he lays Nolee on the dock, cradling her head but averting his eyes from her blank face.

"Keet, I'll go in first." Zelka's hand on his bare arm reassures him. He hears the swish of her robe as it drops onto the weathered wood, then a splash when she dives into the water.

Keet undoes the belt around Nolee's waist. As the robe falls open, her body looks deflated; the soft, warm curves are gone. He bows his head, his tears fall against her pale skin; for a moment, he lets himself think this might be enough to bring her back. Swiping the back of his hand against his eyes, he takes her face in his hands.

"Nolee. Lia. Come back, please." Seen through a watery scrim of tears, her expression stays the same. He kisses her, but her cold lips are unresponsive. Glancing over his shoulder, he watches the rising and falling dorsal fins. He wants to call Zelka away, to drive the strange orcas back into the canyon from which they came.

He screams at the sky, eyes squeezed shut against the helplessness that is crushing him. The exhalations of his family pod circling in the bay reach his ears; they're keeping their distance from the unknown trio. The dogs, quiet now, lie by the gate. Even the wind holds its breath.

Keet takes off Nolee's robe and holds her against himself on the edge of the dock. He kisses her forehead and murmurs, "I'll love you always, Lia, no matter where you are or what you choose."

Zelka swims close, ready to catch Nolee as Keet lowers her into the dark water. Sending a click train toward Nolee's limp form, she wills her to come back. In return, she receives images of a fluttering heart, of lungs fighting for air. Zelka submerges so Keet can drape Nolee's body across her back.

As she swims away from the dock, she hears a splash and then feels the current created by Keet's spin and transformation. Now he swims beside her, his large pectoral fin touching her own; she feels the undertow of emotions coursing from her brother through her own body. Trying to keep Nolee balanced so her head is out of the water, she bumps into him, reassuring him that he's not alone with his fears.

In the dark gray murk, Zelka sees Byree, Yiskal, and Arogem, white eye patches and chins glowing. Closing her eyes, she drifts, bobbing on the surface, pleading with the Water Canyon House orcas to be gentle with the woman who has become so important to her.

A stuttering train of clicks and whistles come from Byree and Yiskal. Arogem is silent.

Keet disappears, and she follows him with sound, watching as he swims at Arogem, his body a weapon to break the being who brought Nolee to this state, to the brink of death. Zelka senses a flicker of a heartbeat in Nolee's thin chest as breath fills her lungs, but then once again, she's still.

Byree dives, then turns her white belly toward the surface, putting herself in front of Keet before he can batter Arogem. Keet stops his rush, large flukes motionless in the water, then returns to Zelka and nudges Nolee's pale hand, veins blue against her white skin.

Zelka, still on the surface, swims toward Arogem, unsure how to transfer Nolee to him. Byree meets her, laying her head against Zelka's side. *Let her go, child.*

And before Zelka can react, Byree moves behind Nolee's limp torso and nudges her into the water.

Zelka dives, Keet behind her, both clicking, desperate to find and raise Nolee once more. Before they can reach her, Zelka sees the white of Arogem's belly rising to meet Nolee's body as he folds his gigantic pectoral fin over her. No air bubbles escape from Nolee's mouth.

Zelka and Keet follow in Arogem's wake as he swims toward the doorway, every rise and fall of his tail counting Nolee's life in slow seconds.

Byree and Yiskal flank Arogem, and Zelka watches their flashing black-and-white tails as they swim with him. She wonders if this is Nolee's rebirth into being human or a slow swim to her death.

In the distance, Zelka hears the agitated whistles and cries of their family pod, Grandmother in the lead.

I'm dying. It's in the slow and stuttering beat of my heart. The space during which I still have a choice is getting smaller. Behind my eyes, I see Keet's family pod, Grandmother swimming in Arogem's wake. She places her rostrum on my limp feet.

"Granddaughter," I hear Grandmother's beloved voice like a faint echo. I turn my head into the warmth of Arogem's body.

"Granddaughter," the voice says again. Then a flurry of squeaks and a rising arpeggio of calls. I understand each syllable. George is silent with fear, and Atma and Nana swim on either side of him, offering comfort. Belle, Poppy, and Tia are behind us, rolling the song of the pod in synchronized harmonies. Does this mean I'm becoming Blackfish?

"Nolee." The voice is clear and strong. I turn my face away from Arogem's warm slickness.

"Grandmother!"

"You have a choice. Make it now."

I push against Arogem, my forehead a round bulge. Part of me is fighting against Grandmother's words. There's a warm pressure on the soles of my feet (are they even still feet?). My body elongates, my arms shorten, my back grows broader. Louder than the voice telling me to choose to be Keykwin, I hear Grandmother.

"Do you choose to sacrifice the love others have for you on the altar of your desire to be something you're not?"

I convulse again and again, tremors that threaten to dislodge me from Arogem's grasp. Each time, a burst of memories appears. A horse's black mane in my face as we run behind my dog Boo, chasing cattle, dust painting the land a golden yellow in the setting sun. My parent's faces lit by Christmas tree lights, and shouts of glee from my brothers and sister. Cradling Abbie after she was born, my body deflated but my heart huge in my chest. My dog Luna dancing around my feet in a flurry of black and white. Abbie smiling at me, her cherubic grin and pink cheeks flushed from her first solo ride on a carousel horse.

Rolling away from Arogem, I bring my arms up and wrap my hands around the edge of his pectoral fin. Its texture reminds me of the smooth, wet tree branches that sometimes wash up on the beach in Osprey Bay.

On a Texas summer night, climbing the trees near our house, opening and closing my hand against the dark, trying to hold starlight in my small fist. Another memory, this one the first house Nate and I bought together, him carrying me through the door, then laying me on the couch in a rush of joy and passion. The ferry that brought me to Camas Island, the smell of the wind and water, the sight of Keet and the solid assurance of his body beside me.

My body reanimates to every memory of our lovemaking, even the sorrow of his leaving and return. Ava smiles at me as we rearrange our new shop, Zelka holds my hand, Jerry and Saila with their arms around each other, Andi offering me a kitten. Keet's shoulder against mine as we stand on the sailboat together on our first date and name his family pod.

Keet. His face alight with a secret before he tells me to close my eyes as he dives into the nighttime sea. The boat rocks under me as I lean against the rail, then hear the sudden exhale of an orca. When I open my eyes, I see that orca trailing streamers of blue light behind him as he swims. When I join him in the water, the bioluminescence shudders, then outlines my own skin in greens and blues. As we glide through the water, I open and close my hands, trying to hold on to light that slips between my fingers.

Lungs bursting for oxygen, I swim away from Arogem, Grandmother's rostrum still on my feet, pushing me upward. Sunlight pierces the bright green water, and pale sea foam flows on top of the waves, an augury of a new life. George surfaces beside me as I break through. Gasping, I fling a weak arm around his body and rest my cheek against his silky, comforting bulk.

"George."

Beneath me rises another orca, this one lifting me from the water into the weak afternoon light. Crying, I collapse against his massive dorsal fin; through my tears, I see the notch at the top. Too weak to say his name aloud, I feel it in the pulse of water against my legs as he carries me back to Osprey Bay. Keet.

My body judders against his. If I don't get out of the water soon, hypothermia will take me. Given how weak I am, it will be a short walk. I close my eyes, remembering the conversation I had with my Aunt Iris as we scattered my father's ashes around the ranch.

"I think being an empath is good. It allows me to connect to people, and animals," I told her.

Iris says, "Nothing is all good or all bad. That's not how life works. Everything has a price, or a consequence."

"And what consequence could there be to my ability to empathize and connect with another being?"

"The consequence, Nolee, is losing yourself."

"I don't understand."

"Why are you so interested in relating to other beings?"

"Well, I get to become someone, or something, other than myself. And the other being is seen, heard, and listened to. Because they matter."

"What is wrong with being yourself? Don't you matter?"

I begin to answer, but she holds up a hand, asking me to wait.

"What is it about yourself that seems so bad that you need to seek other experiences, those you can watch from a distance, perhaps even feel, but aren't yours?"

"I'm not bad, Iris. But I've lived with myself for more than fifty years now. I'm tired of my old stories, and worries. Why not share someone else's?"

"Because you're abandoning yourself."

"Not if I *choose* to be a part of another's world."

She rests her hand on my shoulder "When you were a girl, I watched you learn from your father and my sister that the only person you could count on was yourself. We may not have physically abandoned you, but we abandoned you in every other way. For years, you begged to be seen for who you were, but your father left you behind"

I cover my mouth with my hand, willing the tears to stay in my eyes. Turning away from my aunt and her own grief, a schism opens in what I have called my reality. Everything I thought I knew, everything I thought I was, flies up like charred confetti, snatched away in seconds.

"Nolee, I don't know if this is the only life we get, or if we get do-overs. My faith is strong, but at the age I am now, I'm far more comfortable with mysteries than I used to be."

I take her hand, as much for my own comfort as for hers.

"What I do know is that this is the only life we have right now. It's yours. Please don't waste it by fooling yourself that living another life is better."

My memory is interrupted as someone hauls me out of the water, then bundles me into robes. Teeth chattering, I see only the blur of the evening landscape around me. But Iris's last words are as clear as if she were here with me. This time, I realize she's right.

213

# CHAPTER THIRTY-FIVE

The process of returning to my body is slow, like summers in West Texas: early to arrive and late to leave, heat dragging its heels in the dust before giving in to cool rains and shorter days.

I fall asleep easily but wake up often, sometimes disoriented. This time when I wake up, I sense I'm in bed because of the softness underneath me and the heavy duvet over me. I hear Keet's breathing and roll toward him, falling back asleep with my hand curled in his.

When I open my eyes, it's morning, the light filtered by the dark cloud of Keet's hair. His face is against my neck, and he's murmuring what sounds like a prayer. First, I wonder if I've lost the ability to recognize English, but then my sluggish brain reminds me he's speaking Keykwin. Is he praying? I don't realize I've asked out loud. He jerks away from me with a gasp before pinning my body under his.

"Keet, sweetheart, I can't breathe." My voice is huskier than I remember.

He moves and I sit up, realizing that I'm starving and need the bathroom.

"Be right back," I say as I swing my legs out of bed.

"Nolee, wait—"

My bladder can't wait. But when I ask my shaking legs to support my weight, they buckle, and I find myself on the cool wooden floor. Keet joins me.

"It's been more than two weeks since you walked, Nolee."

"It feels like a couple of days."

Keet asks, "Have you seen yourself?"

I pull the t-shirt up, away from my legs. These are not the strong, round thighs of a middle-aged woman. These are the legs I had when I was ten. "Where did my thighs go?"

"You haven't eaten much since Arogem returned you."

"Returned me? From where?"

"From almost becoming one of his relatives."

A scrabbling of paws outside the bedroom door is Keet's cue to let the dogs in. Fae and Wallace engulf me in whines and yips; laughing, I move my face away from their pink tongues. One arm around each dog, I murmur to them, petting their wiggling bodies, scratching their bellies, and wondering why I thought I needed any more than I have right now. When I look at Keet, he's smiling.

"Let's get you to the bathroom." He lifts me up and walks me to the bathroom, then closes the door once I'm sure I can support myself from toilet to tub. I run a bath as hot as I can stand it. As I get out of the bath, I say, "Good news, Keet." My voice is stronger.

"What's that?"

"I get to eat whatever I want, and right now I could go for a chimichanga."

Laughing, he opens the door. By this time, I've made it to the sink, but what I see in the mirror makes me gasp. My hair is white, the bones in my face are prominent, my round cheeks are gone.

"It's seven-thirty in the morning, Nolee." He stands behind me, toweling off my back before wrapping his arms and the towel around me. I touch my face, run my white hair through my thin fingers. I touch my chest, where the skin lies close against my collarbones. Behind me, Keet is silent, watching as I see myself for the first time since awakening.

"When did my hair go white?"

He sighs. "When you woke up and swam away from Arogem. Believe it or not, you've gained weight since then."

I look myself in the eyes, feeling awe for this woman who dared to return despite her delusions. Despite almost dying. Keet kisses my neck, holding me tighter. His voice is muffled when he says, "Thank you for coming back to me. To our life."

Turning in his arms, I rest my forehead against his chest. "I meant what I promised, Keet Noland. It took me a while, but I figured out what really mattered. You."

The air is cold against my skin, and I shiver. "Let's get you into some warm clothes, then I'll make you something to eat before we go get a chimichanga," he says.

"Anything but salmon."

He looks down at me, hair falling along the side of his face. I reach up and brush it away.

"Why not salmon?"

"Because I'm human, not orca."

Keet laughs, then falls on me in another breath-stealing hug.

"One order of eggs, bacon, and toast coming up," he says, helping me sit upright.

"Do we have any fruit?"

"Yes. I was force-feeding you smoothies."

I grimace. "Somehow, I remember that."

Sitting on the bed, I tighten the waistband on my yoga pants. I feel like a kid wearing her mother's clothes. But this time when I stand, the soles of my feet are firm on the floor and strength is returning to my shrunken limbs.

After breakfast, Keet helps me to the beach and settles me in a chair, a mug of ginger tea on the ground within reach. I look out at a stretch of blue sea. Beyond buoys turned sideways by the wind, it's a shifting bolt of cobalt silk. Closer to shore, it's ruffled, the water meeting itself, separate yet together. I take my phone from Keet and call Abbie. We talk until my stomach reminds me it's time to eat again. Her voice loses its frantic edge as I reassure her that I'm doing great and being well taken care of. We make plans for her to visit at Christmas. I hang up, smiling.

"All good with Abbie?" Keet asks, wrapping another blanket around me.

"Yes. It's good to be separate, and it's good to be together."

"Deep thoughts this morning, Lia." He smiles and leans in to kiss me.

"True thoughts," I say. Cupping my hand against his rough-stubble cheek, I bring his face to mine, inhaling his scent. Almost too late, I realize that most of life happens in the small moments, not the big changes. The scattershot of memories that came to my mind when I thought I was dying had a common denominator: love. The past isn't entirely dead, as I believed. Some of the past is a gift. Those gifts saved me from myself.

"You're smiling," Keet says as he sits down next to me.

"Death is funny, isn't it?"

Keet's smile disappears and his eyes narrow.

"Not sure that's how I'd describe it. What do you mean?"

"It's a visceral fear. But when I was on my way to meet Death, there was only peace. It was so quiet."

Keet gazes out at the waves rolling up on the shoreline, then turns his gaze north, toward the island where Arogem used the secret door. I wonder if we'll ever be able to forget what happened because I wasn't strong enough to be myself. Tears cloud my next words.

"My fear was loud, Keet. It yelled that I was getting older, and getting older meant dying. I thought…" Taking a breath, I wipe my eyes and nose, then go on. "I thought if I could change into someone else, I could pause death, that my fear would stop screaming. Turns out, there's nothing quite like facing death to make you realize life is good *because* you're getting older, not because you're young and think you have decades."

I take a sip of ginger tea, and as the honeyed liquid hits my belly, I'm suddenly tired again.

"I know the walk you're taking, Lia. It's a walk we're all on, even if we ignore it. It's my honor to walk with you."

I open my eyes, offer Keet a drink from my cup, watch as he swallows. "What happened with Arogem?"

Keet hands the ceramic mug back to me and I cradle it in my hands, absorbing the warmth. Long moments pass as I wait for Keet to answer. When he does, his voice is strained. I lean toward him so I don't miss what he's saying.

"When I brought you into the house, Arogem, Yiskal, and Byree waited while I took care of you. You were talking, but I didn't understand what you were saying. There were many names, including mine. You were smiling, so I thought that was a good sign." He rubs his thumb over my knuckles, and it occurs to me that my hands are starting to look like Grandmother's.

"When I came out of the bedroom, Arogem asked to see you, to apologize."

I concentrate, trying to pull a memory of Arogem from the clouds floating in my brain.

"You don't remember?"

I shake my head.

"You were in bed, still shivering. He got down on his knees and begged you to forgive him."

"What did I say?"

"You said that there was nothing to forgive, that he gave you a gift."

"I said that?"

Keet nods. "But that's not the best part."

"Go on," I nudge his shoulder. "Tell me the best part."

"You said he needed to ask my forgiveness as well."

"What?"

"You said, 'your forgiveness depends on Keet's mercy.'"

I burrow into my nest of blankets, drawing them close around my neck.

"Shall we go back inside?" Keet half-rises from his chair.

"Not yet. I need to hear what you said to Arogem."

"I told him I was too angry for true forgiveness, and it would have to come in its own time."

"What did he say?"

"Nothing. I asked him to stand up, so I could say what I needed to say while we looked each other in the eye."

"Was I awake?"

"You were watching."

The clouds are thick in my brain. Keet sees my confusion. "I told him that my feelings about how he wounded you, and our family, would take time to heal, and my anger is a part of that healing. We can't achieve wholeness until we've walked through all the pieces of ourselves and reclaimed what someone took from us."

Suddenly, something clicks in the dark recess of my memory, and a clear picture comes to mind: Keet speaking to Arogem, whose head is bowed under the weight of the wrongs he'd committed.

"You said..." I close my eyes, reaching for Keet's words. 'Instead of forgiveness, which would not be true at this time, I give you mercy.'"

Keet smiles. "You remember."

"I remember being relieved. I think I went to sleep after that."

"You did. I met Yiskal, Byree and Arogem on the beach. They promised we would live in peace."

"Did you believe them?"

"I did, and I do. They were here last week checking on you. Arogem left you a gift."

Shivering, I feel my skin crawl. "What is it?"

"It's your gift, I didn't open it."

"Open it for me."

"Now?"

"Yes."

Keet goes into the house to retrieve the gift, and I gather the blankets even closer. When he returns holding a small stone box, the dogs are with him. Even in the gray light, the box glitters. Turning it over in his hands, Keet pushes against the sides and the top slides off.

Despite my mixed feelings, I lean over to see what's inside. I hold out my hand and Keet drops its contents into my palm: a killer whale carved of stone, white inlaid in black, a swirl of white behind the small dorsal fin.

"This is George!" I trace the familiar saddle patch. As I turn the cool stone in my hands, I feel myself smile. "How can I love this so much and yet be so angry at the person who created it?"

"Because we're able to feel many things at the same time."

"What a messy thing being human is." I close my hand around the carving and lean my head against Keet's warm shoulder.

# CHAPTER THIRTY-SIX

On a small shelf in our living room, I set the new stone orca beside six others. Once a month, I find an effigy of a member of our family pod on the dock. There's George, Tia, Poppy, Belle, Atma, and Nana. The new one is Grandmother, the largest of the carved-stone figures.

Keet wraps his arms around me, softening the ache of Grandmother's absence.

"The only one missing is you, Keet."

He laughs against my hair, nuzzling into my neck. "That one may take Arogem longer."

"Has he said why he's doing this?" I turn to look at Keet.

"No. He's been hanging around with our family pod since…"

"You can say it, I won't break."

"Since he tried to change you to Keykwin."

"They allowed him in?"

"Of course. As Blackfish, we have a more intimate knowledge of each other than we do as human. He feels a lot of guilt for what he did to you."

"He's not the only one."

"I think he's making these carvings to show you he's sorry, and that he's trying to change."

"Like an act of penance?"

Keet ponders the word for a moment. "Maybe."

"What's he trying to change?"

"He realized how angry and self-centered he'd become. That entire experience with you showed him the worst of himself, and he doesn't want to live that way."

I pick up the carving of George and run my fingers over the smooth stone.

"I understand that. It took a divorce and moving here for me to find the person I am."

"It's a tough life when you don't like who you are."

"Or what you've become."

Resting my head against Keet's chest, I listen to the deep drumbeat of his heart, slow and steady. Outside our window is a wide Salish Sea blue sky, and under it, Marissa and Zelka lean into each other, their heads close together as though sharing secrets.

"What do you think those girls are up to?" I ask.

"I think I might know. We need some robes and towels," Keet says, turning to fetch them from the linen closet. Fae and Wallace jump up from their beds and stretch, forelegs out, butts in the air, tails waving.

"Let's go outside, doggies. I think Marissa is in for a treat—or at the very least, a surprise."

Zelka turns her head when she hears Keet and Nolee's front door click open and sees the couple headed their way. Keet carries an armful of towels and a couple of robes, and though it's April, Nolee's wearing a long down jacket, Grandmother's knitted scarf, and a black watch cap pulled down almost to her eyebrows, white hair streaming from underneath. Zelka notices that Nolee's skin is pink, and her face is regaining its familiar roundness. She's heard Nolee say she finds it difficult to get warm—something Zelka has never experienced. Right now, her body heat is amplified by nervous excitement and a jittery fear of what-ifs.

Marissa touches Zelka's cheek. "Come back here, sweetness. I've been waiting almost half a year to find out what your big secret is. Didn't you bring me out here to tell me?"

Zelka gives her girlfriend a shy smile. "I want to tell you, and it also involves Keet. He said he's happy to help."

"Help what?"

"He and I have the same secret."

"Nolee knows?"

Zelka nods, then she and Marissa stand as Keet and Nolee arrive.

Marissa gives Nolee a hug. "Zee says you've been sick most of the winter. I'm glad to see you up and around."

Nolee kisses Marissa's cheek. "Me, too. Better every day."

As Keet sets his bundle at the end of the dock, Marissa asks, "What's with all the towels and robes?"

"These are for later."

"Later?"

Nolee says, "Zee will explain everything."

Zelka takes Marissa's hand in her own. "Em, let's go in the cabin."

"We can't talk out here?"

Keet says, "It would be easier if you gave me a few minutes."

"Wow. Y'all are a mysterious family, but okay." She smiles and allows Zelka to lead her away. Inside, Zelka sits on the sofa, tucking her hair behind her ears. It's past her shoulders now, and she doesn't think she'll cut it ever again. But she might keep putting purple streaks in. Shaking off that distracting thought, she pats the cushion next to her.

"This must be a big deal for you and Keet."

"It's a big deal for our whole family, Em. I love you, and it's time for me to show you all of me."

"I love you too, Zee. Whatever you are."

Zelka hopes this is true.

Through the window, she sees the splash when Keet dives into the water. "We can go outside now." She takes Marissa's hand in hers and they walk outside.

Marissa, eyes wide, points out to the bay. "That's a male orca!"

Zelka smiles. "Do you remember me telling you about my brother, about how he's different?"

Marissa nods as she watches the orca zig-zag toward them, tall notched dorsal fin cutting through the water. Running to the end of the rocking dock, she stops in her tracks. Zelka waits until it stops moving, then goes to stand next to her.

Marissa points to the orca. "It can't be."

"What can't be?"

"I told you about that aquarium I worked at for a little while, right?"

Zelka nods.

"And the killer whale, Odin, who disappeared, the one that I worked with who… I didn't tell you this part. I was the first person he let feed him, and it made the lead trainer furious. Odin would do things for me he wouldn't do for anyone else. I think he saved my job, but he also became my friend. I thought Odin was dead."

Wiping her tears with the back of her hand, Marissa gives Zelka an embarrassed smile, then returns her gaze to the orca bobbing in the current. "Odin had a notch out of his dorsal fin like that. I'm standing here, hoping it's him. Hoping he's free."

Zelka takes Marissa's hand. "Trust me, Em, it's the same orca." As they watch, the dorsal fin disappears, and for a few long moments, nothing happens. Marissa, straining to detect movement in the water, gasps when Keet's head breaks the surface. As he treads water, he shakes his head, flinging saltwater out of his eyes.

Letting go of Zelka's hand, Marissa says, "I don't understand."

"Marissa," Keet calls. "Watch me." He dives, muscular back arching, feet disappearing. Seconds later, the long blade of a male orca dorsal fin cuts through the water, followed by an exhale.

"I don't get it."

Zelka steps closer to Marissa, not speaking. She knows her girlfriend will either accept what she's seeing, or not. If she can't… Zelka's heart thumps painfully at the thought of losing her. Zelka looks over at Nolee, who's smiling as she watches Keet sink beneath the waves, then rocket skyward, twisting the white of his belly to the sky.

"If that's Odin, where did Keet go? Zee?"

Zelka pats the dock beside her. "Em, please sit next to me." Behind her, Zelka hears Nolee leave the dock.

Out in the bay, the orca raises his head out of the water and squeaks. Marissa puts her hand to her mouth. "That's the sound Odin made when he saw me. But Zee?" Marissa takes her hand again, brown knuckles paling as her grip tightens. Zelka grips her hand back.

The orca sinks out of sight and Zelka hears the screech of gulls as they circle above water boiling with bubbles, air rising fast to the surface.

Marissa leans close, her voice hushed in Zelka's ear. "Is Keet Odin?"

Keet's head reappears. Brushing the hair out of his face, he swims toward the dock.

Zelka touches Marissa's chin, bringing her eyes away from Keet and to her own.

"Yes. And I'm the same as my brother. Our people are called Keykwin. In orca form, we're Blackfish."

Marissa shakes her head, her hands trembling in her lap.

"Can I show you?" Zelka asks.

Marissa blinks and nods. Keet steers away from them, aiming for the beach where Nolee waits for him with a towel. Zelka turns back toward Marissa, shrugs out of her sundress, then dives in, thrilling to the cold water against her human skin. Swimming toward the buoys that mark the bay, she pulls herself deeper, through the dark green sea, kelp and small fish floating in front of her. She closes her eyes, and begins to spin, opening her hands to the caress of the water between her fingers. Another fast turn and she's Blackfish, eyes still closed but mind open, the vast soundscape of the Salish Sea reverberating in her head.

When she rises and exhales, she twists to face the dock and sees through a thin scrim of water that Marissa is standing. Before Zelka can swim closer, Marissa cannonballs into the water with a whoop, then rises gasping from the cold.

Zelka ducks under the waves, riding the current toward her girlfriend. When they meet, Marissa places her hand behind Zelka's pectoral fin, and she feels the warmth of Marissa's face against the cool slickness of her orca body. Turning, Zelka swims in a slow arc, then pauses to scan her girlfriend with a long series of clicks that reveal her pulsing heart, the bones of her skull and neck and ribcage, the float of her uterus in the bowl of her pelvis.

Teeth chattering, Marissa laughs. "Zee, whatever you're doing, stop! It tickles! And I need to get out—this water is crazy cold."

Zelka swims toward the dock, Marissa trembling on her back. Getting as close as the cove's depth will allow, she watches as Marissa paddles to it. Once Keet pulls her from the water, Zelka dives and changes; when she boosts herself onto the dock, Marissa, dark curls still dripping, hands her a towel and wraps her arms around her.

As they walk to the cabin, Marissa looks over her shoulder at Keet, arms around Nolee's waist, head burrowed into her hair. She calls back, "I'm glad you didn't die, Odin." Keet raises his head, smiling. "Me, too, Ms. Smithson." They share a laugh, and Zelka asks, "Ms. Smithson?"

Marissa plants a kiss on Zelka's cheek. "Let's go for a drive around the island and I'll explain."

# CHAPTER THIRTY-SEVEN

Smiling, I watch Zee and Marissa twine around each other. Turning to Keet. I put my arms around his waist and pull him closer. "Why did you call her 'Ms. Smithson'?"

Keet rumbles a laugh. "That's how the owner of OceanMagic addressed her. Though the way he said it sounded like an insult."

"Do you think we need to follow them?"

"You're shivering again. Let's go inside and make something warm to drink."

"Hot toddies?"

"Now you're talking."

Several hours later, as I doze on the sofa, my phone pings with a text. "Keet!"

The mudroom door opens, followed by padding paws. Fae and Wallace push their faces close to mine, panting and wagging their tails.

"Zee texted. She'd like us to come over."

As Keet and I and the dogs walk through the cabin's open door, I glance into the kitchen, but they're not there. Then I hear giggling upstairs.

"Zee?"

"Up here!"

Wallace runs up the stairs, taking them two at a time. Fae, Keet, and I follow more slowly.

"We have so much good news," Zelka squeals as she hugs me and then Keet. Marissa sits on the edge of the bed, smiling. Apparently, she's not disturbed by Zelka and Keet's revelation.

"What's the good news?"

Zelka sits beside Marissa, holding her hand. "Em is moving in! I already texted Ava and asked if it was okay."

Keet and I gather them into a laughing group hug. Fae dances around us, yipping, and Wallace stands beside Zelka, looking up at her, tail wagging.

"We're so happy for both of you," I say.

"It'll mean commuting to Whidbey for a while, but that's no problem."

"She might have an orca escort some days," Zelka says, laughing.

We chat for a few moments longer, until the fatigue of talking and excitement hits me.

"I think Keet and I are going to take the kayak out."

Keet looks at me in surprise.

"C'mon. Let's get out on that water while it's still sunny." I'm halfway down the stairs with the dogs when Keet turns to Zelka and Marissa. "You're welcome to take the kayaks out any time. That way, Marissa can be on the water with you without freezing."

After thanking Keet, Marissa says, "I'm planning on investing in a wet suit."

"Good idea!" I call up the stairs.

We put the dogs in the yard and carry the double kayak to the water's edge, pushing off from the rocky shore. I take a deep breath, close my eyes, and enjoy the kayak's gentle rocking as we paddle north. Without discussing it, Keet and I head in the direction of the small island with the underwater door.

"Are you sure you want to go this way, Lia?"

I hear the concern in Keet's voice but have zero sensation of it in my body. For the past several months, while still sensitive to how others process the world, I no longer experience the reverberations of their emotions inside me. For possibly the first time in my life, the only emotional weight I'm carrying is my own.

"Yes."

As we push past The Point, gulls screech, and the wind pokes its fingers under my knit cap. In the dusky green water, small silvery fishes dart around our kayak.

"Keet, let's stop for a little bit."

We glide to a halt, the kayak rocking in a passing boat's wake. I rest my paddle and close my eyes, raising my face to the sun. In a few moments, I feel that we're moving again.

Keet tells me, "Keep resting, I've got this."

My eyes are still closed when I hear a burst of powerful exhalations.

Glancing over my shoulder, I see eight dorsal fins rising and falling. The largest one, missing a saddle patch, hangs at the back of the pod. The smallest one races ahead, squealing with each breath when he surfaces. Keet turns the kayak to face them.

George runs the length of his body along the hand I'm holding above the water. I don't need to translate the joy that suffuses both of us. Scratching his tongue, then his chin and under his pectoral fins, I murmur endearments. I watch as black-and-white forms glide underneath and around us, flashing bellies and blowing bubbles, carefully bumping the kayak.

Then laughter dies in my chest, replaced by a familiar ache when I see Nana and Grandmother approach. They float, one on each side, close enough for us to touch them. I lay my hand on Grandmother's dorsal fin, feeling a sadness that seems fathoms deep.

But down in the depths of my sadness there's another current. This is not only my life, but Life with a capital L. Joy and sorrow. Love and loss. Choosing to be human after coming so close to death seems to have given me a strange sort of inner peace. For the first time, I'm satisfied with everything I have. I'm finished striving, though I imagine I'm not done changing.

"Thank you," I whisper, first to Grandmother, then to Nana. They submerge and leave us, swimming northwest. But one orca stays behind; facing us, his dorsal fin splits the water's surface like a dagger.

Keet touches my shoulder with an unspoken question. I put my hand on top of his as an answer.

Arogem floats closer, raising his head above the water, watching us. Part of me should be trembling in fear, but I can't conjure it. Another part should burn with anger, but that fire is cold. I stare at Arogem, listening as he breathes, picturing the stone carvings in our living room.

"Arogem."

He gives a low whistle. Keet's hand still rests on my shoulder.

"Thank you."

He drifts closer until his rostrum rests against the kayak. I hesitate a moment, wondering if fear keeps me from touching him, then realize: It isn't fear, but rather, a recognition that both of us, Keykwin and human, walk our paths with only the knowledge we have. Our strange connection seems to have increased compassion in both of us. When at last I rest my hand on his rostrum, watching him open and close his eyes, my gratitude intensifies.

Arogem sinks. The last we see of him is an exhalation that flings water vapor into the blue sky, then the white underside of his tail as he dives, scattering droplets that return to the sea.


A week later, Keet and I lean on the railing at the front of the ferry, heading home after a day in Bellingham. A porpoise jumping out of the water reminds me of Arogem. I haven't seen him again, but this morning, I found another stone figure on the end of the dock. Arogem carved Keet's likeness, even the notch at the top of his dorsal fin. Keet laughed out loud when he saw it.

"What are you thinking, Nolee Burnett?" Keet looks down at me, his shoulder warm against mine.

"I like how you've adopted my habit of saying both names." The wind whooshes by my ears, almost carrying my words away with it. "Actually, I'm remembering more than thinking."

"What are you remembering?"

Pewter clouds hang like thick cobwebs across the setting sun, and the sky is striped in yellow, pink, and orange.

"I'm remembering the first time I rode this ferry, wondering what my life was going to be like."

Looking first at me, then at the sky, Keet settles his arm around my waist.

"How excited I was about all the ways the woman I'd hidden away was going to flourish."

Another harbor porpoise leaps out of the water ahead of us, the sun flashing on its back before it disappears into the glittering water.

"I'm also remembering how it felt to forgive Arogem. I wasn't sure I could, but I did."

"So did I."

"We have an amazing life, Keet. I want nothing but what I have, right here, right now."

The rush of water against the ferry's bow and the chug of its motors fills the silence between us. When I first arrived, road-weary, in a car still covered with Texas dirt, I thought it was the salt- and pine-scented air that held all the promise. It turns out the promise was a seed inside me waiting to germinate and blossom into the life I now have.

Tucking a lock of stray hair back underneath my knit cap, Keet says, "Lia, our promises to each other have grown from seeds to trees."

"You're doing it again."

He smiles, puts both arms around me, and holds me tight. "Reading your mind?"

"Something like that, yes."

"Then tell me something you haven't said before."

I watch the sky, now painted in streaks of orange and butter yellow. The prow of the ship points toward the black islands. A line of wavering white rims the waves, a watery road leading to a distant land. Or the yellow brick road I said goodbye to in what seems like a lifetime ago. "I don't regret one thing in my life."

"Not one?"

I shake my head, burrowing into Keet's warmth. "Every choice I've made, and everything that's happened to me, easy or difficult, has led me to contentment, and a life with you."

The ferry's engine rumbles beneath our feet and the wind charges around us. The captain's announcement that Camus Island is the next stop breaks the spell.

Keet and I walk to my car, the same silver Honda that had delivered me here three years ago. Once home, the usual routines take over: emptying the coolers, opening packages for the pet store, and deciding what to eat. The light in the sky has deepened to azure and lavender, and on the beach, I see Marissa and Zee huddled beneath a blanket.

Later that night, awakening in a wash of sweat, I throw off the covers. Slipping on the wool-lined shoes Keet gave me at Christmas, I pick up a blue hoodie, knowing that after the flash comes the chill.

"Where are you going, Lia?"

"I'm hot flashing like hell and I need to get outside. Maybe take a walk along the cove."

He swings his legs out of bed. "I'll go with you."

High tide has narrowed the beach to a sliver, and the waves advance and recede like an endless series of freight trains. The chilly air is a balm against my face. Tossing the hoodie on the deck railing, I walk to the beach, toe off the slippers, roll up my pants, and step into the water. The cold snatches the breath from my lungs, but the relief it offers keeps me standing there, surf rattling against my legs.

Keet and the dogs come toward me over the rocks, and Keet says, "I want to try something I saw Marissa do."

"What's that?"

His grin glows in the moonlight. "Watch me."

On the dock, Keet pauses, head lowered. I bow my head as well to this spring night, in appreciation for the full moon, for the roaring waves, for the life that I came close to losing—a reverie that's shattered when Keet runs the length of the dock, lets out a loud whoop, then cannonballs into the water. I laugh, Fae barks, and Wallace dances away from the waves.

When Keet rises, he is Blackfish, skin gleaming with saltwater and moonlight, leaping into a sky cloaked in stars. If I didn't know I was standing on this rocky beach with my feet going numb, I'd swear I was out there with him, leaping for the sheer joy of it.

# ACKNOWLEDGMENTS

This trilogy began in the fall of 2020, when it seemed the world was locked in depression and uncertainty. I certainly know that's what it felt like to me. Then the orca dreams started, and they wouldn't stop until I wrote them down. Then a new scene would arrive, never in order, and rarely connected. This has been a four-year journey, and it lifted me from despair and into wonder more times than I can count. Writing this series has been one of the great joys and mysteries of my life. While I can point to some scenes that are amalgamated from my experiences, others dropped in from the ether, mysterious and whole.

I'd like to thank and acknowledge my debt to the Indigenous cultures of the Pacific Northwest. Their beautiful Oral Traditions and their Traditional Knowledge are treasured and, I hope, celebrated by this trilogy. I honor and respect their cultural rights as the primary guardians of their unique Traditional Stories. I also honor the wonderful sensitivity reader Maryann Flett for working with me since 2020, helping me recognize my biases and rectify my misunderstandings of Indigenous cultures. She's a benevolent force behind these stories, and I wouldn't have published them without her insights.

I've been writing since I was eight years old, and my mom has been an editor for as long as I've been writing. She's applied her talents to each of these stories, and they wouldn't be what they are without her clear-sightedness, just as I wouldn't be who I am without her guidance and love.

I've spent three springs in the Pacific Northwest, in and around the Puget Sound area. While Camas Island is fictional, it is based on real places. During those trips, I've been accompanied by two women who live in my heart, Hunter Purdy and Dianne Adel. You are both on these pages, steadying me when I fumbled, inspiring me with your courage and ability to tell the truth, as difficult as it might be.

To my business partner and friend Anna Blake—I owe you a great debt of gratitude, not only for our long talks about the art and craft of writing, but for the (mostly) metaphorical Croc kick in the pants to explore indie publishing. It's your fault any of my books saw the light of day, and I hold you accountable for all the joy that's brought to my life, which is second only to the joy you bring to all the lives you touch.

Thank you to Carissa Sorensen, artist extraordinaire, for her talent and heart creating these covers. Another thanks to Jane Dixon-Smith for her mad design skills; she's the reason these books look so good, inside and out.

But none of this would have been possible if it weren't for the steady support of my husband Mark. He's cheered me on through every victory and supported me through every struggle. I wouldn't be a published writer without his belief in me, and for that, my gratitude is endless.

*Find Crissi's books on her website at crissimcdonald.com. You can also find her books at major online retailers.*